I0789025

THE GIRL WHO DIDN'T DIE

RUBY JEAN JENSEN

A Gayle J. Foster Publication

THERE IT WAS— OUTSIDE MY WINDOW!

I looked out into the moonlight. Moving nearer, as if blown by the wind, was a small patch of diaphanous fog.

I could not move my eyes away from it, and the coldness moved over me in wave after wave as if I were sinking beneath the surface of frigid, paralyzing water.

It stopped, as if it saw me, and slowly as I watched, the milky, misty substance condensed again as it had the night before when it followed my car; and now, again, became thick and impenetrable and so nearly the shape and size of a large, tall man that I choked with fear.

I jerked the draperies to close out the sight and shrank into a cold, shivering ball in the corner of my room ...

First printed 1975 in the United States of America

Published by: Gayle J. Foster, Carrollton, Texas

Library of Congress Control Number: 2021922046

Cover Art: SelfPubBookCovers.com/ DesignzbyDanielle

❀ Created with Vellum

CHAPTER 1

The picture of the house was spread out on the coffee table in front of the slightly battered sofa, and Donna paused once again to look at it. Why Sheba wanted to buy the thing was more than she could understand. To her it resembled a large pile of gray boulders more than anything, or a castle out of medieval Scotland. There wasn't even a tree or a shrub near it. None, at least, that showed in the picture the real estate agency had sent.

Well, it was Sheba's money, not hers. The trouble was, Sheba wanted her to go along and run the thing and help make a profitable business out of it. And the voice of Sheba came at her so convincingly that she was about ready to tell her okay, okay, okay, just to get her off her back.

The girl, who looked younger than her twenty-six years, stood looking out the window at falling snow that should have been white but had been turned gray by factory smoke. Her profile was cherub perfect; the kind that is often found in the less serious paintings, Donna thought as she looked at her. Even when she talked with chin pumping, half angrily, always impatiently, always impulsively, her profile was perfect.

"What difference does it make, for cripe's sake, Donna," she was saying. "At least you would get out of this!" She waved her arms dramatically, from the soot-gray snow beyond the window to the surrounding small living room of the three-room apartment they shared. She turned

1

from the window. "How you lived here for three years beats hell out of me. Six months is more than I can stand!"

"I don't doubt that," Donna said, thinking of the marriage Sheba had walked out of six months ago. A very good marriage, too, financially, so she had heard. Sheba's third one. If Sheba got tired of something she didn't waste time considering anything. Like the inconveniences in this giant of an old house, for example.

With a low sigh, Donna reminded her again, "Remember, Sheba, the house doesn't even have electricity. Not having a telephone isn't so bad—but electricity? Have you ever lived without electricity?"

"No, and I think it would be a great adventure. Donna, don't you have any adventure in your soul? Never mind answering that. I can tell the answer from your choice of boyfriends."

Donna picked up the glass of Coca Cola she had just poured, sipped it, and said, "Neil's okay. You don't have to be in love to date someone. But back to your house. Aren't you at least a bit suspicious of a bargain anyway?"

"No, I love bargains. Come on. Go with me."

"I suppose I will. There's really no reason why not. Except, of course, trying to run a hunting lodge without electricity. I suppose we can handle business by mail. But who wants to be in the dark all the time? Dark house, I mean."

Donna swung her legs over the arm of the fat chair and let her feet dangle comfortably.

"So who said it would be dark?" Sheba came away from the window and stopped at the coffee table to look at the letter from the real estate man. "What's wrong with a hunting lodge that is lighted by lamps? Or candles. I can't think of anything sexier than candles. It will be a wild scene when we get all those handsome hunters there." She sat back on the couch with a dreamy smile that shouted her thoughts. "As for bargains— didn't you ever hear of fate? Maybe it's *supposed* to be our house. Waiting for us."

"You choose your fate, I'll choose mine. And even though I'll be glad to work for you, I'll take my destiny elsewhere, thank you."

Donna watched Sheba with amusement, and sipped the cold, sharp liquid. A hunting lodge. It had all been Sheba's idea, and Donna had to admit it wasn't a bad one. As soon as Sheba's money came in from her ex in a lump sum of twenty thousand, there was no holding her back. And, though Donna had no savings to amount to anything, Sheba had generously offered her a partnership. Donna assured her that she would simply take care of the business end, the bookkeeping, actually, and thanks just the same but she'd really prefer an ordinary salary. She didn't tell Sheba, but she couldn't see getting herself tied up indefinitely with this particular house. It might appeal to Sheba, in some dark and mysterious way, but Donna didn't like the looks of it. Of course as bookkeeper, Donna would be handling the bulk of the business, while Sheba had in mind keeping hunters who didn't bring wives entertained. Donna could practically see the dream-men floating about over Sheba's head.

"As far as the telephone goes, we can probably have one put in," Sheba said after a while of dreaming. "And the house has bathrooms, that's the important thing. And heating."

Donna put down her glass. "I wonder what runs those things, too. But what about hunting season, Sheba? That doesn't go on all year. I know because my dad used to hunt."

"But you lived in Minnesota. I'm sure it's different in southern Arkansas. That's a lot farther south, you know."

"Yes, I know. But it wouldn't be difficult to find out about the hunting seasons. We *should* consider these things. And find out all we can first. Buying sight unseen is very risky."

Sheba shrugged impatiently. "But it would take time, and anyway we can think of something else other than hunting during other months."

"Like what?"

"Well, like..." Sheba picked up the picture of the large stone house that appeared to be sitting on top of the world because there was nothing behind it but blue sky. The photo, Donna thought, must have been taken slightly downhill in front to give it the background of sky and the slightly haughty attitude of looking up and away. Sheba smiled. "How about a rest home for young businessmen."

Donna laughed. "All right, you win. It does sound as much a bargain as the real estate dealer claims, so I guess you can't lose. As for me, I'm ready to go. I wonder if it will be warm and sunny. At least it's better than working all my life in a back office as one of a dozen bookkeepers."

"Good! Oh, great, Donna!" Sheba was up and about suddenly, as excited as a child. "Where shall we start? What shall we pack first?"

Donna didn't move. "First you mail the man his check, don't you think?"

"Okay, I'll do that right after I start packing. But why not take it and hand it to him instead?"

Sheba was serious, Donna saw with amazement. If Sheba had her way they would go tonight. Donna took her glass and placed it carefully in the tiny sink. Being in the kitchen for the brief moment it took to cross from the door to the sink didn't prevent her from carrying on a normal conversation with her apartment mate. In fact, they could talk to each other even if one was in the bathroom and the other in the kitchen. And that was the greatest distance two people could put between each other in this apartment.

"Sheba, we can't possibly go tonight. I have to give notice, for one thing."

"They'll be keeping the roads clear. I wonder if I should yell at Esther and Wanda and tell them to start packing." Even as she spoke Sheba began banging on the wall that separated the two apartments. "They'll be glad to get out of here. Wanda has asked me about the deal every day for over a week."

Donna thought of the two sisters, both unmarried, though Wanda was a widow, both middle-aged, one more so than the other, and both as different as high and low. She wondered if they would really like living in an isolated place like the house Sheba was buying when all their lives they had lived in Chicago. They thought they would, but Donna wondered.

Donna returned to the living room to find Sheba standing by the wall, but her fists were on her hips. She was clearly waiting for an answer. Donna felt the same slight amusement and amazement that she always felt when Sheba showed her completely impractical and impulsive side. She liked Sheba, enjoyed being around her; but she couldn't really understand her. They were too different. But they were so different that they had successfully roomed together, to save money, and never got in each other's way.

Sheba went to answer the knock on the door, and the two sisters came in—Esther, taller, older, looking as serious as an eighteenth century schoolmarm, and Wanda, several years younger, short, a bit stocky and plump, round-faced and wide-mouthed. She talked almost as much as Sheba. Naturally it was she who spoke first.

"Heard your call. Is it good news? Am I about to be liberated from that smelly hotel and all those beds I have to make every day?"

Sheba draped one arm carelessly across Wanda's shoulders. "You are! I've made up my mind and I'm buying, definitely. What's more, we're leaving tonight." She glanced at Donna. "That is, part of us. Donna insists on giving her two weeks notice, but—"

Esther interrupted, "I have to give one."

Wanda had stopped. "Me too."

Sheba's excitement began to fade. She withdrew her arm from around Wanda. "All of you cutting out on me?"

"No," Wanda said, looking concerned, her too-fleshy face dropping from smiles to sorrow. "I'd give anything to leave tonight. Except," she added, "my paycheck. And that's what I'd have to give up if I did. It's not much, but I need it."

"You'll be getting paychecks down at our hunting lodge," Sheba said, "Just like here."

"But—"

Esther said dryly, "If I ever want another job in a hotel as a cook, I'd better give my one week's notice."

"Then I guess I'll have to go alone. You'll all have to come on the bus."

The phone rang and Donna picked it up. He had said he would call first, before he came over. The voice on the phone was deep, soft with the unspoken suggestion of constant longing and passion. "Hi, beautiful. What time shall I be over to get you? We'll go for a sleigh ride in the park, with a lot of blankets to keep us warm."

"Oh great," Donna said with small enthusiasm. Neil was okay but she couldn't get very excited about him no matter what he thought of. And she had to give him credit for trying.

"Does that mean you don't want to?"

"I didn't say that," Donna said, though she was thinking it. Right man, fine. But Neil? "It might be fun. The park is probably lovely tonight." But under blankets would be a struggle to keep Neil's hands out from under her dress. It was a struggle even in a theater. It could even be a struggle in a restaurant where one ate by candlelight. Sometimes she wondered why she bothered with Neil. But there seemed no answer—except that he was always there, in the way, scaring off others she might have preferred. But since she didn't strongly prefer anyone she allowed him to remain.

"Want to, then?" he asked, pleading in his voice. "See you in fifteen minutes," she said. "Come on over here to wait if you want."

"You going out?" Sheba demanded with a frown when Donna put the phone in its cradle. "With all these exciting things we have to do to get ready, you're going out with that drip?"

"Might as well."

"How boring," Sheba said. But she had settled back on the couch and put her feet up on the coffee table. Across from her the sisters sat in chairs." If I can't make that trip in one day, I'll drive through the night. It's not that far. You can see on the map it's not that far. All I have to do is drop over to the Mississippi River, drive down across one state or two, then over a ways. It's only about an inch from the river."

"That's right," Wanda said, bending forward to look at the map of the United States that was spread open on the coffee table, and the cross in red ink that marked the location of the proposed lodge. "Only an inch. Or less. Of course, an inch on the map is probably twenty miles."

"Or a hundred," Donna said as she went toward the bathroom to take a look at her face and remove any mascara that might have become streaked by falling snow. "But didn't the agent say the place was about fifty miles west of the Mississippi River?"

"Yeah," Sheba answered. "Right on the border of the best duck-hunting marshes in southern Arkansas."

Donna crossed the room, carrying her slightly musty snowsuit. "Are you sure you want to drive down alone, Sheba?"

"I do want it. And I am serious about going down tomorrow. All the way. No stopping. Tomorrow night I'm going to sleep in my own lodge. My own house. My own huge, beautiful mansion. How about that, girls? I'll bet you'll be wishing you'd gone along."

CHAPTER 2

Sheba held the car carefully and with increasing tenseness on the narrow road, looked around at the moonlit landscape, which seemed to be only a flat nothing with a scattering of tall clumps of grasses shadowed black and golden in the moonlight, and wondered why the man at the cafe back in the last small town had voiced such concern about her night journey. In the quietness of the slowly moving car she heard again his words, but more than the words she heard and felt the tone behind the words. Incredulity. "You're going *where* tonight?"

"To"—she looked again at the page in her small notebook—"to the Murphy place. I just recently purchased it and I'm turning it into a lodge. I understand the land is marshy and great for hunting."

"Well, that's true."

Like a hick he had simply stood, there scratching his head and frowning at the door behind her. Still open at one o'clock in the morning, Sheba was his only customer. He had been preparing to close when she drove up and went in for a much needed cup of coffee. Southern Arkansas seemed damp and surprisingly cold, but she didn't have time to ask if it was always so cold in the winter. "Then," she told him, "it should be a profitable venture. A hunting lodge for duck hunters and so forth."

"Well, sure—but there's a season, you know."

She hadn't followed Donna's suggestions and asked about that, but she wasn't going to sit there in the small, vacated cafe and let the native know she was unfamiliar with hunting seasons.

"Do I have these directions right?" She repeated them to him: "Third road west turning north. Can't miss it. Road winds northward toward a big marsh. The house is located at the end of the road in the high ground of the marsh."

"Well, yeah. But you'd better wait till morning."

She laughed at him "Why? I'm no coward. The heat has been turned on, I bought the house already furnished, and I'm going home, that's all. And if you see any hunters out looking for a hunting range and hunting lodge, send them my way, okay?"

The man turned his head from the door to her but he didn't say another word. She paid her bill and left.

She had no trouble finding the road, but she was beginning to wonder just how far north the end of it really was. Either time was passing slowly or it was a lot farther than the real estate man had led her to believe.

Still, she felt it was the advantage she had been searching for. She was so tired of crowds and cities, and especially of working in the dull routine of the office, that she had been—well, so desperate that she had no qualms in buying a place on description and pictures, everything handled between her real estate agent in Chicago and the agent in the small town of Archer. So what if the house was fifteen or twenty miles off the highway, and farther yet from town? A lodge such as she had in mind needed plenty of privacy.

The area of brown grass was increasing, covering a major part of the flat landscape and coming to the edge of the road where it waved gently in the cold winter wind, the feathering tops softly golden in the moonlight. The marshland, she thought silently; that meant she was coming closer to the end of the road.

She looked at the terrain of the land with growing interest, seeing in it a beauty that was touched with wildness, and something more. Something she couldn't catch the meaning of. A strangeness that was becoming eerie, as if it hid something in its lack of life. She had pictured a marsh as filled with life. Birds of all kinds from ducks to other water fowl. And here there was nothing but the grass, the moonlight, and the wind. But of course that would be changed in the brightness of sunlight and daylight, when the birds would rise from wherever they were, and especially when she became accustomed to the area, birds or no birds.

Over to her left she noticed a spot of fog and was not surprised. The moisture in the marshes would undoubtedly create quite a bit of fog at times. The only odd thing about this tonight was the size of the fog pocket. It was no larger than a large automobile, a lone, heavy spot of fog amid a land in which she could see for miles ahead.

She began to watch the fog more closely and automatically reached over and locked her door. Fog or low-lying cloud? She had driven through clouds in mountains, and from a distance they looked very much like the thing in the marsh, except clouds usually were larger. She gripped the steering wheel tighter in her gloved hands and tried to concentrate on the road, straining her eyes toward the horizon ahead in search of the bulk of the house that surely, hopefully, was not too far away.

The real estate man had assured her by phone that he would have the house ready and heat turned on, and would leave the front door unlocked with the key lying on a table just inside the door. When she had asked him about prowlers and so on he laughed and said, "Out there? Don't worry, Miss Gilbert. We're a sparsely settled area, you know, and the only people you'll ever see out that way are a few stray hunters and local fishermen, and only in the daytime. Uh... if you do arrive in Archer near evening, though, I would prefer that you spend the night in a motel and then I can show you the way out the next day."

She answered, "If I don't have to worry about prowlers, and if the house is that easy to find, I see no reason to—"

The conversation left her thoughts abruptly as something else occurred to her. She had spoken with two people from this community and both of them had seemed concerned about her driving out to her house at night.

Any concern on their part was probably only her imagination, she decided, and turned up the heater. The car seemed to be getting cold.

And very quiet and lonely. So quiet that she could hear the sound of the wind in the grasses above the hum of the car. She reached for the radio... and stopped, her hand hanging motionless as her attention was drawn to the white spot of fog. It had moved.

Was moving.

She stared at it, reluctant to draw her eyes away, watching it come toward the road and gradually change form, condensing into a thick compact whiteness hardly larger than a spread sheet. She couldn't believe what she was seeing. It was coming straight toward the road, straight toward her car, as if it were alive and pursuing her.

She tightly grasped the steering wheel with both hands and pressed hard on the accelerator. The car shot forward on the narrow dirt road, gaining speed rapidly, forcing her to concentrate the best she could on keeping it between the tall weaving grass where the ground was solid. One slip and she would be in the grass, and probably be bogged down until help came.

Until help came? Who would travel this road but she tonight? Or ever? No one, probably, but a few fishermen and the people who would eventually live at the lodge that was not yet a lodge. Her reluctant employee, Donna, and the two neighbor friends, Esther and Wanda, who were coming down South to help with the work as the cook and the housekeeper. For one brief moment she allowed herself to regret that she had not waited for the week that would bring Esther and Wanda, at least, if not Donna too. And then she glanced into the rearview mirror and saw the reflection of the white thing at the back of her car. It was so close that the entire back window was filled with the white of its body.

Panic nearly caused her to jerk the car off the road. She got it safely back and shoved the accelerator to the floor. Then the headlights picked up the narrow, wooden structure of a bridge ahead, a narrow, narrow bridge that didn't look as if it would be wide enough for her car.

She made herself let up on the gas a bit to be sure that she was capable of crossing the bridge safely. No one had said anything to her about a bridge!

The boards rattled and shook beneath her car and she saw in stark terror that a long section of the railing on the right side was gone. She was forced to slow the car even more, almost afraid to look into the moon-reflecting water beneath the bridge. So close, so very close. And how deep? Surely not very deep, not here where no river, not even a creek, had been mentioned to her.

Another glance into the rear-view mirror showed nothing, no fog, no white moving object, and she nearly stopped the car as she turned her head to look for it. For a moment it seemed to have disappeared again into the dampness of the marsh, and relief made her weak. She turned back to conquer the crossing of the bridge and saw that the other end of it was obscured, bathed in the whiteness of the <u>thing</u> that was coming straight for the front of her car.

It surrounded the car suddenly, closing out all but the darkness of its interior. She threw her arms up to cover her face and let out her fear and torment in a long, unheard scream.

Her last sense of consciousness was the sound of the boards splitting as her car lurched to the right and tipped sideways. Because her seatbelt was secured across her thighs she didn't fall, even as the car went slowly down on its side into the water beneath the bridge.

CHAPTER 3

For a while she couldn't remember. She was nothing. A part of nature, nothing more. She felt the dampness of the ground beneath her, the enclosure of dried winter grass against her body, and saw above the pale coldness of the winter sky and brightness of daylight beyond the swirling mists that rose from the water. It hurt her eyes and she closed them. A voice came through to her, causing her to jump with the unexpected.

"Are you all right?"

She opened her eyes again and looked up into the face of the man who was leaning over her. All at once she remembered. The moving... *fog*? And then her car sliding off the bridge into the black, moon-shimmering water. She sat up, twisting her body, drawing her legs beneath her. Her glance quickly took in the flat land, the grass moving with the wind that howled and sang down from the north, the bridge with the broken railing, the dirt road leading to and away from it, and on the other side the three cars parked in a row on the road safely off the bridge.

"She was sure lucky to get out of that alive," one of the men said.

She noticed that a small group of men, some white, some black, stood nearby looking helpless, but her attention passed them quickly to settle on the one tire and part of one front fender that rose above the water under the bridge,

She got to her feet, with someone reaching out to help her, and put her fingers to her lips as she stared at all that was showing of her submerged car.

"Sure lucky," one of the men said again, as if he couldn't believe what he saw.

"I'll say," another agreed in the same awed tone. "You want someone to take you to a doctor?"

After a moment she found her own voice. "Is it ruined?" All she could think of now was how on earth would she be able to run a lodge if her car was ruined. Her money was budgeted too tightly to afford a new one.

"Well, I don't know," someone answered. "We've got a wrecker coming to pull it out and look it over. It'll need some work done on it for sure, but the garage'll let you have one to use in its place until it's fixed. If it can be fixed."

The cold wind began to feel as if it were freezing her wet clothing to her body in sheets of ice and her teeth started chattering.

"Here," said the man who first had spoken to her, a tall, thin man of perhaps sixty with a fatherly voice. He took her arm. "We'd better get you out of this cold. You'd better come back to town and see a doctor."

"No," she said, hearing the determination in her voice yet not quite sure why it was there. "I bought the Murphy place, and I'm—I was—on my way there. The heat is on there in the house and I'll be all right. Is it far?"

"Wal, no ... but..."

She looked around at the men and saw that all six of them were staring at her as if they had never seen anything like her before. She was on the verge of demanding why they were looking at her like that when the drone of a truck on the road drew away their attention one by one.

"It's the wrecker," the quiet-spoken man said. He was still holding her arm. "Come on over here to my car. It'll be warmer there. I'll drive you on over to your house if you're sure that's what you want."

"That's what I want," she said, "if it's no trouble to you. And provided someone will bring a car to me from the garage."

"Wal, we'll have to wait and see about that. The men in that wrecker own the only garage in town."

She waded beside the man through the tall grass toward the bridge. The ground on which the grass grew was not as soft as she had expected, but then she decided that that was because it was frozen solid. The ground of the road was hard and firm too, a silent contrast to the old boards of the bridge.

"I didn't know there was a stream of water here," she said as they crossed the hundred yards or so of grayed boards.

"They's streams of water around everywhere in this part of the country, but most of it's only about knee deep. This under the bridge is part of a lake and that's why it's as deep as it is. Good duck-hunting ground, most of it. The ducks find the marshes a good breeding place."

When they reached the end of the bridge the wrecker had been backed down to the water's edge and one of the men was approaching them, staring at her.

"You in that car?" he said, jerking his head toward the one wheel and bit of fender.

"I was, yes," she answered, seeing him shake his head, dumbfounded.

He kept shaking it as he asked, "How in the world did you get out?"

"I—" She tried to remember what had happened, but her memory of the night stopped when the car slid sideways into the water. "I don't know. I don't remember."

The garage man turned away, still shaking his head, and began motioning to the driver in the truck. A bit farther back, a bit farther, his waving hand signaled. Whoa! Over a bit to the east. Now back again, slow, man, slow... Now, lower...

She watched, fascinated, from the interior of the soft-spoken man's car as her own car was slowly eased up out of the water, drawn up to stand almost on its hood, and then slowly pulled up and onto the road.

All the men had gathered to stand around it, staring at something she couldn't see. Her curiosity overcame her coldness and she got out of the warm, idling car and ran back to see what it was.

They said nothing as she came up, and she looked first for signs of damage, but there was not even a noticeable new dent. Mud clung thickly to one side, but it was the other, the driver's side, which held them staring.

For a moment she couldn't place their interest, then she saw that all four windows of the car were still tightly rolled up and the lock button on the driver's door was still pushed down.

"How in the hell," said the man who had directed the movements of the wrecker, "did you get out of that thing?"

But she could only stare at it dumbly, suddenly afraid to get close to it, as if to do so would reveal that her body was still in there, somewhere, with the boxes, the luggage, and the clothing that had fallen from their hangers.

As if he felt the same dread, overthrown by the pull of curiosity, a man stepped forward and looked into the car.

He spoke as though talking about someone who had disappeared into nothing, "Her purse is still in there. And that's all, besides her clothes and things. There may be more luggage in the trunk."

Sheba nodded her head but no one seemed to notice. They too were gathering close to the car to look through glass that was fast icing over.

"This is the only way she could have gotten out," one exclaimed, pointing to the lock button on the back door.

"She must of got back to the rear seat and opened this door somehow, and then it fell shut again."

"Seems dang nigh impossible to me."

"Well, there she stands, living proof. Lucky, too. I can say this for you, young lady," he looked at her sharply, "you're the only one that ever got out of that place alive. The only one."

"You mean there have been others who drove off that bridge?" She looked at the broken railing and knew the answer before it was given.

"Lordy yes. Been four or five drowned there, hasn't there, George?"

George was the man who had taken upon himself the care of her, in whose car she had been sitting.

"Yep," he answered. "Three of them in one night. One car." He took her arm again and started guiding her toward his car. "I'm taking her home. You fellers will bring her a car out that she can use while hers is getting fixed?"

"Where does she live?"

"The Bleeker place. Or Murphy, I reckon it's called now."

"Oh. So she's the one bought the Bleeker place. Yeah, we'll bring one out. Have it here before nightfall."

She was ushered to the car then, before she could even say thank you, but the wind had turned even stronger and so freezing cold that she was glad to get out of it. She huddled in the car, in her wet clothes, and listened to her own teeth click and chatter as if she were listening to strange radio signals from outer space.

And she had thought it would be warm down here. The temperature might be a lot higher, but the humidity made it cold as a cold hell.

Questions urgently began forming in her mind, but she waited, watching ahead for the house that she hoped to make into a permanent, self-supporting home.

"How did it happen you run off the bridge?" her benefactor, George, asked calmly, as if it were of no special importance.

"There was a fog. I couldn't see—" she hushed suddenly, reluctant to say any more. She had to think it out first, get it straight in her mind before she said any more than that, because it hadn't seemed that much like a fog. Of course she wasn't used to this area ... but still, she had to think it out when she was warm and comfortable and alone.

"Fog," he said, still calmly, weaving his car slowly along between the tall grasses that waved in the wind like fields of spotted wheat through which pools of water reflected a brightening sky. Far off a lone bird rose to flap its way toward the blue. "Yeah, fog. There's a lot of that over the marsh sometimes, especially this time of year, getting in close to spring."

She looked around. "Spring! But it's only January. I don't see any signs of spring." Spring to her meant leaves growing again on the trees. Of course here the only trees she saw were a thin string of pine far away that looked as if it had been half drowned a few times. If the lower branches had needles she couldn't see them from the distance.

"But there's a change coming before long—another six weeks—that's why it gets foggy sometimes. Of course it's always foggier here than anywhere else." He changed the subject abruptly. "You're a mite late for wild-game hunting season, though. It's closed now and won't open again until next fall, early winter."

She didn't want to talk about that, either. She would wait until she reached the privacy of her room to consider her own reluctance to inquire about a hunting lodge going along all year with no let-up. Donna wouldn't be surprised, of course. Hunting seasons didn't, even now, seem as important as simply owning the house.

Yes, owning the house. That was what she wanted the moment she had seen the photo in the thick book of properties for sale in all parts of the country. The house had drawn her like the whisper of a lover.

"I'll think of something," she said with a determination that was fast warming up.

"There it is," he said, pointing one arm past her nose. "You can see it from the bridge, clear, then the road dips a bit and the grass gets taller too."

She turned, wiped steam off the window glass, and saw a large house that looked just as Donna had said, as if it could be a pile of gray stone. It sat high on a round knoll above the brown grass of the surrounding marsh, just like the picture. But the picture hadn't shown the strange, unreal background, or the impact of the house at first sight. But she hardly had time to consider the bleakness of it when the man was asking for her attention again.

"See this road here," he pointed to a thin trail running off left into the weeds as he turned the car sharply right toward the house. "It goes over to that lake. It's the arm of the lake that's under the bridge."

She looked for a lake and saw nothing but the continued spots of water among grass, and the farther on toward the trees it went the thicker became the grass. Or so, at least, it seemed.

"Wal, you cain't see it from here," he said in his slow speech which was not really southern. Just somewhere in between. "And it ain't much of a lake. But it's deep enough. I got me a little paddle boat moored out there to a stake and I go out and do a little fishing once in a while. Don't catch much, but that ain't all a fisherman goes fishing for. That's what I mostly been doing since I retired a couple of years ago. And that's where I was going this morning when I spotted that car of yours with two wheels stuck up out of the water. I got out and started looking around and finally found you. I can tell you I sho was nervous there for a while. I had no idea but that another family of folks had gone under for good. I sho was glad to see Rally come along. He had thought to join me fishin' but he's the one went back to town for help. I reckon it was too much for him. He stayed in town and didn't show up again."

"Another family?" She fixed her gaze firmly on the sunken, whiskered side of the face beside hers. His long nose pointed down the road.

"The whole Murphy family. Almost, that is. The boy wasn't along with them, he was off at school or somewheres. Working maybe. He was quite a bit older than the girl. Never saw him myself."

"Now wait," she said, and rubbed her temple with her cold fingers. "I must be a little groggy, or else I can't understand what you're saying. The Murphys—the people I bought this place from—drove off that bridge too?"

He shook his head. "Not them that went off the bridge, you didn't. They died in the car, in the water. Mr. Murphy, his wife, and his only daughter. The man you bought the place from was their son, Cliff Murphy. He's the one who wasn't living here."

"Oh."

But it still wasn't clear to her and she felt tired suddenly, and confused. She wanted to know more, but didn't feel like asking.

George, though, didn't need prodding.

"I don't think the young Murphy, Cliff, that is, ever did live out here. He just run out for a visit now and then to see his folks. I don't even know where he lives."

"New Orleans," she said automatically.

"Oh yeah? New Orleans, huh?"

She noted the difference between his pronunciation and hers, but didn't ask, and wouldn't have had the chance had she wanted to.

"New Orleans," he repeated. "Yeah, that sounds familiar all right. I reckon I'd heard that and forgot. The Murphys, they didn't buy the place until last summer. Their son was about ten years older than their daughter. I never saw him but I heard he was a mighty nice-looking man; but then all the Murphys were a bunch of good-looking folks."

The pile of gray stone was beginning to look more like a house, but the pictures she had seen had done it more than the usual justice and brought out aspects of attractiveness that weren't visible yet. So far it simply looked like a large, two-story house with an attic high enough for a third story. It had a jutting front and two side wings and looked almost like a heavy, ugly bird that had tried for an eternity to fly and could not.

"Not very pretty, is it?" she stated glumly, wondering why she had felt so drawn to it when now it looked flat out-and-out ugly.

"It's warm in the winter and cool in the summer, they say," he answered. "I wouldn't know. I never been in it." He drove the car up the low rise of land and around a graveled driveway that curved up to the front door. "Want me to come in and see if everything is all right?"

"Thank you, no, you've done enough for me now. I'll never be able to repay you."

"Pshaw. I'm glad I found you before it was too late. You sure you're feeling all right?"

"Yes, I'm fine." She opened the car door to a sweep of cold wind. She could hear it whining and moaning somewhere in the stones of the house and around the corners. "Thank you, Mr.—uh—George. I hope you catch plenty of fish."

"I probably won't, but I'll try. I'll check up on you again before I go home."

"You don't need to bother." Her teeth were chattering again, so she drew back and prepared to run into her house. "Goodbye."

He nodded. She closed the door and hurried, her face down in the soggy collar of her coat.

When she faced the front door, with the sound of his car moving away, she faced one dreadful moment of fear that the real estate agent had forgotten and locked it. She would be left in the awful cold, down here in the upper South where it was supposed to be warmer than this— or so she had assumed—with no choice but to take out after George in an attempt to catch him.

She took her fist out of her water-soaked pocket and unfolded it long enough to grasp the knob and turn.

The door opened smoothly, silently, easily; as if it had been waiting to be opened.

She stepped cautiously but eagerly and with bursting curiosity over the threshold into a hall that was long and wide and fairly warm. She closed the door and leaned against it, looking around.

The house was almost elegant in a shabby, old way. To her left three large archways separated the hall from the living room. The right side of the hall was closed off by a wall into which several doors were spaced, all closed. Ahead, and making a sharp turn up to the right, was a long stairway. At the top of the stairway a banister, almost as sturdy as the one on the stairs, edged a hallway that ran both right and left out of sight into that which apparently was the right and left wing of the house.

That part of the house was gloomy dark, though, and just looking at it increased her sense of coldness.

The thing that most attracted her at the moment was the warmth that radiated from the living room on her left. She went toward it, drawn by the thin light let in between half-opened draperies on tall, narrow windows. She didn't expect to see a fireplace, the agent had not mentioned one. However, he had said there was a very quaint, old potbelly stove. She found it, finally, sitting back in one corner like a fat black spider on a web of solid brick.

"Ah," she said aloud into the silence of the room. "You beautiful thing, you."

Warmth was still there, and a basket of wood and a bucket of coal.

While looking it over from a distance of about four feet she removed her wet coat and shoes and dropped them on the warm brick on which the stove sat. Then she took off her slacks and blouse and spread them carefully. Her pantyhose, panties, and bra would simply have to dry on her.

The stove, she saw on careful, cautious examination, had what looked to be a door with a handle. From its back ran a black pipe up into a brick chimney. The top of the stove was flat enough to set a pot of coffee on. And right in the front, spaced similar to a pair of eyes, were two holes. *Why* the holes? she questioned wordlessly.

Anyway, the whole fat, black, comfortably warm affair squatted on four legs that were bent slightly as though the load it held were too heavy. She liked it.

But she wondered, what were the holes for?

She edged close, closer, to look into the holes, and just as she got her eyes positioned the stove puffed and her face was filled with smoke, soot, and surprise. She jumped back, looking at it as if the thing were alive and unappreciative of having a stranger peep into its innards.

She wiped one hand across her face and then looked at her black palm. But then she began to laugh at her feelings of having been taken by a hollow piece of something. She had read about stoves, and remembered that there was a reason for it to puff out the holes instead of up the pipe. The damper, of course. It was turned crossways to hold the fire.

She turned the damper and then opened the door with gentle caution, easily, well out of the way of the holes in case it should puff again in ironic contempt of the opened damper. Nothing happened though, and within a moment she was looking into the small, black, soot-coated cavern of the stove. At the bottom a few coals still glowed with heat. She added more coals, then closed the door and tried to brush the black from her hand, but it seemed to be there for good. Or at least until she found a bathroom.

The stove, she reasoned, could not possibly be the only source of heat, and on looking around the large, L-shaped living room she found two lukewarm registers. Their presence told her that there was a furnace in the basement.

She went back to the stove, though, and the growing warmth of it, and huddled into one of the half-dozen chairs that had been placed in a cozy semi-circle around the brick hearth. Here would be a good place for the duck hunters to gather in the evenings and talk over their day, she thought languidly, with warm cider or coffee or cocktails or whatever hunters drank.

The thoughts of the way it would be someday, not too long off, when Donna and Wanda and Esther came, and then the guests, put her into a mellow mood. Donna had two weeks' notice to give before leaving her job, and the other two would arrive next week. That gave her only one week to get things in order. But to get things in order she had to have her clothes, and her car... and that reminded her of the fog last night.

Strange. A fog that changed shape, condensed, and moved to follow a car in the moonlight of a cold winter night? To then sweep suddenly around to cover the windshield so that the driver was terrified, blind and helpless?

Was that what had happened to the Murphy family, too?

The cold was returning to her, and she became acutely aware of the faraway sound of wind crying in many pitches, high and low, like several wild things screaming and dying only to rise to scream again. And die again. The stove popped and snapped, too, and made little stirring noises with the burning of its fuel.

Suddenly an answer to one of her problems came to her. During the slack season, which evidently would be spring, summer, *and* winter, she could probably draw guests by advertising in city newspapers as an authentic haunted house.

She sat up in her chair, eagerness making her loathe to waste any more time. Why not! People, some at least, adored the idea of haunted houses; and after all, no one could say she was wrong.

She reached for her blouse, found it was only half dry, and put it on anyway. The long sleeves felt warm, even though the cuffs were still very damp.

Telephone ... but there was no telephone. They would have to have one installed as soon as—

She paused, remembering the marsh grass, the long, narrow, winding road, the bridge over the arm of water that evidently ran from the lake or into it, and nowhere could she remember seeing a line of poles that would transport either electricity or telephone. If that were so, it would cost a fortune to bring in either one. She wouldn't be able to afford it at all.

She ran to a window in the front of the house and pushed the draperies farther aside, her gaze flashing over the flat grassland beyond. The road, yes, disappearing into the grass, and far off to her right a tiny row boat with its one occupant. No telephone or electricity lines anywhere.

The car came into sight then, easing along through the grass, only the upper part of it visible. She fervently hoped that it was coming to the house, and watched until it passed the trail that went over toward George's car parked, nearly invisible, among the weeds at the lake's edge.

She remembered then that she was wearing only her blouse and beneath it her legs might give her visitor a jolt of surprise if he didn't know that her slacks lay drying on the brick beneath the stove.

She ran back to put them on, damp or no, and then went to the front door.

The man who came in was about fifty years old and dressed in a brown suit. He looked her over swiftly.

"I came as soon as I heard," he said. "I'm Dan Fielding, the real estate man who handled this sale. I sure am sorry about what happened. I was hoping you'd stay in town last night and check with me before you came out."

That wasn't exactly what he had told her, but she was in a hurry to get back to the stove. "When you said the door would be unlocked I preferred to come on out. I'm really afraid of only one thing—burglars. I had no idea I would be crossing a bridge and then would drive off it, or you can be damned sure I would have stayed in town. Do you mind coming over to the stove? I'm freezing—every time I get away from it. You didn't happen to bring any of my clothes, did you?"

"No, but I did turn them over to the laundry, and I'll bring them out tomorrow, or you'll probably want to go in yourself by then and pick them up. They'll have an extra car out here for you before I leave while they get yours dried out and in shape. But I'll tell you, there's dry clothes upstairs in two of the bedroom closets. You see, the Murphy women didn't take all their clothes. I guess they were coming back for them, and then had that accident. And the heir just said leave them in the house, so I did. But you might as well use them until you get your own."

She noted the fact of the clothes mentally, but as less important than a few other things she had on her mind. "There's a little matter of a telephone," she said, and led the way back to her chair, where she curled up, wet pants and all. "Is it possible to get one installed? I didn't see any poles or anything."

He stared at her, then dropped his eyes away.

"Well, you know," he said easily, on a clear trail to skirting the subject, "it's things like that that bring down the price of a place and make it a bargain. Also, since you want it for a lodge, it could be an attraction. People coming back out here to get away from the roar and pace of work and city life will probably appreciate the silence of no ringing telephones and—"

She stopped him with a blunt, "So there is no available telephone. What do I do if I want to order supplies or something?"

"You have a car. Just watch the road and be careful. You can't buy supplies around here at night anyway, so you wouldn't have need to travel the road after dark, and you could advise your guests that if they do travel the road to be careful of that bridge."

"I had thought perhaps we could get those things later—telephone and electricity, I mean."

He shrugged. "Like I said about bargains... You see, you're surrounded by marsh here, and there was just no call for electricity or telephone to be brought to this house."

"I see. It will take getting used to—not having a switch to flick."

"There's lamps. All you need to light the house." He pointed at various shaded lamps around the room. "And I saw to it that there's kerosene in the cellar to fill them, and I saw to it that they're all full. What with the energy crisis, you may be glad you have such a simple way of heating and lighting."

"But no power for television, not even for a stereo. Where does the music come from?" In her dreams she had seen herself dancing with good-looking guests. In her impatience to buy the house before someone else did, she'd forgotten that it took electricity to run most modern pleasures such as stereos, and especially television.

He just looked at her and blinked.

"Of course," she added, "it might be fun not to have those things for a change." Donna wouldn't like it at first, but she'd get used to it One thing about it—more dark, more privacy.

He nodded and sighed as if he'd been afraid she'd decided not to buy. "Well, I think for a lodge it would be perfect. People who come to hunt don't care for anything but comfort when they come in because duck season is in the early winter, you know, and it gets mighty cold and damp out there. This icy spell is out of the ordinary, but it still gets cold. But I'll be glad to take you back to town and return the money to you, even though I'd feel sure you'd missed a great bargain. There's a lot of house here for that money, a lot of land too, to say nothing of all the furniture. Even the dishes, pots, and pans go with the house."

He went slowly about the room, from the warmth-creating old stove to the chairs, the tables, the lamps; he gently touched books that were spaced attractively in a wall bookcase.

"It's comfortable here. It's only been a couple of months since the Murphys left. You're the first potential buyer." He snapped to and faced her. "But we're wasting time here. Is your coat dry?" He reached for it and withdrew his hand quickly. "No, it's not. Well, my car should still be warm so you won't freeze on the way back to town. Are you ready to go? I'll get you a place to stay until your car is ready and you'll be free to leave then, anytime."

The indecision had gone. She stood near the stove and felt drawn to it as if it were an old friend. In astonishment she realized that she didn't want to leave. Not today, not tomorrow, not ever.

She had come home.

"No," she said. "It is a bargain anyway, even if a telephone and electricity won't be available. I'll take it. The rest of my money will be available before long and I'll pay the rest then." She glanced up to see that he was looking at her with a strange, puzzled grimace and she laughed. "Of course you've heard about women having the right to change their minds in a hurry." Slowly he answered, "I was just thinking how lucky you were."

"Lucky?"

"To get out of that car alive."

It was something she didn't want to try to think about. As if the terror of the moment might come back again. As if even the memory of the time it required to escape the car might return and let her know a horror she didn't want to know. She sat down in her chair again, curled her legs and placed one palm on an ankle.

"Nobody else ever did," he was saying. "That railing needs to be fixed before you start bringing guests in so that bridge will be safer."

"Yes, I agree with that. Do you know someone who will do it? Does the bridge belong to the county or to this land, this property?"

"Unfortunately it belongs to this property, so you would have to pay for it yourself. But I do know a man who will take care of it for you. I suppose you just want the same kind of railing that was there. A new one would be stronger of course, and if anyone did drive in at night at least they could see the edge of the bridge."

"Yes," she agreed again. Something was building in the back of her mind and she wanted him to leave so that she could think. "If you will do that for me then, Mr. Fielding, that will be enough. I appreciate your coming out to check on me, but I think I can manage all right from now on."

"I said I'd wait until a car is brought," he told her mildly as he wandered toward one of the archways. "If you feel up to it I'll show you around the house."

She sighed softly to herself and got up to follow him, thinking of warm robes, at least, somewhere upstairs in a bedroom.

The house did not seem unfamiliar to her, oddly, and again, as they walked slowly from dim corridor to dim corridor and room to room, she felt safe, secure, at home. Even the clothes in the closet of the room upstairs that had belonged to the girl seemed to fit into her wardrobe. She found among the robes one that was thick and fuzzy and very warm. She hugged it around her and finally heard the words behind the slow, southern drone of Mr. Fielding's voice.

"I don't know what the young Murphy will want to do with these. I'd suggest that you pack them away when your own things get here and then just have someone put them in the attic. Murphy said he'd be coming around in a month or two. He was here after the accident, of course, but I don't think he even came to the house. They were a close family. I reckon it would have been too hard on him to come around the house at that time. I expect he'll be here when he feels up to it. You want me to show you the attic?"

He seemed reluctant, and she could dredge up no interest in it.

"Is it important?" she asked.

"No. There's the door on the left at the end of the service hall. It's just a place for junk, that's all. And there's probably quite a lot of it up there. You might want to get a cleaning man on to it come warmer weather and get rid of the junk."

"Even the junk was in on that bargain price, eh," she said, smiling, comfortable, no longer caring much that Mr. Fielding was there.

He chuckled a tiny bit. "Yeah. Everything but the clothes. Even the dishes in the cupboards, as I told you. You're all set up for housekeeping."

Through the faint cry of the southbound wind came a fainter sound of something bumping, or slamming. She stopped, alerted, to listen; but the man went on talking calmly.

"That'll be the man with the car. The man from the garage. I reckon we'd better go down now. Feel free to borrow a coat and go on into town for whatever supplies you need, and keep the car until they bring back yours. If there's nothing more you need with me I'll go on and take him back to town. I don't expect he'll want to come in. I'll see he just leaves the keys in the car."

She held out her hand. "It has been a pleasure meeting you, Mr. Fielding, and I apologize for yelling about the electricity and telephone. It may cause a bit of inconvenience, but we can get around it I'm sure."

"You don't need to apologize. Besides, if that was what you call yelling I wish you'd show my wife how it's done. Ha ha. I'm just sorry about the misunderstanding. I thought you understood they're not available here except at your own expense. And it would take miles of poles and lines."

"I understand. It doesn't matter. I want the house no matter what."

She followed him into the hallway and watched him go down the stairs and out the front door, then she turned back to the bedroom she liked.

A bit of warm air came from the register. Not enough to keep her comfortable the way she enjoyed dressing, but enough to satisfy the narrow limits of nature.

The thought of going to town, though, was not a pleasant one, and there really was no reason why she should have to go. Even the pantry had been left with canned goods. There was no milk or bread or anything perishable, of course, but she could get along on hot soup.

Quite happily she went into the closest bathroom down the hall and washed the rest of the black soot from her face. Mr. Fielding had obviously been too polite to mention that she looked a bit odd with the dirty face of a child who's been playing in a coal bin. She looked at her reflection and laughed, wondering what he had thought. Perhaps he had attributed her appearance to the brown water she had escaped from. Alive. One of many. Many who hadn't escaped alive.

She stopped, staring at a reflection she hardly saw. O-How many? She wished she had asked.

She turned away from the mirror and the thought and went to a desk in the corner, where she found a scratch pad and a pen. Then she went back downstairs and after putting a few more chunks of coal on the fire she sat down in the chair, put her feet forward this time on a footstool, and wrapped the fuzzy robe around her legs. Snugly, warmly. And then the idea that had been waiting for the silence of aloneness sprang fully to mind.

A haunted house.

If that didn't draw enough guests to keep the lodge going out of hunting season, what would? Swiftly she wrote the first draft of an advertisement.

Spend your vacation in an authentic haunted house. In isolation from society where there is not even a telephone to disturb the workings of the supernatural. Of course you will be protected, hopefully, by the few people who dare live in this house only for your convenience and comfort, but do not—at all costs do not — arrive at night!

Sheba Gilbert put her head against the high back of her wing chair and laughed aloud, and the sound passed beyond the arches and the pillars and was picked up and returned to her again, then again, in faraway echoes.

CHAPTER 4

The blankets and sheets that had been left in the house had a musty, unused smell, but they were otherwise very clean and she brought enough from the nearest linen closet to make her bed. The real estate man had certainly been right, she had to admit to herself as she spread and smoothed blankets and made the double bed by the light of a kerosene lamp, which wasn't as bad as she had thought it would be. The place was a bargain, furnished as it was right down to its beds. Of course, that was because the Murphy <u>family</u>, she now realized, had all died in the water under the bridge one night. They must not have been planning on moving away, they had simply left in a hurry one night for some reason. The son had called? Had had an accident, perhaps? But how could he call when there was no telephone?

Well, anyway, there was nothing to be gained from worrying about other people's problems. She left that sort of thing up to her room-mate and friend of six months, Donna Walker, now employee—practically, anyway—of a hunting lodge that would have to draw its guests in a somewhat unorthodox manner.

Donna, her exact opposite.

Sheba sat down on the side of her bed and thought of Donna. They had worked for the same business firm, and had seen each other often. And at first Sheba hadn't really liked Donna. She was too queenly, too self-contained. She looked as if she wouldn't be caught dead in a singles' bar or with a pick-up. She looked as if she didn't have a wild bone in her long and perfect body. After the first look at her, in which Sheba had noted her beauty and her poised and graceful and very proper attitude, she had felt that she had at last met with some competition. But she hadn't. The men still liked her best— smaller, curvier, and not in the least poised or graceful or reluctant to take on any man who appealed to her. Donna hadn't been interested enough to even be envious. Neil was her constant escort. But Donna wasn't interested in him either. She wondered about Donna— was she frigid or something? She didn't know. Donna never talked much about sex.

Gradually, with lunches now and then and their contact at work, a friendship had grown. And finally they decided to share an apartment because Sheba wanted more money to spend than she could scrape out of her salary alone while covering her total rent, and it turned out that Donna wasn't exactly adverse to a little extra money herself.

One thing about it—they sure didn't step on each other's toes.

But it had taken some talking to get Donna interested in leaving a secure job for this lodge business. And talk Sheba did, because she had in the back of her mind a houseful of men practically all to herself— certainly enough to play around with. It would be like having a vacation all year long. So finally Donna had sat down with a notebook and pen and figured out possible profits; then she gave in to Sheba and agreed to become at least an employee if not a partner.

But she had insisted on giving her boss two weeks' notice. How silly, Sheba thought. What bull. Girls are always around to replace other girls. But if that was what Donna wanted, then let her go ahead and drudge along for two more weeks while her less conscientious buddy slept late for a change.

Sheba stretched out between warm blankets and relaxed. Nine o'clock, ten o'clock, who cared when she got up? There wouldn't be anyone to know.

But when she did wake it was many hours from nine o'clock. The night was still, so still that only the whine of a soft wind came to her suddenly alert mind. She sat up in bed, listening, looking at the moonlight that fell through her bedroom window so brightly that her entire room was light. Had some soft sound not made by the wind awakened her? She was afraid of burglars, of men coming into the house in the dead of night to sneak, steal, or kill. *That* kind of man she didn't want around. She wondered if she had forgotten to lock the door.

But she distinctly remembered locking it before coming up the stairs with her kerosene lamp in hand. There were other outside doors, though, and she hadn't even checked them. She had simply assumed that they had *not* been unlocked. And if someone wanted to enter the house, might there not be other means of access? Such as a basement window?

Quietly she got out of bed and tiptoed across her room to the door. She felt beside the knob, found the button lock, pushed it, then put her ear against the door and listened carefully. After a moment she decided the silence itself had awakened her; or a dream she couldn't remember. She went back to bed, but instead of getting in she changed her mind and went around it to look out the window.

Tonight, as last night, the moon was bright and unveiled by even a trace of cloud. The landscape was a soft, feather-topped, golden sea of grass that moved gently with the wind. Far away a black line of trees that sent spiked tops toward the moon and stars drew an end to the golden sea like the blunt sweep of a child's pencil.

Below, moving nearer as if blown by the wind, was a small patch of diaphanous fog.

She stared at it as if she couldn't move her eyes and all the warmth that had been in her body swiftly drained away. The coldness moved over her wave after wave, as if she were sinking beneath the surface of frigid, paralyzing water. In breathless, silent terror she watched the fog that was not a fog, but something beyond her comprehension.

It stopped, as if it saw her looking down, and as she watched the milky, misty substance slowly condensed again, as it had last night when it swiftly followed her car, and now, again, became thick and impenetrable and so nearly the shape and size of a large, tall man that she felt choked with the realization of it. She took one step backward, and abruptly it moved, coming straight for the house.

A sound of terror broke from her and she jerked closed the draperies at the window, closing out the light of the full moon. Then, sobbing under her breath, whimpering like a trapped animal, she backed into the darkness of the nearest corner and scrunched down, cold and shivering in her thin nightgown, staring into the darkness of her room.

After a while she could see the outline of the door and she stared at it, her ears sharply attuned for any sound of movement in the hall. But how would it sound when it moved? Would there be any sound at all?

What did it want with her now that it had let her live?

The tears finally came, wetting her cheeks in helplessness. She put her face down on her knees and sat there, cold, stiff, terrified. And finally the room was light again and morning had come.

She rose from her long-held position as if she couldn't believe she had lived through the night.

Slowly she went about the room seeing that nothing was changed after all, and she drew open the draperies to see that the landscape was even more golden in the sunshine, grasses still waving in the stronger wind of daytime, the trees pointing yet toward a sky that was a clear, deep blue. Above the marshes a few birds flew. But she looked at them without interest.

And then she opened her door and looked into the hallway. There too she expected a change of some kind, a sign at least of her night of terror, but there was none. The air in the house was colder than she liked, but a register in the hall had a bit of warm air oozing out.

She decided to get out of the house as quickly as possible, get to town, make her phone calls, and not spend another night alone. Last night she had laughed at her ad of a haunted house, but today she wasn't laughing.

She was outside and on her way to her car when the pickup truck came inching its way over the bridge and toward the house. She waited.

The man who got out was a tobacco chewer. He spat neatly out of one side of his mouth. "I hear you want a railin' put up," he said. "And I'm here to do the job. Just wanted to check with you first so you'd know what I'm doin' down there on your bridge all day. Take me all day probably."

"That's fine," she said, smiling, loving the comfort and security of another human. "I don't care if it takes you two days. Just send me your bill when you're finished. My name is Sheba Gilbert, and I guess you know the address as well as I, or better. I don't even know where I'm supposed to get the mail."

He nodded back south. "There's a mailbox down at the main road where your road here turns off."

"Way back there?" she cried.

"Tain't fur. Only about six mile."

"Six miles," she repeated, remembering the long, long ride of the night she had arrived. "Is that all? It seemed at least sixteen."

He never once smiled. His eyes wandered off toward the tree line and the bridge and squinted there as if thinking out the best method to make the railing. "Always seems farther the first time you drive a road. After you get used to it it won't seem no ways at all. In fact, it's not a bad walk for a young woman like you, or an old guy like me for that matter. Good for a body to walk six mile comin' and goin' now and then. Well, just came by to let you know what I'm doing hammerin' on your bridge. That's needed fixin' a long time now."

"What happened to it in the first place?" she asked, mainly to keep him with her for a few more minutes.

"Well, the owner—the first owner—this is really the old Andrew Bleeker place, you know. The Murphys just bought it a year or less ago. Andrew Bleeker was the son of another Andrew Bleeker, who settled and built this house here on this rise. That was back in last century. But anyhow, the bridge was old to start with, and Andrew Bleeker Junior, he lived here by hisself, you know, for years. And one day about thirty or thirty-five years ago, maybe longer, he just straight out drove off the bridge. By the time we got to him he was drowned and gone and nobody ever fixed the <u>railing</u>. Should have, for sure, because everybody—and, lady, I mean *everybody* who has ever drived cross that bridge at night went off it! They just can't seem to see where they're a goin', or somethin'. Beats me all to hell they can't keep on the bridge. Pardon the language. Anyway, it sure needs a railin' all right."

"Yes."

The conversation was ended so far as she was concerned. She didn't want to hear any more about anything that reminded her of that strange apparition that started out looking like a fog and then was capable of change.

"As I said," she told him as she started walking away, "just send me the bill, please. I'll be going into town and won't be back by the time you quit work."

She drove carefully across the bridge, afraid to look at the water or the edge of the bridge that wasn't protected. Narrow, it obviously hadn't been built for cars. Probably it was the work of the first Andrew Bleeker, and was built for horse-drawn carriages and buggies.

The first thing she did when she hit town was find the post office and mail the letters containing the advertisements to major newspapers around the country. An advertisement for guests, ostensibly, a tongue-in-cheek invitation to a haunted house, directions included; and now, inwardly, a cry for company, for the presence of other humans to help her face the fear that had been uncovered during her one-night stay in the house.

Next she went to a phone booth where she placed a collect call to Donna Walker at Smith, Smith and Webb.

The well-modulated voice of Donna was not quite so well modulated as usual when she accepted the call after a brief pause of surprised silence. "Sheba! Why on earth are you calling collect? Is something wrong? Where are you?"

"Well, I'm here in Archer, and I'm calling collect because I'm in a phone booth and I don't have the change handy to pay for this and besides, I don't want to waste all day dropping in clinky little coins. And yes, something is wrong."

"What on earth is it? And why haven't you called sooner? I expected to hear from you last night."

"I was just too tired to drive back to town. Our house is down a private road that's six miles long. It's never used by anyone but sportsmen. There are no other houses out there," she babbled, her thoughts on her car, the fog, the house, the bridge. But her tongue babbled on without telling what was on her mind.

Sheba finally paused long enough for Donna to say something, had she been so inclined, but she heard only silence on the phone, a silence that seemed distinctly puzzled. "Listen, Donna, you've got to come down right away. Today."

"I *what?*"

Sheba gave in to tears again. They ran into the corners of her mouth. "Please, Donna. The house is not what I expected. There's something—" She stopped, knowing it wasn't the time yet to tell Donna, that she was afraid to be alone, and then to tell her why. Not over the phone. But she was desperate for the security of the others.

Sheba could almost see Donna's eyes widening and her eyebrows lifting slightly as they did when something came close to overwhelming her. It took a lot to make Donna react outwardly.

"I was only trying a little joke." Sheba tried to laugh. "Sorry it bombed out. Actually, it's not bad at all. In fact, I think it will be a very successful place. But I need you. And I mean today, not two weeks from now. I want you please to tell Mr. Webb that your friend and partner needs you more than he does. Also, bring Esther and Wanda with you and come today."

"Today!"

"Yes. Fly down. Come to the closest airport and I'll pick you up there. I'll pay the cost myself. You can—uh—get in touch with Mr. Fielding, the real estate man, as to the time you'll arrive, and I'll be waiting."

"Sheba, why? You said something is wrong. What is it?"

"Well... I had a wreck. I just sort of drove off a bridge."

"What?"

"I'll tell you when I see you. It wasn't serious at all, but will you please come on down?"

"Were you hurt?"

"No, but listen, I'll tell you when you get here. Now will you come on and stop arguing with me?"

"I'll try." Donna's voice had gone back to the soft, even texture of smooth velvet that was typical of her. "We probably can't get there today, but I'm sure we can be there by tomorrow. It will certainly put a hole in our budget to buy three plane tickets when we had planned on bus fare."

"Do you always have to consider the money angle, Donna? I said I'd pay for it personally." Sometimes Sheba felt so frustrated by Donna's practicality that she felt like crying, and this was one of those times. "I tell you we will make enough to pay it back and more. I have a great idea. But I can't handle it alone."

"All right, but I'll cover my own traveling expense. I guess we can take Esther's and Wanda's out of the expense money. I'll be looking forward to hearing your idea and I'll see about plane flights and let Mr. Fielding know when we will arrive. See you then?"

"Yes. Come as soon as you can, okay?"

"Okay. See you tomorrow."

Sheba hung up the phone and leaned back in the warmth of the booth that captured through its panes of glass the heat of the sun. She felt suddenly as if she could sleep. Just knowing that Donna and Esther and Wanda would be arriving took from her all the tension of the long night. But first she had other chores.

She didn't bother to go to the garage. They would let her know when her car was ready, no doubt of that. She found the laundry without trouble, the only one in town, and got her clothes, all freshly pressed, laundered, cleaned, and on hangers or in neat little bundles.

The woman behind the counter kept looking at her as if she were something hardly human, and finally she said, "They weren't in bad shape at all, considering."

"Good. I was afraid some of the things would be ruined." She paid the required cost and picked up bundles and hangers, but the woman wasn't ready to let her leave.

She adjusted her glasses to look more closely and more boldly at Sheba. "You sure had a close call, they tell me. I expect that was a terrible thing. I know it would scare me plumb to death—going off the Bleeker Bridge. I went out to see it once, in the daytime after the Murphy family was found there, but I didn't get close to it."

Sheba rested her bundles on the counter again. "The what? What did you call it?"

"Bleeker. Bleeker Bridge."

Perhaps it was the woman's voice, the inflection when she spoke the words, but it carried an ominous sound that was short, unavoidable, and definite.

The woman adjusted her glasses again, pushing them back up to sit higher on her nose. "You can't cross that bridge at night, no one can. No one ever has. It's been called the Bleeker Bridge as long as I can recollect. And that's a long time. "

"Because of the man who owned it, I suppose," Sheba said.

"Partly. Because he owned it, and because he was the first to drive off it. That was back in the thirties. Thirty-one, thirty-two. But even before that folks around here called it Bleeker's Bridge."

Sheba smiled and picked up her bundles again. Something about the woman was beginning to get on her nerves, as if in some way the woman was disparaging that which now was Sheba Gilbert's bridge. "It's not so bad. A bit narrow is all."

But the woman seemed set on explaining something whether Sheba asked or not. "They called it Bleeker's Bridge because he was one of them kind that wouldn't let a neighbor cross it if he could help it. In those days, before he was drowned there, nobody ever crossed that bridge to hunt or fish on that lake back in there."

"Maybe," Sheba said, her patience going, her smile gone, "he didn't approve of hunting. A lot of people don't."

"Him? Ha! You could hear that shotgun of his blazing anytime a bird big enough to shoot at came around. In those days hardly any birds set down on that marsh, or that lake. Still don't, I guess. They knowed better. No. The reason he wouldn't let a neighbor across was plain and simple. He wanted to be left alone. He was a hermit if ever a hermit lived. Owned an automobile all right, and came to town often enough. And was civil enough here in town, but just try and get out there and you'd liable to get your hat shot off."

Sheba suddenly decided that the woman was an out-and-out gossip, and she didn't like gossips. But she couldn't turn and walk out or she might pick up the same reputation of unfriendliness that her predecessor, Bleeker, had acquired. For him it might have worked all right. For her, owner of a lodge, it would never do.

"Well, times have changed," she told the woman with a forced smile. "The place will now be known as the Gil-Walker Lodge, open year round for guests." She had chosen the name before Donna turned down her offer of a partnership, and kept it now because she liked it.

"That's what I heard. But duck season don't last all year, you know."

Sheba shrugged. "They can fish, or just rest and enjoy the peace and quiet. However, for clarity, we have to start out by saying that Gil-Walker Lodge is actually the old Murphy place."

Suddenly a smile lighted the woman's face. "The Murphys. Now there was a fine family." The smile died as suddenly as it came. "Too bad. Too bad. Lovely people. They only lived there a few months, you know. About three, I think. Then they too died under the Bleeker Bridge. You know, it's a funny thing. I know of eight people who drove off that bridge at night, first old man Bleeker himself, then a young couple out driving around at night, then a man who had been over on the lake fishing, and the three Murphys, and now you. And you're the only one who got out."

Sheba gathered her things into a large bundle in her arms without trying to adjust them neatly to prevent wrinkling. Over her shoulder as she went out the door she said, "Yeah, so I've heard."

So it was funny, she thought, trembling with anger. Everyone was treating her as if she were an oddity of some kind just because she'd escaped the car. It seemed almost as if they hadn't wanted her to. As if in some way she had ruined one of the most fascinating aspects of the area. After all, what did it have to its credit? Two or three small towns, scattered far apart. A lot of marshland. A refuge for wild life set aside by the government. *And* Bleeker Bridge.

And she, a stranger from up North, had come down and ruined the mysterious image of the old Bleeker Bridge.

Aloud she muttered, "Well, too damned bad."

As she tossed the clothing into the back seat of the car she decided that never again would she talk of it— not if she could avoid it in any way.

She turned on the radio, loud, and drove over to the office of the real estate man. He too was easy to find in this one-street town.

"The closest airport?" he repeated her question as he leaned back in his chair. "About thirty miles, I'd say."

"I've asked my friend and business manager, Donna Walker, to call you to let you know when she is to arrive tomorrow. I hope you don't mind."

He shook his head. "Naw. Anything I can do to help. I'll be glad to drive over and pick her up for you."

"No, thanks. I can go. But I'm going to spend the night here in town in a motel and I was wondering if you would call me and let me know?"

He peeped at her from one half-closed eye. She couldn't tell if he was amused or simply curious.

"Didn't like it out there by yourself?"

"Oh sure," she said quickly. "But I have to be here to go after Donna whenever she can make the connections and since that carpenter is working on the bridge I thought I might as well stay in town while I wait. And besides, getting in touch with me out there, since there is no telephone, would be a bit awkward, wouldn't it?" *That* should take care of any amusement he might be harboring.

He opened his eyes. "Yes, I reckon it would." He leaned forward and picked up his desk phone. "Let me call the motel just down the road here and see if they have a vacancy. This time of year they surely will. Then I'll know where to call you when I hear from Miss Walker."

Within a few minutes he had reserved a room for her and written down the phone number, and she was in the borrowed, late-model car again and on her way to a room that was small, warm, and comfortable.

She turned on the television for company, locked the door, stripped, and took a long, hot relaxing bath. Then, curled in her own robe, she lay on the foot of the bed and drowsily watched soap operas as she waited for the phone call that would tell her when Donna, Esther, and Wanda would be arriving at the airport.

In the evening she dressed and went down to the cocktail lounge and spent a couple of hours dancing with a man who was passing through, but she didn't take him back to bed with her. There hadn't been much man-choice in the lounge, and he wasn't her bed-partner type even though he did a hard sell on himself. She had seen him slip his wedding ring into his pocket. Not that it mattered. He just simply wasn't her type. Any man who slipped off a wedding ring wasn't her type. If he was married—so? She didn't give a damn. If she wanted to go to bed with him she would. It was as simple as that. Men who took off wedding rings gave the impression of thinking that all women wanted to get married.

So she went to bed alone, tired, quite happy from the evening of flattery and compliments.

Sheba was waiting at the small airport the next morning at ten o'clock when the miniature jet circled in and came smoothly down on the runway. It stopped not too far from the high, woven wire fence where she had gone to wait, shivering in the wind. The first face she saw peeping down from the opened hole in the plane's side was the round, wide-mouthed face of Wanda. Sheba raised her arm and waved, but Wanda was looking at everyone but her. Behind Wanda came Esther, taller, older, a face stern in comparison to Wanda's; her eyes too were turned toward the crowd waiting for arrivals. Sheba decided that if she wanted to be seen she'd have to go back and join the crowd. Going to stand by the fence hadn't gained her a thing but cold feet and fingers. But just then the model-perfect face of Donna appeared as she moved down the steps behind Esther. She smiled as she said something to Esther, and then she raised one arm in greeting to Sheba.

The separation seemed more like four months than four days, Sheba thought as she ran back into the shelter of the tiny airport terminal to wait for them.

Wanda reached her first, wide smiles, excited brown eyes, a short, stocky, strong body with muscled arms used to hard work that now was ready with a quick hug. "You poor baby," she said. "Way off down here all by yourself."

Esther was not the type to hug anyone. She stood stiffly back, looking on, but around her mouth was a pleased little pinch of wrinkles. Donna leaned down slightly and kissed Sheba's cheek.

Sheba put off explanations for as long as possible— until they reached the car. After that nothing could be put off. Donna took one look at it and stopped, as if she weren't burdened with two heavy suitcases and a shoulder bag.

"You didn't!" she said. "You couldn't have. You wouldn't do that to us with less than a thousand dollars' expense money left in the bank."

"No, I didn't, I couldn't, and I wouldn't even if I wanted to," Sheba answered.

Wanda laughed. "Now that's what I call a conversation. But when you left Chicago didn't you have a sort of ancient whitish thing that rattled?"

Sheba opened the trunk of the new green job the garage had so graciously loaned her. "If you think it rattled there you should hear it down here on our six-mile private lane." She laughed at the expressions on the faces of the two older women.

Esther said in her solemn and quiet way, "Six miles? Isn't that pretty far out?"

"Sure," Sheba replied. Now that she was no longer alone her confidence was returning. "But that was what we wanted, wasn't it? Whoever heard of a hunting and fishing lodge that wasn't far out? And speaking of far out, this place really is. It's wild—you'll love it."

Esther said dryly, "I'm glad to hear that." Her sarcasm flowed in the same current as her humor and hardly anyone other than her younger sister was able to detect the direction of the flow.

So Wanda answered, "Sure you will, Esther. Just think, life in the country. In a big mansion yet! So what if you have to do the cooking— you had to cook in the city. Me, I'd as soon make beds and do laundry here as in town. I think I'm going to like it."

Sheba thought briefly of the problem of the laundry and decided to not mention to Wanda just yet that all laundry would have to be taken to town to a laundromat, probably, since there was no hope of electricity or natural gas to run machines. But let trouble take care of itself each in its turn. First was the matter of the car.

Donna paused before she got in. "You didn't say where you got this car," she reminded Sheba. "Was yours ruined? I assumed your car was all right too when you said you weren't hurt."

Sheba sat behind the wheel, looking out over the hood. Briefly, now, she thought. Anything to get it over.

"I'll tell it as we drive, okay? We have to stop at a grocery for supplies and we want to be sure to get home before dark."

Donna got in and fastened her seatbelt.

Sheba backed out of the parking space and headed for the highway, her mind busy with the possibilities of describing to their satisfaction the bare surface of the truth. She didn't want to scare them away before they even got there. "What happened was this, and when we get there you'll see how easy it is to do, so that's why I want to warn all of you, first, to not drive the lane at night."

From the back seat came Esther's cross-sounding comment: "Me, I don't drive. You don't have to worry about me."

"It sounds to me," Donna said, "like you're putting us off. What happened to your car?"

"Well, I drove it off a bridge into water, just like I told you, so the car had to be dried out."

After a brief, puzzled silence from everyone Wanda blurted out, "My god. How deep was the water?"

"It covered the car."

"Oh my god!" Wanda's imagination was clearly expressed in the horror in her voice. "Did you get *out?*"

Esther said, "Of course she got out, Wanda, who do you think's driving this new car?"

"Well, but I mean—my god!"

Donna had turned to look closely at Sheba, as if examining her for injuries. "Why didn't you tell me that on the phone? That it *was* serious."

"I was afraid you wouldn't come if you found out that was all it was, because it really wasn't so serious."

"All? Not serious!" Wanda cried again. "My god."

"Wanda, do shut up," Esther said.

"But in the *water,*" Wanda said, as if anything greater than water in a bathtub was too much. "It must have been terrible for you. No wonder you wanted company."

Sheba relaxed. A few more words, then cut it off. Forever. She didn't want to talk about it or think about it, and she never would. "Nothing was really damaged. All they have to do is dry the car out, I guess. Meantime, the lodge uses this one. That's all. And yes, another thing, the bridge is on my property, and had a broken railing. But a carpenter has already built a new one. Now, how was the trip down?"

From the back seat came Esther's wry comment: "Bumpy."

Sheba deliberately kept the conversation light. Trouble loomed ahead, in the form of such technicalities as hunting seasons and off-season expenses such as salaries and so on, but that could wait. They stopped for groceries and a late lunch in Archer, then drove on out to the narrow road that turned north, twisting lazily among the waving grass on what Sheba now knew was high ground.

Brightly, Sheba pointed out their mailbox, and the miles of marshland and the few birds that dotted the wide blue sky like tiny periods on a large sheet of paper. Still brightly forcing an enthusiasm she didn't feel, Sheba drove slowly across the bridge while Wanda sat on the edge of her seat and swore she'd never drive across it anytime, night or day. The new railing had the bleached look of new wood, and the bright heads of nails glinted occasionally along its length.

"Is this the only way to the house?" Donna asked.

"Yes. But it really isn't so bad once you're used to it. There's the house, see. You'll love it."

There were appropriate comments from Wanda. She seemed to have good-naturedly forgotten the long, narrow bridge that lay between her and the world outside.

Sheba put it off for as long as she could. Together the four entered the cold house, and together she and Esther went into the muddy basement and started a coal fire in the monster furnace. Esther was the one who remembered how things of that nature were done and she took over without complaint. By that time they had learned that there was no light power available unless they got rich, which was unlikely, but there were no complaints, to Sheba's surprise. Or Donna might have told them how it was. Sheba decided that they said nothing probably because they didn't really know what it was like to make a house run without the convenience of a switch.

In the large kitchen, later, the room beginning to be warmed slightly by a fire in the black iron cookstove as well as a small amount of warmth drifting up through pipes from the furnace, they sat down to a light meal of soup and sandwiches.

Night was falling rapidly. The kerosene lamp on the table sent out a yellow glow that was so limited most of the kitchen looked huge, shadowed, coldly mysterious. Sheba stepped into the twilight of the pantry long enough to bring out more lamps, light them, and place them in various parts of the room. Near one end, where the back stairway rose against one wall to the rear wing of the second story, a lamp hung in a holder to light the lower part of the stairs. Sheba removed the globe, twisted up the wick, and held to it the match, which was now burning low.

From the rustic table far down the room a comment came to her ears; "Sheba lights those things like she's lived with them forever."

It caused Sheba to stop, her gaze caught by the rising yellow flame on the wick. The match, forgotten, burned her fingers and she dropped it hastily. It went out before it reached the step on which she stood. The comment stayed in her mind, comfortingly, as if it reminded her of something she could no longer remember.

She went back to the table and sat down.

"Have you got any hunters lined up yet, Sheba?" Naturally it would be Wanda, Sheba thought, to bring it up.

"Actually," Sheba said, "hunting season is closed until next November or December. I don't even know for sure when it opens." As she had expected, Donna didn't look too surprised. *Amused* would be more exact, and perhaps a little thoughtful. Sheba added quickly, "But I've taken care of that little matter. I'm not as inefficient as I seem at times, girls. I don't think we'll have any trouble keeping plenty of paying guests."

"Oh yeah," Wanda said. "No hunting, nothing else to do out here, and a jillion kilometers from nowhere."

Esther said quietly, "Wanda, do shut up."

Donna pushed away her coffee cup and leaned on her elbows. She smiled slightly and with a level gaze looked at Sheba across the yellow glow of the lamp. "Explain yourself, dear. I tend to agree with Wanda, but we'll listen to whatever you have in mind."

Sheba reinforced her drooping courage with a deep breath. "I have already advertised it in several large newspapers and other appropriate places. Girls, hold on. We're calling our lodge an authentic *haunted house*—open to guests."

They stared at her, all three of them, as if she had gone mad. She spread her palms upward helplessly.

"It's only until hunting season opens! And saying it doesn't make it so!"

The sudden loud cry and drifting moan of the wind filled in their continued silence, and all of them gave evidence of being aware of it. Wanda pulled her coat tighter. Esther turned her head slightly, as if listening. Donna picked up her cup again for the remaining bit of warm coffee to help still the shiver that visibly passed over her.

And Sheba watched them, one by one, seeing their discomfort.

But not feeling it.

"I don't know if I want to go to bed," Wanda said in a low voice, looking over her shoulder into the corners of the room, looking at the unshaded windows.

Esther drew herself up and spoke down to her little sister. "It's not haunted, Wanda." She sounded slightly disgusted. "It's only being advertised as such."

Donna said, "Isn't that a bit fraudulent?"

Sheba spoke hastily, without thinking, as she got up to go after another cup of coffee. "Fraudulent! Let me tell you—" She stopped, on the verge of telling them her experiences. She changed it, without really knowing why. "Let me tell you it *could* be. I mean, I can't prove it is, but neither could a ghost hunter prove it isn't. Besides, I was thinking we'd get a few thrill seekers."

Wanda brightened considerably. "Say, yeah! And maybe we could give them a few thrills, too, by dragging a log chain around in the attic or something. It does have an attic, doesn't it?"

"Yes, it does," Sheba said. "I haven't been up there, though. I understand it's still full of things—including the personal possessions of the last people who lived here. The Murphys."

"Why?" Donna asked. Sheba didn't look up, but she felt Donna's demanding gaze and heard Wanda repeat the *why*. She made it as brief as possible. "It seems they—father, mother, daughter—were killed in a car wreck. And their stuff is still here, that's all. As well as the things of the original owner."

For a moment the faint whine of the wind was the only voice in the house, then Donna asked, "It wouldn't have been on the bridge, would it?"

"Well, yeah. They drove off it at night, just as I did. Only they didn't get out. The only other member of the family, a son, is supposed to come after their things." She brought her coffee back and sat down. "But about Wanda's log chain... Anything to change the uncomfortable subject. She smiled at Wanda, a slightly wicked and teasing wish to be frightening pushing it out. "Who's going up there alone at night to drag it? You?"

Wanda's round, brown eyes grew more round. "Me? I don't even know where it is."

Esther said, "Obviously above us, Wanda."

"I'll show you the door," Sheba said. "Would you like to see it tonight?"

"Good gracious no. Maybe we can think of something later."

"And maybe," Esther said, "we'd better forget it."

Donna said lightly, "You know, I think you might have something there, Sheba. This place is certainly a fitting candidate for a ghost or two. An imaginative person out for a vacation that's different might take the wind, combine it with the natural creaks and groans in an old house, and come up with enough ghost to satisfy anyone."

"Yeah," Wanda agreed, looking toward the stairway and up the service wing where hers and Esther's bedrooms were—two rooms that she and Esther had chosen so as to be closer to the kitchen. Two rooms among many others that had been left closed. "Even me. Remind me to not go up to my room alone after dark."

Esther said, "Don't be ridiculous, Wanda. There are no such things as ghosts."

Softly, Sheba asked, "Are you sure, Esther?"

Donna interrupted anything that Esther had been prepared to say by suggesting that they leave the kitchen. "Let's try the living room, which doesn't sound like a good name for our guests. Shall we change it to *parlor*? Or *lounge*?"

"*Parlor* would fit a haunted house better," Wanda said.

They went down the hallway, Donna in the lead carrying the lamp that had been on the kitchen table. They speculated on appropriate names, looking straight ahead as though uncomfortable on their journey through the longest hall Sheba had ever seen in a house. In her hand she tightly held a small box of matches, and when in the living room she finally had lighted about half the lamps and the room was cast with a soft glow of light, Wanda came up with her final suggestion on a name.

"*Sanctuary!*" she said, settling herself in a chair near the stove, lazy in the warmth that spread from its fire. "The only unhaunted room in the house. Sure, the sanctuary."

Donna kicked off her shoes and put her feet on the hearth. Esther sat straight and stiff in a wooden rocking chair.

"Sanctuary?" Sheba put the matches into her pocket and joined them by the fire. "If we did that do you know what would happen?"

"Yes," Donna said. "Everyone would be bringing blankets and sleeping on the floor here."

"When you put it that way," Sheba said, "it might be fun."

They laughed, all except Esther, who began to rock. The subject was changed then and the conversation interspersed by slightly eerie snaps and creaks from the rocking chair.

Wanda finally looked at her sister. "Do you have to rock, Esther? It's giving me chills."

"Maybe we ought to go to bed," Esther replied.

"You're probably getting cold. Fires don't last all night unless you feed them."

Sheba's eyes had begun to feel slightly heavy and she was glad to break up the evening. She went around blowing out lights, and the four of them went up the front stairs, each with her own lamp. On the second-floor balcony Sheba said good night to the others and stood waiting until Esther and Wanda had gone through the door that led back to the service quarters and Donna had gone into the bedroom that was next to Sheba's.

Suddenly aware that she was alone, that the downstairs was a black cavern over the edge of the balcony, Sheba hurried on into her own room. She locked her door and began preparations for bed.

The house was quiet. The feeling was one of isolation. The others seemed far away, still back in Chicago, and Sheba, clean, makeup removed, in her nightgown, took in the dimness of her room and then looked out the window. The landscape was just as it had been the night before, except there was no fog.

She kept looking, covering the field of vision available from her window, looking and searching and hoping it had gone. Hoping and thinking that maybe it hadn't really been there at all—not the way she remembered it. It could have been a most natural thing, only a pocket of fog and nothing more. Something as harmless as a low-lying cloud.

Her arms had grown cold, chilled by the air in the room that seemed to be growing very damp. She turned, leaving the draperies open, to go back to her bed and rest, finally, without fear. And then she saw it and she stopped, the fear rising in slow, cold waves up her legs, body, arms, and face to paralyze her. She was unable to call out or even to move.

Slowly, oozing in around the narrow cracks of her door, a milky mist was coming, filling in the space of the door with its silent, white form, filling the corner of the room, condensing until the door was invisible behind it, coming nearer to her...

Finally she was aware of all strength and consciousness leaving her and she knew she was falling, falling, falling as the white form reached her and touched her face with its cold dampness.

CHAPTER 5

Donna woke instantly, knowing that she had been sleeping only a short time. Had she heard something fall? She didn't really think so. At least there was no sound now. Even the wind seemed to have settled for the night.

She turned over in her bed and reached for a match to light the lamp on the side table. Now that sleep was gone, it was totally gone. Probably for hours. She knew that from experience, which was one reason she kept magazines in her room. An article that was short and not too interesting was usually all she needed to finally get so bored she would start yawning.

Her hand groped for and found the fragile globe on the lamp. She set it aside carefully and put a lighted match to the wick on the kerosene lamp, watched it as it rose brightly, then turned it low and replaced the globe.

She sat up, pulling her blankets up under her arms and looking about the room. She had chosen it because it was large, with huge, rather masculine furniture that had a faint look of old Spanish. The room was no beauty now, but she had plans for it. It was even less a beauty in the dimness of her light, since most of it was in a state of mysterious shadow.

She smiled, thinking of Sheba's wild idea of calling the house haunted. Here, in a room like this, at night, even the most skeptical person would begin to believe such things possible.

Putting aside the oddly uncomfortable thought, she leaned over and reached for the magazine she had earlier placed on the low shelf of the bedside table. But her reach was suddenly halted and frozen as her eyes caught a slight movement at her door.

The knob was turning.

Not quickly and without hesitation, as one of the girls would have turned it had she wanted in, but very, very slowly. She watched it, all at once very glad that she had thought to lock it.

The knob continued its slow turn, easing stealthily around and finally, as Donna held her breath, it stopped. Whoever was trying to enter had found it locked, and in a silent prayer Donna asked God that the one who wanted in had no key to unlock that door.

As she continued to stare at the knob there was one rather quick, determined push at the knob, a slight jerking back and trying again, and then the knob was released suddenly and it whirled to its original place.

It didn't move again.

Neither did Donna move. Her arm still hung stiffly over the side of her bed, her fingertips touching the edge of the magazine she hadn't picked up.

She listened for footsteps, for the opening of another door.

And the fear and wondering eventually got to her as she pictured Sheba helpless and asleep in a room that might be unlocked. She got out of bed as quietly as she could and went softly toward the door. Only the thought of Sheba gave her courage to turn that knob herself and let the button lock click open. She looked out into a wall of darkness, and immediately closed the door and ran back for her lamp.

With the light she returned to the door, opened it, and stepped out into the hallway. There, for a long moment, she stood without moving, looking beyond the limits of her light into shadows too deep and too black to penetrate. The silence was so intense that the inner sounds of her own body, her short gasp of long-held breath, the thud of pulse in her temples, began to be the only source of sound and movement in the world.

Sheba's door was still closed, and at last she quickly approached it and turned the knob. To her great relief she found the door was locked.

Faintly, from somewhere in Sheba's room came a low moan, a soft cry that was in some way more than the cry of a nightmare. A cry of danger, a cry for help? But her door was still locked! Or had it been locked *later*—later after someone had entered the room?

Panic seized Donna and all she thought of was reaching Sheba. She called out, "Sheba!" and knocked hard on the door. *"Sheba!"*

Silence answered her, and she jerked at the door, twisting it violently as if the act in itself would unlock it.

"Sheba, answer me! Open the door!"

Sheba's voice, sounding younger, fainter, finally answered, "Donna?"

"Yes! Open the door, Sheba. Are you all right?" Donna heard the soft bare steps come toward the door, out of natural rhythm, as though stumbling. Then with a small click the door was pulled open. Donna stared down into the white-white, pinched face of the girl in front of her.

Sheba looked up at Donna for a moment, then her eyes closed and she swayed and put out one hand against the wall to steady herself. Donna quickly crossed the threshold, closed the door behind them, and with one arm around Sheba's small waist guided her back toward the bed.

"Sheba, you look ... hideous. What on earth is wrong?" Sheba sat on the side of her bed and for a moment held both hands over her face. When she finally uncovered her face Donna thought that Sheba appeared to have been through a private hell from which she had returned exhausted and weakened.

"Why don't you lie down?" Donna asked, with the private thought that unless Sheba mentioned something about a prowler in the house nothing would be said about it. Sheba looked ill enough. Knowing about the turning doorknob tonight would be too much. She placed her lamp on the table and helped Sheba into bed.

In a whisper, her eyes large and dark and worried, Sheba said, "I've got to tell you something, Donna." Donna forced a smile that she hoped was reassuring and sat down on the side of the bed. "Of course, dear. What is it?" At times like this Donna felt older than Sheba, not younger, even though there was a four-year difference in their ages.

Sheba's hand gripped Donna's hard, hurting. "You've got to promise to believe me, because so help me it's true."

"I'll believe you," Donna answered, keeping her voice low, wondering if she had locked the door. Her glance swiftly covered the room, but the shadowed corners seemed innocently unoccupied.

"I think I fainted," Sheba said, still whispering. "I never fainted before in my life, but something scared me so much that I think I did ... faint."

Her eyes pleaded for understanding, and instantly Donna knew that there was more to it than someone trying to enter her room. She nodded, watching Sheba closely, the question of the door being locked or not gone to the back of her attention to quiver warningly.

"There *is* a ghost, Donna. It came into my room tonight. I saw it. I've seen it before."

Donna kept her lips closed. Her own opinion was not important—the important thing was Sheba's extreme fear of something that had caused her to faint. She nodded for Sheba to go on and talk about it.

Sheba's eyes went from Donna to the door, and remained there. "It's like a milky mist, a fog. It oozes. I saw it the first night I came here. It came and closed over the front of the car and I couldn't see where I was going. That's why I drove off the bridge. And that's all I remember because I came to the next morning on the bank. Some men found me and helped me. Then that night I saw it from the window, and it was thick and small like—like—I don't know. Anyway, it came toward the house. Tonight I looked out the window and I didn't see it, then I looked at the door and it was coming in around the cracks in the opening of the door-frame, Donna —like a mist, white and..." As though she saw it again, she stopped, unable to continue talking.

Donna turned, her stare taking in the close fit of the door. She knew Sheba's terror was not imagined, but there had to be a logical explanation.

She said soothingly to Sheba, "This is a damper climate than we're used to, Sheba. Couldn't it really be a mist? Out on the marsh there would be fog, naturally. And perhaps some of it would seep into the house at times."

Sheba's cry was the cry of a frightened and misunderstood child. "You said you'd believe me! You promised, Donna."

Donna turned back to try to comfort Sheba. "I believe you. Is there more?"

"Yes. It came in and filled the corner and became a thick, white thing that moved toward me and finally touched me. That's when I fainted."

Donna thought of her doorknob turning and wondered if there might be some connection. Perhaps some madman in the area, in the house itself, conceivably, wanted to frighten them away and had some method of surrounding himself with ... with what?

"What are you <u>thinking</u>?" Sheba begged softly.

"Did you notice your doorknob turning during that time? Had you locked your door before it happened?" Better that Sheba know the truth than to think the fantastic.

"I didn't see it turn, why?"

"Had you locked it?" Donna repeated.

Sheba nodded. "Yes. Why?"

"Because, Sheba, something man-made might be happening, because my doorknob *did* turn. Someone tried to enter my room."

Sheba stared without comment into Donna's eyes. "Are you sure?" she asked after a long silence.

"I'm sure. That's why I came to see about you."

Sheba lay small in her bed, her dark hair a striking contrast against the white pillow, her dark eyes an equally striking contrast against her white skin. But the expression in those wide-open eyes seemed to Donna to hold an increasing amount of hostility. The smooth, nearly unreadable surface of her face suddenly broke into a twisted mouth and desperate yet angry eyes.

"You don't believe me!" she cried. "You said you'd believe me but you don't. You think I'm just putting you on. Making it up. You don't believe me at all." She flopped over and pulled the blanket up to cover her face. Huddled, she lay with her back to Donna.

Stunned at a behavior she had never seen before in the six months she had lived with Sheba, Donna felt foolish for a moment. There was a touch of guilt, too, as if she had done something wrong. After a moment she put out a hand and gently touched Sheba's back.

"Sheba ...She wanted to assure her that she did believe the thing about the ghost, but she couldn't force it out. Even the thought of it made her feel like staring blankly at a wall because ghosts were something people dreamed up on Halloween. They didn't really exist. How could it be possible? Probably Sheba had had a dream. In this house it would be easy. "Sheba... do you want me to stay here with you the rest of the night?"

Sheba jerked away from Donna's hand without answering. For a few more moments Donna sat looking at the back of the dark head that was bent into the blankets, but there seemed nothing more to say. Quietly she left the room, taking her lamp, locking Sheba's door behind her. At least Donna was safe from whoever had tried to open her own door.

She stood in the narrow corridor beyond which was the blackness and depth of the stairwell and the long, dark hallways that reached into areas yet unexplored. She had no idea how many rooms were in the house, but she did remember that the brochure had said eighteen bedrooms. Down the corridor beyond the closed door of the service quarters there were at least six bedrooms, and although the thought turned Donna wet with cold, nervous perspiration she knew that she had to go see if Esther and Wanda were all right. Because even if Sheba had dreamed up her ghost, the turning of the doorknob was no dream. And whoever it was knew that the room was occupied.

She tried to walk without sound, but the boards in the floor creaked softly with each step. When she finally reached the closed door and put her hand on the knob she felt the dampness of it. As if the fog and mist of the marshes had come in to dampen everything.

She looked over her shoulder into the darkness that seemed to have moved in closer and closer, as though the fog had risen into the house to push the light from her lamp into a small tight circle around itself.

Tomorrow night, she promised herself, there would be lights left burning in the hallways, upstairs and down. No more of this.

She wiped her sticky, wet hand on her robe, and then raised it to touch her cheek. The cold dampness on her skin was not perspiration caused by anything, not fear, not nervousness. It had simply coated her just as it had the door and walls, and still it hung heavy in the air. She felt almost as if she were smothering in it, as if she had walked into invisible webs in a forest path and was forced to stop and disentangle herself.

Quickly she touched the damp doorknob again and opened the door. To her relief the fog had not moved into the back of the house, and she closed the door behind her and walked briskly down to the bedroom where Esther had put her things. The snores coming from the room were comforting and familiar. She had heard them often enough through the thin walls of the apartment back in Chicago. She went on to the next door. There was no sound at all.

The head of the long, steep stairway that made three sharp angles down into the kitchen was only about twelve feet away from Wanda's door, and the sight of it dropping away so steeply into total darkness captured Donna's attention and held it. She found herself listening intently for steps on those stairs, slow, stealthy steps that would go with the kind of person who would come to a locked bedroom door and try to enter.

She forced herself to turn away, to put her back toward the stairway and not think of it. Softly she knocked on Wanda's door and just as softly called, "Wanda?"

Then she thought of the possibility of waking Esther, so instead of knocking again she tried the knob. Wanda usually snored too, more quietly than Esther, true, but she did snore. And there was no sound from her room.

The door opened, to Donna's surprise. She looked for a moment at the pale light that spread itself on the floor, then she pushed the door wide and saw Wanda, sitting stiff and straight in her bed, a magazine in her hands, her mouth open in a large O and her brown eyes in nearly the same state of immobile horror. In another second she would be screaming the house down. "Wanda!" Donna said, slamming the door behind her. Instead of screaming, Wanda collapsed, groaning. The magazine fell from her hands and her face crumpled as she leaned back against the stack of pillows behind her. "Oh my heaven and earth!" she squeaked breathlessly. "Did you ever knock *me* out of ten years' growth."

"I'm sorry, Wanda, really I am. Why wasn't your door locked? Didn't you hear me knock?"

"Yes, I heard you knock. I not only heard you knock I heard you walking down the hall and I heard you stop at my door and stand there for a long time before you opened it."

"Well, didn't you hear me call your name?"

"Yes, I did that too—but I wasn't sure it was you." She raised her hands to the visibly pounding pulse in her throat. Then she opened her eyes and fixed them rather weakly on Donna. "Was that you earlier too? Walking in the hall?"

Donna stared at her, feeling the goosebumps rise on her arms and the back of her neck. "Earlier?"

"Yeah." Wanda's round eyes gradually grew larger again. "It wasn't, was it?" She sounded as if all her hope had dissolved into the still night.

Donna shook her head. Then she placed her lamp on the top of a tall chest of drawers and came near the bed to sit on a chair. "But that's why

I'm here. I wanted to be sure everyone is all right. I could hear Esther snoring, so—"

"Yeah, thank God. I never thought I'd see the night when I'd appreciate those snores of hers. I thought my husband snored, but he never could have kept up with Esther. The only thing that kept me from running out of here—jumping out my window or something—was Esther's snores. Did you hear someone walking too?"

"I—uh—saw someone turning my doorknob, but my door was locked."

Wanda closed her eyes again for a brief moment. "Oh my god, if whoever that was had turned my doorknob you wouldn't have found me here. All I heard was someone walking by. That was enough, believe me."

"But why didn't you have your door locked?"

Wanda pushed up into a sitting position again. "It won't lock! There's no lock on this door."

Donna looked at the door and saw the difference immediately. And she knew that the locks on the bedrooms up front were recent editions, because even the knob on Wanda's door was old, dark with rust; it was probably the original doorknob. "Put a chair under it then," she said. "When I leave."

"I never thought of that. Actually, I was afraid to move. Did you say somebody tried to get into your room?"

"Yes. I had my light on too, and I saw it—the doorknob—move. But my door has a modern deal on it with a push-button lock, and I had locked it."

Wanda's voice dropped to an urgent whisper. She leaned on an elbow toward Donna. "Well, what did you do?"

"I waited awhile, then I got afraid that some of you— that he— Well, anyway, I took my lamp and went to check on Sheba, then I came down here."

"Sheba's okay?"

"Yes." Donna decided against telling Wanda anything else about Sheba. There really was no point. With deliberate vagueness she said, "The house seems to be filled with fog. Probably from the marshes."

"But you came through all these dark halls alone after you knew there's someone else out there?"

"Well—yes."

"Weren't you afraid?"

"I was literally petrified. But I had to know. Can you tell me just what you heard?"

Wanda settled back and looked at the door. "Sure. I couldn't get to sleep." She nodded back toward the wall between her room and Esther's. "Who can sleep next to that in a house like this? It sounds good to me now, but at first it didn't sound so good. I kept hoping she'd turn over before she drew the attention of all those ghosts Sheba was talking about at supper. Anyway, I was sitting here reading, or trying to read, when I heard a board squeak out there in the hall. I couldn't hear very well, on account of Esther, who didn't pause even long enough to take a good breath—I think she snores both in and out, mostly out—anyway, then it creaked again, closer, and again. That's all I heard. No real footsteps, just the creaking in the boards as it walked." Donna noticed the pronoun. Instead of *he* or *she*, Wanda had referred to the walker as *it*, without seeming to notice. Donna saw the beginning of a puzzled scowl on Wanda's face as she concentrated on remembering.

"It didn't go downstairs, though. I swear to you it went up." Her round eyes came questioningly to settle on Donna. "Is there a stairway out there that goes up?"

Donna moistened her dry lips. The dampness was entirely gone from her skin. "Not that I know of. But when daylight comes we'll take a look. For the rest of the night we'll just assume that whoever it is will stay up there, wherever he is, and leave us alone. It's probably someone who has taken up refuge in what he thought was an empty house. When I leave you put a chair under your door just in case, okay?"

"You can bet on it!" Wanda said as her heavy, muscled legs came out from under the blankets. "I'd offer to walk you back to your room, but if I did I'd have to spend the night there, so I won't offer."

Donna smiled. "That's all right. I made it down here I can make it back."

Wanda padded to the door on large, flat feet. Her white flannel night-gown wrinkled down to mid-calf. "Tell you what I will do—I'll stand in the hall just outside the door and watch till you get to your room okay? You can leave that door open down there and I'll be able to see, and if someone jumps out at you I'll start screaming for Esther and her night-stick. Did you know she keeps a nightstick under her pillow?"

"No, I didn't, but thanks. I'll leave that door open and I'll wave back at you when I reach the front hall." She went rather quickly along the hall, looking straight ahead, not sure that Wanda had helped her much at all by offering to scream if someone jumped out at her. The thought of someone jumping out from the darkness helped her to hurry along.

At the turn in the front hall she looked back and saw the form of Wanda, far, far down another hallway, a pale, ghostly outline against the black of the stairwell behind. Donna raised her hand and waved, and Wanda stepped back into her room, leaving the hall black and without depth or life.

Donna went into her room quickly, locked her door, and put her lamp on the table. Then, feeling a bit foolish, she got down on her knees and looked under the high, old-fashioned bed. But all that occupied that shadowed space was enough lint balls to fill several dustpans.

It seemed that she would never get to sleep, but she did. And when she woke the room was light and the yellow glow of her lamp was beginning to look slightly sick.

A sound rose suddenly from the warm air register by the wall: a loud clanking of metal against metal as a door slammed shut. A few more rattles then, and a familiar cough. Esther, Donna decided with relief, already dressed and down in the basement to start the furnace going again. Donna padded barefoot across the room to look down at the register, marveling at the way sound from the basement carried up to the rooms. But of course it would. The heat wasn't forced, because there was no power behind it. The heat simply drifted up, right along with every sound down there.

Esther cleared her throat, plainly and clearly. And suddenly the house didn't seem so large and frightening as it had last night.

Donna took a towel and cloth and made her way out to one of the four bathrooms on the second floor.

When the rooms were full of guests, she thought, there would be a bathroom problem. If they were ever full.

The bath turned out to be somewhat of a shock. The water was cold and so was the room. Even the air that had started drifting up from the furnace hadn't warmed. But it woke her and refreshed her, and she ran back to her room feeling better. Feeling alive, young, and on the verge of a great adventure. She looked out the window and saw the brilliant colors of a rising sun above the swirling mists of remaining fog, and in the pale blue of morning sky the rising of a few birds from the marshes.

She dressed in slacks and sweater, made her bed, threatened the dust motes under the bed with a later annihilation, and happily left her room. No back office today where she would be faced with boredom day after day. No back office ever, ever again!

She looked about her at the house almost fondly. It was huge and needed a lot of cleaning. The wall paper needed changing too, because the dampness was ravaging it, taking out the color until it looked as if color had never been one of its attributes, bringing it loose from the walls and ceilings in many places to hang unattractively.

But if they were going to advertise as a haunted house which now that it was daylight sounded like fun, the old, hanging wallpaper wouldn't repel as much as it would attract. It would lend a kind of ugly authenticity to *haunted.*

A memory struck her suddenly, an electrical shock through her brain. They were supposed to be alone in the house, the four of them. And they weren't. The room: all had to be looked into as soon as possible.

The thought sobered and slowed her, so that by the time she reached the living room Esther was already there poking at a fire she was trying to get started.

"Well, good morning, Donna. You're up early."

"Old habits are hard to break, I guess. Did you sleep well, Esther?"

"Yes, thank you. Very well. The springs on my bed are as old as the house, I'd say, but I think the mattress is new. Anyway, I slept very well. Is Sheba up?"

"I don't think so."

"Neither is Wanda. I tried to open her door, but she had it blocked tight with something. Wanda always was the flighty sort. And of course being married all those years and having a man around at night makes her more nervous now that he's passed on and she's alone except for me. I told her to get herself a billy club and keep it under her pillow like I do, but she says she would be too scared to use one anyway."

Together they went back to the kitchen where Esther had built her first fire of the morning in the kitchen stove. In the early morning light Donna could see the uncleaned corners, the cobwebs waving lazily from the high ceiling, pushed in their slow swing by the updrift of the air from the furnace below.

Or so, at least, Donna surmised.

Esther, in her energetic efforts to get breakfast together, did not seem to notice the cobwebs. Occasionally she glanced toward the stairs at the end of the kitchen. And occasionally she wondered aloud if the girls were going to sleep all day.

Donna opened drawers until she found a musty stack of once-white cotton dishtowels. With two over her arm she began going through the cupboards, bringing down plates to rinse and wipe. On the stove the coffeepot began to make irregular sounds of perking, and the arousing aroma of coffee filled the air to compete with the smell of musty cupboards and linens. Added to that then was the smell of bacon, and when Esther had lifted it from its iron skillet and left it to drain, she set the pan to one side on the large coal and wood-burning cookstove, wiped her hands on her apron, and set out for the stairs with a long-legged stride.

"I'm going to wake up Wanda, anyway. She must not have set her alarm. Do you suppose I should call Sheba or let her sleep?"

"Why don't you call her and ask if she wants to come down now or if she'd like to be left to come down when she pleases. There's probably no great hurry about getting the house ready for anyone. We'll be lucky if someone is here a month from now, I suppose." She wiped a plate and placed it on the table, adding, "If ever." But Esther had already gone up the steep stairway and was out of sight where it, like the one in the front hall, turned sharply, angling almost back over itself.

Esther's footsteps along the upstairs hall came faintly to Donna's ears and then faded to silence. Donna stood there, listening, remembering the prowler of the night before and the rooms that must be checked out carefully before the day ended and they were helpless in the dark again.

CHAPTER 6

He entered the apartment house where he had lived off and on during the past year, since he'd accepted the position as research assistant to Dr. Clavin Steven, in the field of paranormal phenomena. Oddly, he had been offered the job because of his complete skepticism. Dr. Steven had wanted someone who would doubt everything he saw to the point of investigating it thoroughly. In Cliff Murphy he had found the skepticism, and it had resulted in some stimulating arguments, which they both enjoyed. Sometimes, though, Dr. Steven seemed a little annoyed that his assistant continued to be so bullishly skeptical.

Until they ran across a poltergeist occurrence that frankly had Cliff stumped. That, Cliff recalled, was the month his mother, dad, and sister had gone up north a way and bought an old stone mountain of a house that had been empty for forty years.

The thought of his family, their funerals still so fresh in his mind, brought down about him the familiar curtain of regret and despair. Why hadn't he dropped the poltergeist thing and gone when his mother called for him?

He stopped at his mailbox and picked out from the holder below it the rolled newspaper. From habit he unrolled it and glanced at the headlines before he ran on up the one flight of stairs to his floor. The headlines in the paper meant nothing to him. His mind was still on the *why*— Why hadn't he gone when he was called? He knew why. It was the same personality trait that Dr. Steven had found desirable for the position of assistant. A tenacious trait of sticking to anything until it was solved—even a frustrating puzzle of wooden blocks. He couldn't stand not knowing why a certain thing was the way it was; and when the poltergeist thing had come up he had found himself unable to prove fraud and, frankly, unable to solve the thing. So he had put off going to see his family. And now it was too late.

One year, it was said, eased the sharp pains of loss of loved ones.

Meantime, he had been taught, get your mind on other things.

He smiled a "good evening" at the neighbor next door, an elderly lady who had stepped out into the hall to pick up the paper that was delivered to her door. His own apartment was adequate, he felt, and that was all. A place to sleep, eat occasionally, sometimes think. A place to read.

With a cup of before-dinner coffee at his side he sat near a window and opened the paper. He covered it lightly, reading only that which appealed to him. From habit, though, as he sipped the coffee his eyes swiftly swept the ad section. His attention was arrested suddenly, and he read again one rather lengthy ad.

Spend your vacation in an authentic haunted house, in isolation from society where there is not even a telephone to disturb the workings of the supernatural. Of course you will be protected, hopefully, by the few people who dare live in this house only for your convenience and comfort, but do not—at all costs do not—arrive at night! Write to Sheba Gilbert, Rural Route, Archer, Arkansas.

It was the name that caught him. Sheba Gilbert. The name of the woman who had bought from him the house where his family had lived.

He leaned forward, elbows on knees, and read the ad again. Haunted house... in isolation ... Archer, Arkansas. It had to be the same house, there was no doubt, no possible mistake. He had understood that the place was to be turned into a hunting and fishing lodge. Then why in the hell was she advertising it as a haunted house?

A vision of his mother's last letter came between him and the newspaper, and with it the feeling of sick guilt that he so often felt when he remembered that he could have gone on, then, as she'd wanted, instead of replying in a letter to tell her that in another month he would take his vacation and be up to see them, but right at the moment he was trying to puzzle out how things could move in a certain room when nobody was moving them.

He let the paper drop to the floor and leaned over, reaching for the telephone. Within the minute Dr. Steven was on the line.

"Is it all right with you, Doctor, if I take that vacation now?"

A pause, and then, "Of course, Cliff, whenever you want."

"There's something I have to see about. Something that bothers me considerably."

"Can I be of any help?"

Cliff paused, but slightly. His pride said no, because to take a trip north to investigate this would show that his skepticism had been overcome. Cliff remembered the aging man's words of a year ago: *I'll have you eating crow, young man. I'll bet my library of psychic-phenomena literature against your convictions.* But what did pride matter now?

"Well, Dr. Steven, I would like to speak with you."

"Fine. Why don't you come over to my club for dinner. We can take as long as we like there and not feel rushed."

"That's very kind of you, sir, thanks."

"Thirty minutes?"

"Yes, sir. I'll be there."

The club was one of those old places where time seemed to stand still. Cliff had been there before and found himself surrounded by brown leather, dark wood, linen cloths, and old, heavy silver. There was no music in the background, just a low murmur of voices coming from other tables that were all rather widely and comfortably spaced about the large dining room. The waiters went about in silence, and spoke in raised tones only for the hard-of-hearing. There was a smell that was warm and comfortable in the dining room, but it wasn't food, and it wasn't polish that kept the wood glowing in its dark tones. It might have been the leather. Cliff didn't know, but he liked it.

Dr. Steven was waiting at the same table as before, and the moment Cliff sat down a waiter brought his favorite drink. Cliff marveled at Dr.

Steven's ability to remember the name of a drink that had been mentioned only once in his presence.

"Is that all right?" Dr. Steven asked.

"I can think of nothing better at the moment. Thank you."

Dr. Steven leaned his elbows on the table and created a tent of his fingers over his own drink. "We'll have some time to talk before our dinner." And then he waited, letting Cliff take his own time.

"Do you recall me telling you when my family bought an old place in the middle of a marsh last summer?"

"I remember."

"I don't know if I also told you that their car accident occurred on the property, at night. They drove off a bridge into the water."

"You told me they drove off a bridge into the water and were unable to get out, but after you returned from the funerals you seemed disinclined to talk about it—as people often react after multiple deaths, and as you know. If a person who grieves can escape it by trying to put it out of mind then that is what should be done."

"But that wasn't what I was trying to do. I didn't talk about it because I felt I might have prevented it if I had gone up there last fall after I received a letter from my mother. I didn't go. I put it off. I told her I'd be there for Christmas." He looked down into his drink. "The truth is, I thought it was nothing serious. After they died, just a week later, I began to wonder. But I couldn't bring myself to go out to the house then, not even for their clothes. I immediately put the house up for sale and decided to forget it because frankly I was stumped for an answer. My beliefs stood between me and what my mother's letter hinted at. Three months later the house was sold, at a price far less than my folks paid. But I was glad to be rid of it."

"Three months?" the doctor said. "But that was this month, wasn't it?"

"Yes. The first payment, one fourth of the total, was sent to me last week. The buyer of the house was Sheba Gilbert, and the real estate agent up there told me she was going to turn the place into a hunting and fishing lodge, a year-round thing. But tonight I read this in the paper."

He unrolled the paper, which lay on the seat beside him, to the ad section, took a pen from his pocket, and circled the ad. Then he pushed the paper across the table to the doctor.

Dr. Steven read it quickly and then glanced up in silence.

Cliff felt in his inside pocket, but the letter wasn't there. He searched through all his pockets before he gave up. "I was going to bring Mom's letter, but I changed coats, so I guess I left it in the other coat."

"The letter was written in the house?" he tapped the ad with a finger.

"Yes. Her last letter to me. I wanted you to see it, but I also would like to leave tonight, so I can't give you what she said word for word. Just a gist of the contents."

Dr. Steven nodded, a quick little jerk that meant he was listening.

The compassion that lay beneath Dr. Steven's sharp-edged exterior came to the surface in eyes that were baby soft. "I've gathered that it has something to do with this house, and their deaths, and the fact your mother wanted you to come up. Were you never there? Don't I recall that you went up to see them once or twice?"

"Once. I went about six weeks after they had bought the place. Dad was doing a lot of raving about how good the fishing was, and Mom was having the time of her life trying to get that cold old monster redecorated. My sister, Judy, hadn't said anything beyond the fact that she would be glad when school started because it was so lonesome out there."

"She was in college?"

"Yes. Or would have been. Her first year."

"But she didn't go, did she?"

"No. That is, she went, but for some reason she went home. She had stopped writing me letters, and Mom mentioned that she seemed preoccupied about something and didn't want to go back to school. I wrote and asked if she was sick, but Mom said no, that she only wanted them to move out of the house and that she wasn't leaving again until they did. I knew she didn't like it there very well, and I knew also that as the baby of our family she had been a bit spoiled, *so* I assumed it was just her way of trying to get the folks to move back to Little Rock. By refusing to return to school until they did, she would have a weapon of sorts, because they wanted her to finish. Mom's letters began to sound somewhat disturbed because of the pressure Judy was putting over, and once I received a letter from Judy. In it she said she hated the house and wanted the folks to leave because she had a terrible feeling something would happen to them if they didn't. She wanted me to write and persuade them to sell it and go home."

"But you didn't," Dr. Steven said softly when Cliff paused.

"No. Instead I wrote to her and told her to let them retire there if that was what they wanted." He paused long enough to take a drink and receive another sharp nod from Dr. Steven.

"Then in October—I think the letter was written in September—I received my last letter from Mom. She said that the fogs were rising over the marshes and seemed to be filling the house at night to a point where the new wallpaper was coming loose. That was the way the letter started. There was something about it that sounded melancholy as hell, and I knew right away that something was not right with Mom. And finally she said that Judy had started having a terrible fear at night that her room was being invaded by something that was, in its way, aware and alive. She said Judy had completely refused to sleep in a room away from them, so they had put up a cot for her in their room. Judy, it seemed, had become convinced the house was haunted, and whatever it was was going to kill them all because she, Judy, was trying to protect her mom and dad from it. Mom was confused, and said Judy was so convincing that when they wanted her to see a doctor she pleaded instead for them all to get out of there—or to have me come up and investigate the house and see what it was."

Cliff paused, remembering his surprise at the contents of the letter, and his reaction. Now, while under the soft, watchful eyes of Dr. Steven, he emptied his glass in one more swallow.

"You didn't tell me," Dr. Steven said.

It sounded like a gentle reproval. "I know. We were just on to the poltergeist thing and I was out to disprove it. You know how I felt about so-called ghosts. How I feel about them. In Judy's case I was concerned because I felt she was sick. I wrote back and told them to get her to a doctor whether she wanted to go or not, and that I would be home at Christmas. When a letter didn't come right away I assumed they had gone to take Judy somewhere. Then the sheriff called me, telling me they had been found. I went up right away, then. Too late. Their luggage was thrown carelessly into the car, as if they had left in a hurry. I went into the house only long enough to pick up a photo album that Mom always kept on her night table, and her jewelry box, which she usually never left anywhere. The house hadn't even been locked. I left right away. I couldn't bear to go back, so I offered it, and everything in it, for sale. With the exception of some personal things that had been packed away in the attic. But I had no intention of going back after them for several months."

"So you've carried around the burden of guilt," Dr. Steven said as though talking to himself. He picked up the paper again and looked for a long time at the ad. "

What do you think?" Cliff finally asked.

Dr. Steven looked up. "I think first you should stop feeling guilty. Then I think you should go and investigate this. It's too much of a coincidence. If it looks authentic, let me know, and I'll drop everything and come immediately. Find out, first of all, exactly how your parents died, if you don't know."

"They drowned under the bridge."

"Yes, but the details. When? Had anyone else ever drowned in the same place? If I remember right, you did say it was a bridge that was on the property?"

"Right. Not far from the house."

"And all evidence pointed to them leaving in a hurry?"

"Right."

"Investigate that part of it, find out what the old-timers in the area say. And then move in on the house. Go through the things your family left there, in search of more definite clues to this fear of your sister's. She might have been more receptive to whatever it was than any other member of your family. And, perhaps most important of all, find out why the new owner is advertising the house as haunted when her original plan was to convert it into a hunting and fishing lodge. The idea had to come from somewhere, and there, I feel, perhaps lies the beginning of the answer to what sounds like a case of psychical disturbance;" Dr. Steven leaned back in his chair and motioned for the waiter. "Let me say now that I am very sorry about your family, but try to put away your sense of guilt because it will damage you, and to no purpose. You are a non-believer, and that is certainly your privilege and makes you also one of the crowd of humanity. Hardly anyone else would have acted any differently from you, and even had you gone, it probably wouldn't have done any good. Not then. Not feeling as you did. If in all honesty you can bring up some facts to substantiate the possibility of some force beyond the seemingly natural, then let me know and I'll come right away. Right now, we'll have our dinner. I know you're eager to be on your way."

Cliff thought it over, and after the waiter had gone, he asked one more question: "Do you think I should tell them why I'm there, or go simply on the purpose of sorting out the things I want to take with me?"

"It might be better not to tell them. Not at first, at least. If it's a hoax of some kind you'll be much more apt to discover it if the perpetrator isn't aware that you're in this special line of work. Whatever you do, good luck, and be careful. There are all kinds of people in this world. There are also all kinds of evil forces, stronger sometimes than the forces of good, that lie in wait in places that are sometimes the most unexpected." He paused, waiting while he sipped his drink, then repeated his warning: "Be careful."

CLIFF ARRIVED in the town of Archer, population about two thousand, shortly after noon the next day. He stopped at one of the cafes and sat at a booth. When the waitress brought his steak, he asked her, "Have you lived here long?"

"All my life."

"Did you ever hear of the Bleeker house?"

"Oh sure."

"What do you know about it? What did you hear?"

She shrugged, put one hand on the table, and her body into a kind of twisted relaxation. "I don't know. Some people bought it last year and lived in it awhile, but then they were all drowned in their car. Now somebody else has bought it, and it's supposed to be a lodge for hunters and fishermen. The rest of my life it's just been an empty old house. I mean, no people in it. They say it's a great big one, but I've never been out there. My dad, he goes out to go fishing sometimes."

"Did you ever hear about it being haunted?"

"The house? No. Nobody ever dared get that close to it, I guess. It's the bridge. Dangerous to cross, even in the daytime. At night, though, they say nobody ever drove across it and lived. But that's just a lot of ole nonsense."

He smiled at her. "Why is it nonsense?"

She shrugged again, blushed, and lowered her eyes to look at her hand that was spread palm flat on the table. "Well, who believes that old stuff?

Besides, the woman who bought it, you know? She drove off the bridge too, but she lived."

Cliff leaned back against the padded booth, his smile gone. *"She* drove off the bridge?"

"Yeah. A wrecker had to go out and drag her car out, but she was okay. They say they don't know how on earth she got out, but she sure did. So that proves it was all nonsense, that old stuff. Who believes that old stuff except superstitious people? I'm not superstitious."

"I can see that." He pushed his cup toward her. "How about warming the coffee for me?"

"Sure." For the first time she threw him a smile, then she went after the coffee.

Cliff spent the afternoon wandering around town, and finally wound up at the garage where he found Sheba Gilbert's car. It was white, slightly dented from many old bumps from other cars, and somewhat of a wreck for a job no older than it was. He decided she wasn't a very careful driver.

"Nothing really wrong with it," the mechanic said, wiping his hands on a greasy rag and walking around in Cliff's tracks. "Just needed a good drying out, mostly. We done a few other things, too."

"What's she driving now?"

"One of the cars off the lot. A slick, green number." He grinned lasciviously. "Fits her better than this one. Man, is she hot."

Cliff looked at him closely. "She is, huh?"

The mechanic merely gave a sideways jerk of his head, which spoke more clearly than his words had. Cliff returned his grin. "Is she easy, too?"

"I wouldn't know about that. Me, I got this wife at home. Ball and chain for sure. All I do is look when she comes around."

"Does she come around very often?"

"A couple times. To see about her car. I figure the longer I hold it the more I'll get to look at her anyway." Cliff laughed, then walked on around the car, looking in. "I hear it was a pretty unusual thing that she got out of this."

"Oh, man, unusual! I was there, see, the morning they found her. All that was sticking out of the water was the front fender and tire. But the strange thing was that the doors were all locked, and all the windows were still rolled up."

Cliff moved back from the car and looked at the mechanic to see if he could detect a glimmer of exaggeration. It sounded pretty farfetched, unless... "You found the girl still in the car?"

"No. Hell no. She was out there on the road watching me pull the car out."

"Now wait," Cliff said with a brief wave of his hand. "The car was submerged, and the girl was standing on the road—"

The mechanic interrupted him with a vigorous nod of his head. "Right! She sat in George Pyle's car while we pulled it out. I asked her myself how she got out and she said she didn't know. But she was out, anyhow, and the car doors were all locked. We figured she opened a door and jumped before it went completely under and the lock got pushed back somehow."

"She hadn't been in the water?"

"Oh yeah, she had. She was soaking wet."

"What time of day did this happen?"

"It happened at night. George Pyle and another guy, George in his car, and Rally Smith—you know him?"

"No, don't believe I do."

"Well, Smith, in his pickup, went out early on that morning to go fishing on the lake. George, he keeps a small paddle boat moored out there. And they saw the car. Then George found her, they said, on the bank."

"Just sitting there?"

The mechanic paused, thinking. "I don't know. I guess I never asked about that."

"Where can I find one of these men?"

"George is the one you'd want. Smith went back to town for help and stayed at home. He's not in the best of health. George lives about six blocks out on south Third. The gray house. You can't miss it. Only gray house on the block."

Cliff thanked the mechanic and left, found Third Street and drove south. The house was as easy to find as the man at the garage had said, and Cliff drove into the driveway, hoping the owner hadn't gone fishing again. Within a minute a man slightly past middle age came around from behind the garage. Like southern natives, he was friendly without being nosy, and they discussed the fact that spring must surely be on its way because Mrs. Pyle's shrubs were beginning to bud. George Pyle didn't ask his visitor what he wanted or who he was. Cliff knew he wouldn't. Old customs deemed it impolite. Although George Pyle might come near to choking on curiosity, he would never ask.

After a few minutes Cliff brought up the subject he was after. "You do a lot of fishing?"

"Try to."

"I was told you found Miss Sheba Gilbert the morning after her car went into the water under Bleeker's Bridge."

"Right, I did." George's eyes fixed themselves narrowly on Cliff's bearded face. "I'd started out fishing that morning. "

The man was becoming suspicious, and Cliff decided it was time to identify himself. "My name is Murphy. It was my family who lived there last, and I'm on my way out to pick up some things they left there. But it seems to me there are some pretty curious things about the accident—not to mention other things I've heard about—and I thought you might know."

George's eyes widened and smiled. He held out his hand for a rough, friendly handshake. "Say, I'm glad to meet you. I fished many a day with your dad. He was a friendly man, your dad was. Liked to fish about as well as anyone I ever met. He told me to go right ahead and keep my boat out on his lake and go there whenever I wanted. I saw him pretty often out there." He coughed and looked at his feet. "I sure was sorry to hear about their accident."

"Yes. Thank you. I understand they weren't the first to drown under the bridge."

"No, no. That bridge, it's so narrow you can't hardly keep on it in daytime, and the railing was off on one side—I reckon you know about that. Anyway, when Andrew Bleeker drove off it back in thirty-two he broke through the railing. Then what with this and that, the rest of it disappeared. It just wasn't safe at night. There's been four cars went off that bridge at night since Andrew Bleeker did. Most folks around here got to feeling kind of superstitious about it and wouldn't even think of crossing it at night. But I guess Miss Gilbert didn't know that."

"So you were the one who found her?"

"I was the one. I was driving across the bridge just after daybreak, on my way to the lake, when I spotted this tire sticking up out of the water. I stopped and got out and started looking around and finally found her in the grass on the bank. Stretched out on her back, asleep, unconscious, or something. Rally Smith drove up behind me and then he went back for help. I tried to rouse her and couldn't. I was about ready to get her back to the hospital when help came back. Gawkers, anyway. And all of a sudden she was up like nothing was wrong. She wouldn't go back to town, so I just took her home."

"She was all right?"

"Seemed to be."

"She didn't know how she got out of the car?"

"Said she didn't. She said the bridge was foggy and she couldn't see. I don't doubt it. Lot of fog over the marshes sometimes."

Cliff waited a moment, but George seemed disinclined to offer any opinions. After awhile Cliff asked, "Have you ever heard any rumors about that house being haunted?"

The man laughed. "When a house stands empty as long as that, and especially when it's had a man in it as mean and ornery as Andrew Bleeker was supposed to have been, it always seems to get that tale going on it."

"But you don't believe it?"

"Naw. Never was much said anyway."

Cliff drew the discussion back to Mrs. Pyle's yard, talked a few minutes longer, then left in search of the sheriff.

The jail cell and sheriff's office looked like some kind of small joke. Visible from the outside, on the three windows, were strong and very healthy bars. Parked in front was a car that clearly read *SHERIFF* on the side. But the car was almost as big as the entire building. The building was freshly painted. Probably because the deputy didn't have much else to do, Cliff thought.

The man behind the desk looked capable of his job and more, to Cliff's faint surprise. He was a tall, thin but strong-looking man, the kind who should have been wearing a handlebar mustache. His chin was so freshly shaved it shined. And his blue eyes, when he looked up at Cliff, could easily have fit the clichéd description of flint-hard.

Cliff glanced around, saw a couple of straight-backed chairs, and one jail cell. Empty. There was a door to another room. Closed.

Without invitation Cliff sat down and looked at the sheriff, who leaned back in his chair and almost smiled at Cliff. Almost.

"I believe I know you. Murphy. Just met you once, but I'd never forgot that face—nor," his eyes slid down to Cliff's beard and up again, "all that hair."

Cliff laughed. His dad hadn't really approved of it either and once had asked him if he was trying to go Indian again or something.

"What brings you back to town?"

"I've got some things to pick up yet out at the house, and I wanted to ask you a couple of questions if you don't mind."

"Ask away. I'll let you know whether I <u>mind</u> after I've heard the questions."

"I'd like the details on my folks' accident."

The sheriff looked past him. "Details? They were found about seven o'clock one morning, and the coroner said he thought they had been in the water a couple of hours. They had drowned. These things you were told at the time, as I recall."

"Yes." Cliff pushed away the mental image that rose to his mind. Why was it necessary that he ask now, again; and feel again the ache of knowing the terror of their deaths. Dr. Steven had said find out—but why? "That's all you know about it?"

"It's hard to know anything else in a case like that. The car went under. They didn't get out. That was all."

"How about the other people drowned there?"

"Same thing—except they were all found sooner."

"The first one was Andrew Bleeker?"

"Yeah, that's what I hear. But that's not even on record. The tale was that his car was found but his body never was."

Cliff paused a moment, surprised and not knowing why. "Then how does anyone know he was drowned?"

"Assumed it. A few years later some human bones were found over in the lake. Fished up by somebody. Just a few—enough to know it had been a man. Not all was found."

"Was the lake dredged?"

"Just a little, I think. Not much. Not much point in it considering he had no family. I can remember that myself. That was about the time a newlywed couple came in and rented the place. I can remember seeing them there together, watching what was going on. I guess the reason I remember it so clearly is that a few weeks later she murdered her husband."

"*What?*"

"Murdered her husband."

"I know what you said, but—" Cliff ran long, brown fingers through his hair. "Funny. I never heard of that before."

"Not so funny, since you've only been here a couple of times."

"I'm sure my folks didn't know that. At least they never mentioned it to me."

"They might not have known it After all, it happened in nineteen thirty-five. That's a long time ago." The sheriff's chair scraped on the wood floor as he pushed it back and went to old filing cabinets in the corner of the small room. "Not many murders ever take place around here." He pulled out a folder and opened it. "Her name was Mona Railings and she killed him in the middle of the night, while he was in bed asleep, with an ax. She was sitting downstairs with blood all over her a few days later when his folks came along." Cliff frowned. A thought, something his mother had said or written, was in some way reminding him of a connection somewhere, but it was so formless and vague that he didn't even know in which direction it was heading. "I'm sure she didn't know it," he said again.

"Strange thing," the sheriff said, reading to himself. "The only thing they could get out of her when she was questioned was that *he* had made her do it"

"Who? Surely not her husband!"

"No. After long questioning, it says here, the person referred to as *he* was then said by suspect to be Andrew." The sheriff looked up, straight into Cliff's eyes. "Andrew Bleeker."

"The man whose bones—or so was assumed—were dragged out of the lake," Cliff said. "And she had watched the operation and probably saw the skeleton. Right?" To him it was clear. An unbalanced mind to begin with.

"Right." He looked down at the folder again, read quickly and silently for a minute or so, then folded it and put it away. As he closed the screeching drawer he said, "Andrew Bleeker. They couldn't get her to say anything else."

He came back to his chair.

Cliff asked, "Was she convicted?"

"It was decided she was insane."

Suddenly the thought that had stirred so deeply in Cliff's mind burst forth. A few sentences from one of his mother's letters: *Judy is at times nearly hysterical after one of her nightmares, saying that she is terrified that she will kill us. That something is wanting her to kill us. Of course it's only nightmares, but we have to face the truth. She has never had nightmares before...*

Cliff stood up, suddenly anxious to leave. "Could you tell me where I might find this woman? I think I'd like to talk to her."

"She died a few months later in the state hospital. Back in thirty-six."

Cliff stared for a moment into the sheriff's steady eyes.

"So the case is closed."

The sheriff's nod was slow and final. Cliff motioned goodbye with one hand and went out to his car.

For a while he sat, thinking it over. All of it could be suggestion. First, the murder after watching the bones brought out of the lake. Second, in the case of his sister, Judy, she might have heard of the murder and been influenced by it. He wished he had gone on home when they needed him. He wished he had known about this other incident. But the feeling that not even his family had known persisted—and if that was the case ...

He decided he had been under the influence of Dr. Steven too long. He was developing an imagination toward something that was logically impossible.

The car started smoothly under the turn of the key, and rolled smoothly and slowly into the empty street. He drifted along, thinking, yet not thinking, because what was coming to his mind was not of his own making, it seemed. It was a fantasy. The kind you read for entertainment because there's no danger in it, no reality.

He drifted about town the rest of the afternoon, and finally went to a restaurant for dinner. When darkness had finally fallen over the town he went to a movie. At eleven o'clock he left the theater and drove out to the road that led to the old Bleeker place. He turned north toward the dangerous bridge that crossed the waiting waters, and drove slowly and carefully.

The clock on the dash of his car pointed at twelve midnight when he approached the bridge.

A thin moon vaguely outlined the posts of railings, one brighter and newer than the other, of a bridge that was half as wide as the road. He slowed the car as he drew nearer, and finally stopped it just as his front tires rattled the old boards of the flooring.

He sat still for a while, car lights off. He had turned them off several hundred yards back because he didn't want anyone at the house to see his arrival. He didn't know what he was looking for, he only knew he didn't want to be seen.

The night was still, and only the thinnest of fog was beginning to rise in still waves from the water and the lake and the marsh where the grass grew. He got out of the car and went to stand on the edge of the bridge in front of his car, leaning back against the warmth of the hood. The bridge, quite long and very narrow, seemed only what it was: a man-made thing of planks, old and rattling, loose, but still strong. The house, though, a great, shadowy, formless mass about a quarter of a mile away, drew his attention and held it. And as he watched, the mists from the surrounding marsh rose up to obscure and hide it until it was lost from view.

Although he felt surprised at the ridiculousness of his own thought he couldn't help the chill of conviction that in some way the house had drawn a curtain over itself, to keep itself safe from the prying eyes of an outsider.

And he wondered if Sheba Gilbert was in the house alone.

CHAPTER 7

Through the stillness of the house broke the faint sound of metal against metal, clanging, knocking, somewhere in the front. Donna, in the room across from the living room, a room she had decided would be her office, stood nearly frozen with the unexpected sound, listening. She had come down, still in her robe, to take another look at the room after working with it in her mind. The knock came again, and the location of the sound suddenly dawned on her. It was the front door.

A metal knocker on the front door—someone wanted in?

She hurried, as if to hear the sound again would shatter her beyond help, and opened the heavy outer door in the entrance hall.

The man who stood there held a suitcase in his hand and smiled down at her without speaking. She noted swiftly that he looked extremely neat and well-dressed even though he wore slacks and a short jacket of beige suede. The pale colors of his clothes contrasted perfectly with his dark complexion, black hair, and very dark brown eyes. She saw that he wore a short, neat beard, a moustache, and center-parted hair that hung to his shoulders. The effect was unexpectedly masculine and virile. He seemed to have risen from nowhere—a part of the mists that swirled slowly and thinly about his feet and over the porch, mists that were being pushed away by the rising sun.

After a long moment of waiting his eyebrows lifted slightly. "This *is* the haunted house, isn't it?" he asked in a voice that fit his appearance as well as his clothes fit his large and well-muscled body. "Have I come at the wrong time? I saw your ad in the paper and it said don't come at night, but it didn't state any specific daytime hour for arrival."

Her cheeks had grown warm with embarrassment. She had been staring at him as if she had never seen a man before, for more reasons than one, and he seemed quite aware of it. To her further embarrassment he seemed amused, but she was not. He obviously was used to having a strong effect on women and she decided to burst the bubble of his egoism a little. She had a thing about handsome men—she flatly didn't care for them.

"I'm sorry. I wasn't expecting anyone so early." She pulled the door wide open, remembering that she was, after all, Sheba's business manager. "But do come in. Are you interested in a room, or are you just out looking around for haunted houses?"

"I'm interested in a room," he said, his eyes steady on hers.

She glanced away, feeling vaguely uncomfortable under the strength of his gaze. "For how long, please?" Rapidly through her mind went the fact that not only did she not have a guest book ready, she didn't have anything else ready. They hadn't even agreed on rates yet, and she wished Sheba had waited to place her ad. But then, who expected a guest so soon?

"Indefinitely," he said.

She turned and looked at him, wondering why, but knowing that she couldn't ask. People who ran a lodge of any kind, or even a rooming house, didn't question guests on why they wanted to stay there! The question trembled in her throat, but instead she merely repeated, "Indefinitely."

"Yes."

He was still looking at her.

"Oh. I see. Well, would you mind leaving your luggage here in the entry hall until I can get a room ready for you?" She motioned toward the wall and watched him place it carefully where she indicated, but all the while she felt his eyes on her. After a moment longer they passed her and moved slowly on toward the stairway and up. And the seriousness in his eyes then as he stared so penetratingly into the upper portion of the house made her ever more aware of his extremely soon and early arrival. And the expression, though private and closed in, seemed too intense for a mere thrill seeker. She said, to break into his hidden thoughts, "First, you'd probably like to join us for breakfast. We're eating in the kitchen."

Suddenly he was smiling at her again. "We?"

"Yes. There are four of us. Sheba Gilbert, the owner, and I—and the two ladies who will be taking care of the house and the guests." She stopped, wondering why she was telling him. Even though he would have to meet them. Even though he would have to know, she felt that in some way she was exposing herself.

Holding herself straight, she walked ahead of him, careful to keep her hips from wiggling as Sheba often teased her of doing on purpose. For the first time she was actually, strongly conscious of her rear and that he was probably looking at it. With an effort she kept her hands at her sides and did not reach back to adjust her robe to fit less tightly around her hips.

The distance to the kitchen seemed enormous, and she entered, going ahead of him because he held the door and silently waited for her to go on. She heard the warm and familiar voice of Wanda, talking as she yawned, and Sheba answering in a voice wide awake and eager.

Donna saw them in one hasty glance: Esther at the stove basting eggs; Wanda in an old bathrobe that couldn't possibly have belonged to anyone but her deceased husband; Sheba in a sheer and lovely peignoir set that belonged anywhere but in this kitchen, in this house. Donna wished she hadn't been wearing that particular outfit on this particular morning, but she was, and her attractiveness was there for the guest to see.

Hurriedly Donna said, "We have a guest."

She might as well have fired a gun into the air, so suddenly was their attention drawn to the man who stood slightly behind her. As she had stared, they stared. And Donna remembered she hadn't thought to ask his name.

She put a welcoming smile on her face and turned just enough to get him in her view. "I'm sorry, I can't introduce you until I ask your name."

"Murphy," he said. "Cliff Murphy."

Another brief moment of silence, then Sheba cried softly, "Murphy! Are you the man I bought this house from?"

"I am," he said, and although he smiled he said no more. The subject obviously was closed so far as he was concerned.

But Donna wondered why he had come, now, so soon after the sale.

And why he had not explained who he was in the beginning, instead of asking about the house as if he had never seen it before.

She wondered, but she knew she wouldn't ask. Then she looked at Sheba and saw an expression that was not usual for her when a handsome man was in the room. Her face had gone blankly cold and her eyes, as steady as his, had pupils shrunk to pinpoints.

Wanda was hardly noticed as she fumbled nervously with the front of her tacky, overbig flannel bathrobe. She backed toward the stairway, mumbling something about, "I'd better go up and get dressed... I didn't know anyone was here... I was planning to get dressed anyway..."

"Wanda, do shut up and go on," Esther said, and calmly went back to basting eggs. Donna wondered if any man had ever impressed Esther in any way. Except, of course, the kind for whom she kept the billy club. "Mr. Murphy will be wanting a hot breakfast and a room gotten ready."

"Yes, sure," Wanda said, and clomped up the stairway.

Donna excused herself and followed Wanda, going on to her own room where she hastily dressed and arranged her long hair in a bun on the top of her head. Cliff Murphy was seated at the table eating and complimenting Esther's cooking when she returned to the kitchen.

Esther's long, narrow face was flushed with the pleasure of Cliff Murphy's praise of her cooking and the heat of the stove. She was so intent on seeing that everything was just right for her male guest that she kept only a cup of coffee sitting safely on one edge of the stove for herself. Cliff Murphy evidently had in some way broken through her tough shell. Wanda had come back dressed, and Sheba was not in the room.

As hostess, Donna thought privately as she ate her own breakfast and listened to Esther tell of Chicago and the apartment house the four of them had lived in, Sheba was forgetting her duty as well as her manners. Of course, she probably only went to get dressed.

But she didn't come back.

Cliff Murphy settled back in his chair with his third cup of coffee, and Donna began to be aware that perhaps he was waiting for her to do her part of the job of showing him the bedrooms available. The whole thing was awkward and frustrating and she wished again that Sheba had waited to place the ad until at least the bedrooms were ready. Or at least until she had seen them herself. As it was, she didn't even know what to offer him in the way of rooms.

"I expect you would like to see the rooms now?" she said. "I arrived only three days ago and haven't seen all of the house yet."

"I know which one I want," he said. "That is—if it's not occupied."

"Oh, of course. I'm sorry. I'd forgotten that you lived here. You know the house, then."

"I do know the house, but I didn't live here. My parents and my sister lived here for about three months. I came down for a couple of weekends."

She waited for more, but he was looking into his cup of coffee. He had told her all he was going to tell her.

"You came for their personal things, I gather," she said.

"No. I'm not a collector of material things. There are some photo albums I want, of course. But if you're referring to their clothes, the answer is no. I'd much prefer that some of you took care of that and gave them to the Salvation Army, or a church for people who might need them."

"Wanda can take care of the packing," Esther said cheerfully.

Now that he wasn't looking at her, Donna felt free to contemplate him as he continued to look into the black of the coffee. There was more than one way to ask a question.

"Then you came for the photo albums," she said. "Do you know where they are?"

"Yes. They were in a box in the attic. I'm not sure which box. I'll have to look." He glanced up at her suddenly. "I came over here the day after the funerals on my way back south, and took most of the recent albums, and my mother's jewelry box, but I forgot that old album. Besides, your ad intrigued me. May I ask why you chose to call it a haunted house?"

"That's only a gimmick," she said, realizing that he had turned the questioning back on her in a far less subtle form and that he would get results where she could not. "Anyway, I didn't do it. My friend and employer, Sheba, did it."

"What was her reason?"

"Well, it's supposed to be a hunting lodge, and since duck season isn't open we had to do something else."

"And you came only a few days ago? If so, the ad must have been placed before you ever saw the house."

"Before I saw it, yes. But not before Sheba saw it. She came on down earlier. Last week."

"Alone?"

The way he spoke the word made the very fact of being alone in the house sound dangerous.

"She was alone, yes. Why?"

"Then she was the one who decided to call it haunted."

"Yes." He was confusing her. *Hadn't she told him that?* His eyes, so steady and demanding, asking so much of her, seemed almost to be trying to pick her brain and her thoughts as his questions otherwise served to distract her. "But as I said, it's only a gimmick."

"Of course." He smiled, but it was a surface smile. "But where did she get the idea?"

Esther and Wanda had drawn close and were listening intently. Donna looked from one to the other and tried to laugh. She shrugged, motioning with her hands. "She just thought it would be fun."

Wanda said in a voice so low it was almost a whisper, "Donna, did you tell him about the prowler?" Donna gave her a sharp look of reproval because they had agreed to keep it from Esther, the nervous one.

Esther asked loudly, *"What* prowler?"

Donna looked back at Cliff Murphy and saw a tightening of muscles around his eyes and the quick glance he darted at Wanda, movements so small that they were hardly noticeable. But it was enough to bring to her mind that he had stood on the porch outside the front door with the mists of early morning rising about him, and there really was no proof that he had only arrived at that time. She didn't recall seeing a car in the driveway.

She quickly got to her feet to get him out of the room before Wanda said more.

"Mr. Murphy," Donna said, "would you like to put your car away? There are garages in the back, I think. Two or three."

He unfolded his legs from under the table and rose. "I already have," he said. "And I'll take the bedroom at the front of the house on the southwest corner, if that's all right."

Donna didn't know where it was for sure, but she did know it wasn't hers or Sheba's. They were both on the east. Anyway, she had to get rid of him so she could talk to Wanda alone.

"What prowler?" Esther asked again, but Donna had no intention of talking in front of Cliff Murphy.

"If you'll excuse us," she said. "Wanda and I will go up and get the room ready."

"Of course. I'll go get my things."

Donna waited until she and Wanda had climbed the long, twisting flight of back stairs; then, speaking quickly and softly, she said, "Wanda, for gosh sakes don't say anything about that night to anyone. Not even Esther. And especially not to a guest."

"Why? He knows the house, and he could help us look around."

"We can look around by ourselves. I've been looking the best I can, and I have to know the lay of the house anyway if I'm going to be renting rooms. As for you, they all must be cleaned. Since there's been no more evidence of someone being here, they probably left."

"Well, all right," Wanda agreed reluctantly. "I guess if you run across somebody hiding you can always scream for help. Especially now that we've got a man in the house. And if I have to go alone to clean rooms I guess I can, though I can say I'm not sure I like it one bit. Anyway, show me where that room is and I'll get it ready for him. Sheba showed me the closet where the linens are. It's as big as my old bedroom in the apartment. There's plenty of cleaning equipment, too. Even a vacuum cleaner, though I can't imagine why."

"I suppose the Murphys simply brought what they had, even the electrical appliances."

"When Sheba bought the house did she buy that stuff too?"

"Yes. Furnished right down to the dishes, was the way it was worded."

Donna led the way from back hall to front, then around the narrow balcony that surrounded the front stairwell to the corridor that went into the front wing of the house. She found only two bedrooms there, both very large, both corner rooms, one facing southeast, the other southwest. She left Wanda in the southwest bedroom and went back the way she had come, closing behind her the door to the service wing.

With the door closed, and the only light coming from the open stairs to the kitchen below, the hall was cast in a perpetual gloom of near-dark, as if the sun had gone forever behind a black cloud.

Donna stood quietly in the hall, by Wanda's door. The footsteps, Wanda had said, went past her door and up, not down. Up. Near the open fall of stairs was a closed door. One of several she hadn't gotten around to during the busy days. Donna opened the door across the hall from Wanda's and saw the narrow steps leading upward.

The attic door. For the first time she faced the path Wanda had said was taken by whoever walked the dark halls that first night. She had put it off, without telling Wanda. Afraid? Yes. Subconsciously giving a way out for someone who might have been living in the house he considered vacant? Possibly. Two more nights had passed without incident. She could only hope he was gone.

Reluctance to enter that narrow, confining, musty, cobwebby space brought little ripples of apprehension along her arms. But to back out and call for company, as though for protection, was to admit she was a coward.

She didn't really believe anyone was up there—not now —even though he had gone up another night. Could it have been Cliff Murphy?

She climbed a few steps and stopped again, wondering about him. If he had been in the house these past nights, which was very likely, why had he tried to open her door?

As soon as she finished looking into the attic, she promised herself, she was going to town for supplies and to ask the real estate man all he knew about Cliff Murphy. All she knew was that he lived somewhere in New Orleans. Or at least that's what Sheba had said, and the lawyer who had handled his part of the sale and signing of the papers was in New Orleans. She hadn't thought it important to know anything about the previous owner, until now.

She climbed the rest of the steps warily, brushing aside a few strings of webs that hung down from the ceiling.

The attic seemed infinite, stretching away from her in all directions and cluttered with years of stored items ranging from broken chairs and tables to boxes tied with rope. There was one large painting in an ornate frame standing against a supporting post like a sentry on guard, far back in the shadows.

She walked in the thick dust that coated the floor. Dust that was tracked lightly in places by feet tiny and clawed, as the feet of mice. She passed by several boxes and two old chairs, and saw tracks made by feet larger than the feet of mice. Rats? Or perhaps squirrels?

Footprints in the dust.

And a prowler who had climbed these stairs one night. A prowler who must have left his own prints, who could at this moment be hidden somewhere in the shadows of the low-ceilinged, large attic.

Looking carefully and cautiously in all directions, she went back to the top of the stairs. The dust there was less noticeable, as if it had been swept in recent months or weeks. Moving slowly and as quietly as possible, she looked for prints that hadn't been made by small animals. And for a while she began to think that the prowler had not entered the attic at all, because the only footprints were her own.

Slowly she circled farther back into the darker areas of the attic, and there she found it. And she stopped, staring, with no real sense of successful discovery, only a kind of confused blankness rising in her mind. The print was not that of a man, not even that of a shoe. It was small. The single, bare foot of a girl.

For a long while Donna stared down at it, and gradually her mind began a tentative sorting out of the women in the house. Wanda was short, not a large person, but her feet were wide and substantial, her bones heavy. Esther, tall and thin, had a problem finding shoes to fit her long and very narrow feet.

Sheba. Only Sheba could have been in the attic barefoot. Only Sheba wore size-five double-A shoe.

Donna knew the shape of Sheba's feet better than she knew her own. Hadn't she seen them on the coffee table, ankles crossed, often enough! Narrow, high-arched, tapered. There was no mistaking the footprint.

And that first night? Sheba had said she fainted, but had she? And why, for gosh sakes, had she tried to enter a bedroom so stealthily without calling out? It wasn't like Sheba at all. There was no reason.

Of course, Sheba had spent another night in the house, to say nothing of daylight hours, when she might have made the print.

Yet all logic was against it. Why would she have gone barefoot in the chill and dampness of winter into an attic at any time, day or night?

Donna sighed with the unanswered questions that rose so disturbingly to her mind and attempted to settle them with the decision to go down and talk with Sheba and ask her.

Later. After she followed the prints to see where the girl had gone.

They went straight on back and stopped in front of the painting that leaned against one of the supporting posts in the attic.

Donna stood where Sheba had stood and looked at the painting. It was a full-length, very large painting of a man in a hunter's outfit, a shotgun by his side. He had the moustache and beard of the seventies, but the painting obviously was older than that. The smile on his lips was thin and arrogant, as arrogant as the straight-backed stance of his body, as the lift of his bearded chin. The arrogance was in his eyes, too. They were narrowed as if against the light of the rising sun, or perhaps the rising moon.

"Bleeker," a deep voice said in slow pronunciation. Donna screamed instinctively and whirled to face the sound, and then nearly fainted as she saw the large bulk of the man standing within arm's reach behind her. Cliff Murphy. Anger immediately filled her, helped along by her pounding heart.

"What in the dickens do you think you're doing sneaking up behind me like that!"

"I'm sorry," Cliff Murphy said. "I wasn't sneaking, I swear. I came up the stairs when I saw the door was open and right on across the attic and not once did it occur to me that you hadn't heard me."

Donna relaxed a little. "Okay. I'm sorry too. For yelling at you, I mean. This is the first time I've been up here. You obviously have been here before."

"Oh yes. That's why I know who that is." He stepped forward to stand beside her. "Old Andrew Bleeker. "You've heard about him of course?"

"Bleeker? No, I haven't. At least, not that I recall. Who is he?"

"He was the owner of this place before my parents bought it. There's quite a legend behind him and his life here. He was a loner, they say. A very cruel man who wouldn't let anyone cross that bridge of his. That's why it got the name of Bleeker's Bridge. A few kids used to try to come over to the lake and fish, but he was always on hand with that shotgun."

The tone in Cliff Murphy's voice brought Donna's attention up to his face. He didn't seem to notice that she was looking at him. His eyes too were narrowed, as narrowed as the eyes in the painting. He looked at the man, almost on the same level, so large and lifelike was the painting. And it seemed to Donna that there was something in Murphy's feelings for the man that were dangerous and personal.

"You knew him?" she asked.

"I never met him," he answered, surprising her. "Actually, he's been dead forty-two years. Not many people around here really remember much about when he drove his car off his own bridge and drowned. But he was one of those characters that a neighborhood never forgets, and there are many unpleasant stories about him. One of them is that he once had a young and very lovely bride, and was himself a fairly decent man when he married her. Someone came along and stole her away, and it turned him bitter and made him hate people, all people. But there's another tale that says it's not true she ran away. He killed her to keep her from running away. It didn't turn him cruel, he started that way." He smiled at her suddenly. " Anyway, your friend seems to have bought herself a painting—and a bridge. Did you know about the legend that claims anyone who tries to cross that bridge at night will drown in the water beneath it?"

The smile had disappeared as he talked, and even in the shadowed attic she could see the swift movement of emotional pain that crossed his face.

She hadn't heard it, but to reassure him and somehow help him in the memory of his family and the deaths, she said, "But that can't be true. It isn't even logical. It's an old and narrow bridge, that's all, and hard to cross even in daytime. There can't possibly be any—uh—mysterious power that possesses the bridge at night."

"That's what I thought too," he said, and began walking back toward the stairs in an aimless, strolling way. "But so many have actually died there at night that there seems to be a percentage of deaths far above chance. There's no proof that anyone has crossed it at night and lived. Not since the death of Andrew Bleeker."

"Sheba did," Donna said, and he stopped and looked back at her.

Smiling.

"Ah, but was she really in the car? My sources of information tell me the car was found locked from the inside with all windows rolled up. How did she get out?"

"I wouldn't know. I wasn't there." What was he trying to do? Pick her brain? What did he expect of *her*? "Why don't you ask Sheba?"

"I did."

"What did she say?"

"Nothing. Your friend is extremely rude at times. She gave me a spoiled-child look and left the room. Didn't even tell me to go to hell."

Donna laughed despite herself. "I'm surprised."

He responded to her laughter with a wide smile. "So was I. So that's why I'm asking you."

Her amusement vanished. "And I want to know why it's so important to you? I mean—does it bother you that she didn't drown?"

His smile vanished as quickly. "It arouses my curiosity because she was in the water, obviously, because she was wet. And the information I got in town was that she said she lost consciousness as the car went off the bridge and had no idea how she got out of the car. Yet the doors were still locked. And those doors wouldn't automatically lock if they were pushed open and allowed to fall back. So how did she get out?"

"The only thing I care about is that she did! I suppose she was so terrified she simply doesn't remember how it happened, and what I want to know is why the devil you care? And furthermore, I don't want you bothering her about it because you can see for yourself that it upsets her, otherwise why would she have refused to answer your question? Sheba is a very outgoing and friendly person, ordinarily, but, Mr. Murphy, you turn her off completely. I don't know why, but I don't blame her."

After a silent moment he said, *"Man,* why so much heat? You know, you're really very beautiful. When you're mad your cheeks turn pink as a newborn baby's bottom."

"Well, thanks for the analogy," she said furiously, now aware of the burning on her cheeks. "If you'll excuse me—"

He interrupted her casually, as if she hadn't said a word, "Are you Swedish? As fair as you are... I've never seen hair as pale and lovely. You don't have it bleached, do you? I like my women natural."

"I'm *not* your woman!" She resisted a strong impulse to stamp her foot for emphasis.

"Our kids would really be a wild combination, then. My mother, if she were still here, could say they're Swedish, Spanish-Indian, and Irish, which is why they're so extraordinarily beautiful—and of course she would, even if they weren't."

Her fury cooled a bit, but she reinforced a determination to ignore any suggestion of a sell. If he was trying to make out with her, he had a strange way of trying. She answered haughtily, "Our kids are nonexistent and will continue so. Now, as I said before, if you'll excuse me I'll get on with my work."

He shrugged, but he didn't move except to put his hands in his pockets. "What work?"

She felt like swearing. "If you'll look around you, you'll see that something needs to be done." And furthermore, she added to herself, I am in no way about to tell you what I'm up here for, nor what I want to look for when you're gone. "Now will you kindly leave?" He waited until she was within reach, then he laughed and closed one hand rather tightly around one of her arms.

"Oh come on, don't be so uptight. You got work to do, I'll help you. I didn't come here to make enemies. I need friends. Why is it every time I try to find out something around here the only two women in the house who will talk to me don't know anything?"

She paused. "I don't know anything either," she said. "And I don't know why it matters so much to you."

"Let's just say the—uh—supernatural intrigues me. Look," he released her arm and used the palm of one hand to emphasize his point with the finger of the other hand, "you have to admit, don't you, that Sheba's getting out of that car was a bit strange?"

"I don't know what you're getting at," she replied, frankly puzzled. "All I know is that she did. She lived."

"She lived," he repeated. "A girl who didn't die. Under a bridge that is avoided by all who know about it because it's so dangerous. The odds are too much, Donna."

"Odds? I'm beginning to wonder if you're a gambler, the easy way you keep mentioning odds."

"In a way I am. Not with money, however. But would you do me a favor?"

Slowly and with reservations, she said, "I don't know. What is it?"

"I simply want you to persuade your friend to talk to me about it. I promise not to upset her. If she would let me, we could bring out what really happened that night."

"And that's what you want to know? What happened—how she got out of the car?" He seemed obsessed by it. She was disappointed to think he might be a little off mentally, but it fell right in with the kind of person who might hide in the house for several days before he made himself known. She decided to check up on him, if she could.

"I want to know more than that," he said in all seriousness, so that she was almost ashamed of her thought that he was their prowler. "I want to know what causes the accidents. Why so many people have driven off the bridge."

"Mr. Murphy, I'd like to ask you something," she said.

He nodded. "Shoot."

"Where were you before you came here?"

"New Orleans."

"When did you leave there?"

"I left there Monday night about eleven o'clock, and I arrived in town here the next afternoon. I spent the night in town and came out the next morning. Why?"

"I'm going to prepare a guest book. Will you sign your address?"

"Sure. What's the matter? Why all this suspicion all of a sudden? You want to check me? I'll furnish references if you want them. I assure you, I'm not your prowler." She looked away, uncomfortable. The rise of trust was strong and unexpected, and now she knew she didn't want to believe this man capable of anything abnormal. "I know you're not our prowler. I really don't think there was one—just noises in the house." Now if she could only keep Wanda quiet!

"Look," he said, "I know you want to get out of here and go on back downstairs. But can we get back to the bridge for a moment?"

"All right. Sheba also said the railing was missing. She had a new one put on one side."

"But railings can't be all the reason. Of course it would help. Sometimes when you get away from the larger cities and into the so-called backwoods areas you run across strange old legends that have some fact to them. And the legend of the bridge—that no one who crosses it at night lives, since the death of Andrew Bleeker— seems to be one with a lot of truth in it. I want very much to hear Sheba's side of this."

"Okay, I'll see if I can persuade her to talk about it to you."

He must be a superstitious man, she decided, which only proved how the outward appearance of a person could be misleading. He looked anything but superstitious. He dressed well and obviously was not short on money or education. But to believe in an old legend like that? "May I ask you another question?" she said.

"Of course."

"Do you really believe this thing about the bridge?"

"I believe," he said slowly, as if wondering how much to tell her, or perhaps making up something as he went along, "that I should have paid some attention to it when I first heard it. If I had, my family might still be alive."

"Oh, I see." And she was sure she *did* see. Some form of guilt lay beyond his superstition about the bridge. "You think you might have prevented their deaths?"

"I might have," he answered, smiling again briefly and with a twist of irony to his lips. "My mother called for me and I put off coming up here. Then it was too late. I sold the property to your friend with misgivings, but I wanted to be rid of the place. I couldn't even bear to take any of the things that had belonged to them, my family. Then I read in the paper the ad about the haunted-house bit and rooms for rent. So I decided to come on out and see why you had decided on that. So that, Miss Donna Walker, is why I am here."

Donna's astonishment had grown in her mind like a creeping fungus as he talked. "But that was only a gimmick! A sales pitch, that's all."

"Was it?" he asked. "I would like very much to talk with Sheba about it if you could persuade her."

"Well, I can try. She probably will when she takes the notion. Why not?" Donna felt a frown of confusion draw her eyebrows. Sheba had told her the first night of a thick, white, mist-like substance that was capable of movement and destruction. She had called it a ghost—and Donna had felt Sheba was really only imagining it. She still thought so. But at least Sheba would be glad to know that she had a willing and non-skeptical listener in this man who, after all, had a reason for wanting to know. Though it did seem a bit late to worry about it. On the subject of ghosts they at least would be compatible. Things like ghosts were a long, long way from her own world. And she wanted them to stay that way. "I'll go down and tell Sheba you'd like to talk to her."

"Thank you. I'll be down later. If it's all right with you, I'd like to look around up here for a while."

"Yes, of course it's all right with me. Besides, you said it was still your attic." She glanced teasingly at him. "In fine print."

"Uh—in-fine print, yes. I'm afraid I was just talking. To keep you with me, maybe. There's another thing..."

She paused, ready to leave. "Yes?"

"About the prowler—I heard you mention something about one. Have you been disturbed by someone since you came here?"

She had a sudden urge to go down and stuff something into Wanda's mouth. Did she have to trust every man who smiled at her? "A prowler?" Yes, she thought, if you can call Sheba a prowler. If you can go by footsteps. "No prowler, Mr. Murphy," she said.

"Call me Cliff, okay?"

"Well, okay, Cliff, do you—" She stopped, reluctant to finish asking him if he knew anything about somnambulism, because she felt sure that the only way Sheba could have come barefoot into the attic at night—and not remember it—was in a state of sleepwalking. And if that were so, there certainly was nothing to worry about. The house had probably made her a little nervous, that was all. And now she was settled, more at ease.

"Do I what? he asked.

"Nothing." She smiled a friendly smile to make up for any earlier rudeness. "Make yourself at home here in the attic and I hope you find what you're looking for."

She went down the stairs, glad to get out of the attic, but unable to get away from the sudden burden of mental pressure that was still confusing her. Ghosts? In Sheba's dream she had seen ghosts. Cliff Murphy spoke of odds. All her life she had lived in the mentally nonthreatening world of seeing-is-believing. And she wasn't ready to open herself up to worlds unseen, worlds that threatened one's sanity and beliefs. Let Sheba imagine her ghosts. Let Cliff Murphy search for a reason for the deaths of the ones he had loved. Couldn't he just accept that a simple fog had obscured the vision of the driver and sent them irretrievably to their deaths?

No. She knew you don't just accept death. Not for a long time after, at least. She had gone through it herself with the death of her mother when she was fifteen. It had taken years to accept it. Even after her dad married again, two years later, she still felt that he was being unfaithful to her beloved mother.

But it took a long time. And Cliff Murphy was still too close to the actual deaths.

Donna closed the attic door behind her and went from the service hallway through into the wider expanse of the center part of the house. She paused there, listening.

A door closed softly somewhere around the balcony and down the wing to her right, and Donna went in that direction. As she drew nearer she could hear movements in a bedroom whose door stood open. Outside the door was a service cart piled with linens and cleaning equipment. Inside the room, Wanda was bent over the bed, pounding the mattress with the back side of a short-handled, stiff-bristled brush. Dust rose, puffing up in small clouds with each whack of the brush, and Wanda paused to cough. She then used the brush as a fan against the dust from the mattress.

"Dusty, isn't it?" Donna said.

With a loud squawk Wanda whirled round to stare pop-eyed at Donna, then with a groan she sank down to sit on the edge of the mattress.

Donna said quickly, "Say, I sure am sorry. I didn't mean to scare you." But then she began to giggle softly. "You did look funny. Cliff Murphy did that to me just a while ago upstairs, so I know how you feel."

Wanda fanned her face with the brush as color rushed back. "The minute I stop looking over my shoulder someone sneaks up behind me. The very minute! These mattresses are a mess, especially on this side of the house, for some reason. They're molded, mostly, but this one I think is as old as the house." She got up and poked the end of her brush at, and into, spots that stained the lumpy mattress. "See, it looks like somebody peed on it. Stained. Look at the moldy places. You'd never think they'd be dusty too. I was surprised. When I hit it the dust poured out."

"I know. I saw it. We may have to replace that mattress."

"I wouldn't doubt it. It stinks, too. Of course, most of them do. On account of the damp, I guess. I've made up three rooms besides Mr. Murphy's and the new one Sheba's moving into."

"Moving? Sheba's moving?"

"Already moved by now, probably. But then, her things were mostly still packed anyway, so all she had to do was carry her suitcases."

"Where did she move to?"

"Across the hole of the stairs, whatever you call it. Around on the other side of the balcony, anyway. The first room on this side of the balcony at the top of the stairs. There, by the lamp in the wall bracket at the corner. Didn't she tell you?"

"No. Actually, I was looking for her."

"Well, she's there, in her new room. So far as I know." Wanda went to the doorway and looked cautiously up and down the hall, then she asked in a low and secretive voice, "You say you were up in the attic?"

"Yes."

"Were you looking for that prowler?"

"Well, that's what I had in mind, yes."

"Did you find him?" She immediately answered herself. "Now that's a silly question. If you had you wouldn't be standing here looking so calm."

"You're right. I didn't find him." She didn't want to mention the footprints that could only have belonged to Sheba. "But I don't think you have to worry about anything. Probably whoever it was is gone and won't return."

"I hope so. But just to make sure, I'm not going to leave my door open at night. I'm glad that Mr. Murphy is here, though. Just having a man around makes me feel more—well, at home. Safer, I guess. What do you want me to do about this bed?"

"Just skip this room. If the house should begin to fill up, we'll do something about it then. The main thing is getting things dusted and swept as well as you can. I'm going now to see Sheba."

Donna went back along the hall and turned right, going around the balcony to the first door. She knocked. After a long moment of silence Sheba's voice gave her permission to come in.

Donna entered a room she hadn't seen before. It was larger than the one Sheba had moved out of, but most of the bedrooms were not especially roomy. Most of the floor space seemed to be taken up by large, bulky furniture. The one window near the opposite corner of the room let in very little light.

"But this room isn't nearly as light and pleasant as the one you had," Donna said, looking around.

"I know. But I didn't like that other room."

Sheba was hanging clothes in the tall wardrobe that took up a portion of one wall. Donna had noticed that most of the rooms had these large, bulky, black affairs rather than closets.

"Now I'll be on that side of the house all by myself," Donna said lightly.

But Sheba didn't respond as Donna expected. Quietly, without a word, she went on with the business of putting her clothes on hangers. Donna began to feel like an intruder for the first time since she had begun living in the same house with Sheba. She felt that Sheba was resentful about something and would rather be left alone. With growing discomfort, Donna watched her.

"Sheba, I want to talk to you," she finally said.

"Go ahead and talk," Sheba replied.

"Are you mad at me about something?"

"Of course not. Just because I decided to move to another room you think I'm mad? Don't be silly."

"Okay. But I came to find you because Cliff Murphy wants to talk to you. I told him you would."

"What about?"

"About the night you drove off the bridge. Did you know his family drove off that bridge and drowned?"

"Yes, I knew that."

"Did you know that others have too?"

"Yes."

"Well, did you know you're the only one who got out alive?"

"So I heard," Sheba mumbled, turning to get more clothes and keeping her back to Donna. Deliberately, it seemed.

"Well, because of that he wants to talk to you. He says he's interested because his folks died there, and he's here to investigate what happened. He'll be interested in hearing what you told me the first night we were here."

Sheba stopped and stood very still for a moment. Then she asked, "What are you talking about? What did I tell you that night?"

"The—the ghost. You know..."

"The ghost!" Suddenly Sheba was laughing. She turned, looking at Donna, and her laugh seemed merry and natural. "You must be kidding."

Donna stared at her, the confusion moving through her mind again as insidiously as the mist-like fog of which Sheba had told her that night. Sheba was trying to pretend that the night had not existed. Why? "You're saying you don't want to talk to him about it?"

"I'm saying I don't even know what *you're* talking about, so how could I possibly talk to him?"

Sheba's laugh dwindled away and she went back to hanging up clothes.

Donna continued to watch her, wondering about her change in personality. After months of sharing an apartment with Sheba, could it be that she really didn't know her moods at all? There, they had seldom been together for more than an hour or so at a time.

"Sheba...

"Yeah?"

"Have you been up into the attic?"

"No, I haven't." She shook out a long, blue dress and put it on a hanger. Her face was relaxed and pretty, with no sign of anxiety, worry, or annoyance. "The first day I was here the real estate man took me through the house, all except the attic. He showed me where the door was, but didn't seem interested in going up, and I wasn't either. I told him I'd look into it another time. He seemed to think it needed a lot of cleaning out." She suddenly looked up at Donna as a thought occurred to her. "Why? Have you been up there?"

"Yes, I was. Are you sure you haven't?"

Sheba's large eyes were innocent in her denial. "Of course I'm sure. Why? What's the matter?"

"Nothing," Donna said, going back to the door. There was no point in further questioning. Either Sheba was lying, for some strange reason, or Donna was herself mistaken about the prints. She decided to go look again to make sure. At the door she paused long enough to ask, "What shall I tell Mr. Murphy?"

"Tell Mr. Murphy?" Sheba replied blankly. "Why... tell him we hope he enjoys his stay here. What else?"

"I mean about your accident. He wants to know if you will talk to him about it."

"About the accident? Well, I don't know what good it would do, but I suppose I could. Just tell him I'll be down to the living room later. When I'm finished here."

"All right."

Donna closed Sheba's door and went back to the attic stairway and called up into the musty twilight, "Mr. Murphy?" She climbed the steps to see him sitting on his heels looking into an old trunk. When he saw her he stood up and dusted his hands.

"Sheba said she would be down to the living room later to talk to you."

"Good. Perhaps I'd better go on down."

She started to tell him there was no hurry, but decided against it. She wanted to be alone for a while because she didn't want him to know what she was looking for or why.

When he was gone, his footsteps echoing hollowly on the steep attic steps, she went slowly back toward the painting that stood in the shadows; a large, hulking monster that emanated brutality as surely as if he stood there alive, waiting, just waiting for whatever came within reach.

Donna could see the possibility of the man killing his young wife to keep her from running away to freedom. The eyes, the face, even the posture of the man suggested truth behind the last story.

She avoided looking at it again and kept her eyes on the floor in search of the footprints. She found, to her dismay, that her own footprints, and those of much larger men's shoes, obliterated all other prints near the painting. She looked carefully, searching for that other, small, bare foot. And did not find it. Had they, she and CliffMurphy, walked about so much?Or had the obliteration taken place after she'd left the attic? It seemed almost deliberate.

And it seemed she was becoming inordinately suspicious of everything and everybody.

She went back toward the top of the steps, to the place she first had seen the lone, small print of a bare foot.And foundit again, untouched. She squatted, sitting on her heels as she had found Murphy, and in the musty, smothering gloom of the attic she carefully with one finger traced the outline of the footprint. And the name of the owner shouted itself in her mind.

Sheba... Sheba... Sheba...

But why had she lied?

CHAPTER 8

Cliff Murphy was waiting in the living room when Sheba finally went down. She had put it off for as long as she politely could, taking more time than she needed in putting away clothes, arranging them just right, then rearranging. But finally she had to go down, because he was, after all, a paying guest. And he wanted to talk to her.

She stood for a while by a pillar at the edge of the living room, looking at his back. He seemed to be absorbed in something beyond the confines of the house, something in the sun-bright landscape. His posture was relaxed, with the thumb of one hand hooked in the pocket of his trousers.

Sheba was aware of his attractiveness, but not drawn to it. The feelings he aroused in her were different from any she had ever known. She saw his good looks as distantly and impersonally as she saw the good looks of an actor or a male model, and at the same time was aware of a deep and growing animosity. She wanted to ask him why he had come. Now that he had sold the property, now that his people were gone, *why had he come?*

At any other time she would have dismissed her feelings and said he was Donna's type of man, not hers. As she had Neil. But Cliff Murphy wasn't in the same league with Neil. Cliff Murphy was... well, dangerous to have around. For some reason. She didn't know why, but she knew he wasn't to be trusted.

As if he had suddenly become aware that he was being stared at, he turned and looked at her. And instantly the smile that seemed to Sheba not really a smile but only a practiced copy made to fool people into thinking he was friendly and harmless came to play lightly across his lips. He crossed the room toward her.

"Miss Gilbert. May I call you Sheba? I hope I'm not taking you away from something important."

Sheba said automatically, "Our guests are important." He stopped at a chair near the pot-belly stove and put his hand on the back of it. "Then may I ask you to sit down and talk with me for a while?"

She nodded, and went to sit in the chair he was more or less holding for her. Even his politeness seemed to her to be only the beginnings of a trap he was preparing to spring. A trap that would maim and destroy her. Instinct told her to be careful. Very careful.

"What did you want to talk about?" she asked cautiously.

He sat down in a chair that faced hers, and his eyes were level and steady and dark. There was no smile anywhere now. Especially in those searching eyes. Sheba looked down at her hands and twisted the rings on her finger. She still wore on the same finger, two of the diamond rings given her by her ex-husbands.

"You're aware that my parents and sister drove off the bridge and died there?"

"Yes."

"That others have? That no one came out alive but you?"

"Yes." She was getting so tired of that phrase, and suddenly the anger rose and burst out. She returned his gaze steadily. "You know, I think everyone is disappointed that I didn't die too! Now your silly old superstition is broken, isn't it? Is that why you don't like me, because I lived and your family didn't?"

She expected some reaction, but got none. Instead, he calmly asked, "Do you feel that I don't like you?" For one stunned moment she didn't know what to say. Then the words were bursting from her again, unplanned: "It doesn't matter! What matters is that I'm *here*, and I'm here whether you or anyone else like it or not! I can't help it I managed to get out of that stinking water alive!"

"Sheba, I'm glad you did. I wish everyone had. But since they didn't, and you did, I would like to ask you about it. Do you feel like talking about it?"

"Of course I feel like talking about it!" she replied crossly. "I have no guilty conscience about being alive."

"Miss Gilbert, please. I didn't intend for one moment that you should be made to feel guilty. If I've hurt you, I apologize."

"You haven't hurt me," she muttered, looking at her hands again. "What is it you want to know?"

She expected that he would ask how she managed to get out, but he surprised her.

"What caused you to drive off the bridge?" he asked.

She looked up at him again, silent and thoughtful. Her mind quickly played back over the night when she had tried to tell Donna about the ghost-fog, but Donna hadn't believed her. Even after promising that she would. And Donna didn't know how helpless and afraid it had left her. Then. In the beginning. After that came the hot fury, the anger at being put down as someone who didn't know a fog from a cloud or a... well, a ghost.

To hell with all of them.

If Cliff Murphy thought for one moment that she would tell him the truth, then he was more conceited than he looked. And that was going some!

"What caused me to drive off the bridge?" she repeated, keeping her voice emotionless. "Well, there was no railing. And that bridge is narrow. And I was trying so hard to keep on it that the first thing I knew I was driving off. I tried to pull the car back and couldn't, so I threw the door open and jumped, just as the car went down."

His eyes continued to penetrate hers as though he was trying to read her mind. She wondered briefly if he might be capable of it, and drew up a mental barrier between them. Let him see her hostility, her distrust of him. He would see nothing else.

"So you never really got into the water," he said softly, as though pondering on many things at once.

"Uh..." Her story would be easily checked, she remembered, and added, "Well, I did get wet."

"I understand some fishermen found you unconscious on the bank."

"You've already asked someone in town about this," she cried in sudden anger. "Then why are you asking me?"

"Because they don't know anything. You do. But there seems to be some confusion in the story. They said you didn't know how you got out of the car, and also that it was a fog that obscured your vision and caused you to drive into the water."

Sneaky, she thought. That was what he was. "What are you, anyway?" she asked. "It sounds to me like a third degree you're giving me. Why?"

The smile was there again, and he changed positions in the chair, putting one foot up to rest his ankle on the other knee. "All right, I'll tell you. There's some evidence of psychic disturbances in this house and on that bridge. And I'm a, well—interested in unusual happenings. I was planning to come up and look into the things that were beginning to upset my sister when the accident occurred. But after that I would never have come back at all if it hadn't been for your ad. I figured that if you also called it a haunted house, you must have a reason."

"You're a ghost hunter," she said.

"Something like that."

"And every ghost hunter I ever heard about goes and proves there is no such thing. Well, let me save you the trouble. There's nothing here to interest you."

"You're not asking me to cut out, are you?"

I'd like to, she thought, but when you're making money only by people being around, you don't ask them to leave. "No, of course not Stay as long as you want." She ignored his smile.

"And do you mind if I hunt ghosts and ask questions?"

"Well, you're wasting your time," Sheba told him coldly. "I put that ad in the paper simply because we needed guests to take the place of hunters until duck season opens. That's all."

"You've seen nothing unusual here in the house?"

"Nothing."

"And it was only a fog that caused you to run off the bridge?"

"There was a bit of fog, yes," she said, wishing she hadn't told anyone anything. "But it was the railing being gone that really caused it. I really have to go, Mr. Murphy. The house isn't ready for guests, and I have to help get it ready. There's a lot of cleaning to do, and Wanda can't do it alone."

He stood up when she did, but remained by his chair. On the way out of the room she was sure his eyes were steady, watching her retreat from him. And he was bound to know that she was retreating, and was probably wondering why.

She was careful to not look back toward him when she reached the foyer.

In the three days that followed she worked almost at Wanda's elbow, partly to protect herself from the continued presence of the man. Wishing he would go away didn't help.

She tried to warn Donna about him. "Did you know he's up in the attic?" Donna sat like a fair-skinned, platinum-haired queen behind her desk. "He's been up there for hours!"

Donna gazed at her calmly. "I knew he was up there, yes."

"Well, what's he looking for, anyway?" Sheba demanded. "Does he think we've got a body hidden up there or something?"

Donna laughed. "Oh, Sheba. The personal items he's looking for are up there, that's all. There's a lot of junk up there, and he's having some trouble finding the album."

"What album?"

"One that belonged to his family—an old one, he told me.

"I don't believe him."

Donna looked solemnly at Sheba and tapped the end of her pencil on the open journal in front of her. "Hey," she said at last, softly, "he's a guest, Sheba. We can't be so hostile toward a guest. Especially when he's not doing any harm to anyone. He really has a right to look for things he wants, you know. Besides, he's interested in your ghost."

"You didn't tell him what I told you!"

In quiet contrast, Donna said, "No, I didn't tell him. I figured if you didn't want to talk about it to him you had a reason. What I should have said is he *would* be interested in your ghost."

"Stop calling it my ghost." Sheba whirled to leave the room but her tension and frustration became almost more than she could tolerate. She whirled back again. "Besides, I think you were right and I must have been dreaming or something. It was probably that room, and the moonlight.

"I'm glad," Donna said sympathetically. "I was afraid you were going to be unhappy here."

"No," Sheba replied truthfully. "I love it here. But I wish you'd be careful and not get so friendly with that Murphy character, Donna. I don't trust him."

"I don't know why it bothers you so much," Donna said. "He isn't hurting us by being here, and after all, Sheba, you can't be too picky if you're going to run a—" A knock on the front door, the clanging metal against metal of the old-fashioned knocker, interrupted the conversation. Together they went into the foyer.

Three people stood on the porch, one woman and two men. They were young, alert, and obviously looking the house over the best they could as they waited. The one in front, a man, spoke.

"Is this the haunted house that was advertised?" Donna smiled and pulled the large, heavy door wide. "Yes. Come in."

The men picked up luggage that had been set down on the porch and the three of them walked into the foyer to stop in a small group aside from Donna and Sheba.

The girl was a nice-looking blonde dressed in blue jeans and short jacket to match, and the man who kept one hand on her arm was about her height and dressed exactly the same way. The other man had quite long, very clean hair, and eyes that immediately went from a quick glance around the part of the house visible from where he stood to take in the figure of Sheba. There was no question which he liked better. She watched him, saw his coldness and the unspoken question in his eyes, and remembered that it had been some time since she had been in a man's arms. Murphy, and his irritating presence, dwindled in importance.

She smiled, the special kind that answered unspoken questions, and put out her hand. His hand was warm and moist as his fingers clasped tightly around hers.

"I'm Sheba Gilbert," she said, "And this is Donna Walker. We're here to see that you enjoy your visit." His fingers pressed, telling her he caught her message. "Call me Dennis. And these two are friends of mine, Diane and Randy."

Donna, smiling, motioned toward the guest book that was open on a table. "Would you sign your names here please? Then we will show you the rooms we have and you can take your choice. We're newly opened, and have only one guest registered. How long will you be staying with us?"

"That depends... Dennis said, "on how long we're wanted."

Diane gave him a glance and laughed, then she walked over to look up into the open area above the stairway. "Tell me," she said, "is it really haunted? It really is just a big put-on, isn't it?" the girl said, wandering hesitantly toward the living room, her chin out first and her feet slowly following, as though to give herself a running start backward just in case.

Sheba glanced at Donna and saw the forced smile on her face, and the glance she returned to Sheba spoke clearly her opinion of the young crowd the ad had drawn. But Sheba didn't care. At least it would be a welcome change. Already she felt more alive, younger, carefree. She was going to like this group.

"Actually," Dennis said, letting go of Sheba's hand to get a cigarette and light it, "we're just the beginning. We're the suicide mission. This weekend, if we come out alive, we'll bring you so many you'll have to pitch tents.

"So many *what?*" Donna asked coolly.

Randy cackled, and Dennis said, "Hey, humans, man what else?"

"Well," said Donna, her smile gone, "the spirits of the undead do draw some very strange objects at times. I just thought we should be forewarned."

"Man, you don't mean it," the girl said.

"Ah, but I do. Let me tell you about it," Donna said and she had their full attention. "After dark, when you hear things begin moving about in the hall and in the attic overhead, when you hear the screams of lost souls coming in from out of the marsh, be very sure that you stay in your rooms. Above all, don't try to come out to investigate. That is one of the important rules of the house... because if you open your doors we can't be responsible for what happens to you. Until dark," she said softly in the thundering silence of the huge foyer, "*until* dark, you are quite safe."

After she had finished her eerie little speech the silence was broken by a hardly audible but very outstandingly deep chuckle from the darker, narrow corridor that went back into the depths of the house. The girl whirled and gasped, the men's heads, turned sharply; even Sheba felt a tingle of spooky surprise.

She saw, leaning against the newel post of the stairway, Cliff Murphy. He came forward and bowed slightly. Dressed in black, he was the perfect ending to Donna's speech. A touch of sensual, handsome evil.

Donna said, "Cliff Murphy. The only other guest." Sheba expected a wisecrack of some kind, but the new guests seemed stunned into silence. Dennis now looked a bit immature beside Cliff Murphy, Sheba decided, but not enough to hide his own sensuality. He'd do, for a start.

Murphy said, "Let me further introduce myself. Murphy, psychic investigator. Parapsychologist."

"You're kidding," the girl gasped, her gasp a question, her rounded eyes a question.

"No," he said, and offered her his arm. "Shall we go into the living room and talk of ghosts." It was no question. It was a softly spoken command. His smile looked wickedly teasing.

She didn't take his arm. She kept staring at him as if she wasn't sure but that he was, in some dangerous way, a part of the house. And Sheba wasn't so sure either. She watched the small transaction with growing interest.

"You've seen ghosts?" the girl asked as though wondering whether to believe. "In this house?"

Murphy's answer was the continuation of a smile that could easily have been interpreted as hypnotic. Sheba drew back toward Donna.

"Aren't you interested?" Cliff Murphy asked.

The girl slowly put out her hand to his arm. "I'm not sure," she said. "Really, I thought it was all a big put-on. We all did."

"We'll go prepare three rooms for you," Donna said.

Randy felt he should explain something. "We're on a limited budget and can only afford two rooms."

Donna nodded agreement. "Fine. I'm sure we can find one with twin beds so that you two guys won't have to sleep together," she said pointedly.

"Uh... thanks," Randy said, then took off after Murphy and his girl.

Donna and Sheba went back to the kitchen, where Esther was poking fuel into the stove and Wanda was sitting on the edge of the table holding a cup of coffee with both hands. Donna told Wanda to prepare for three guests, and told Esther to make food.

Esther said, "Get off the table and go get rooms ready, Wanda."

Wanda obeyed, leaving her cup on the table. "Rooms coming up. Three? Where shall I put them? The kids, I mean."

Donna said quietly, "Two rooms, not three. But make sure one of the rooms has twin beds—just in case."

"Just in case what?"

Sheba said lightly, "Don't bother. If the sexy one gets scared to sleep alone I'll keep him company."

Esther turned back to the stove, shaking her head in disapproval. "What is this world coming to."

It wasn't a question, merely her opinion, so no one bothered to answer her.

Donna said to Sheba, "In that case, why don't you go up and help Wanda pick the rooms?"

"But I was going to mix them some drinks."

Esther muttered in an undertone, "Probably not old enough to drink. Are they twenty-one?"

"Who's to know? If they're big enough, they're old enough. Besides, this is a private club. House."

Sheba arranged bottles, glasses, and a bucket of ice on a cart with small wheels, one of their additions to the house, and pushed it along the hall toward the living room.

Dennis said to her as he came to take the cart, "Are you ever a beautiful lifesaver. And I'm the best bartender in the county. Would you let me mix you my special?"

"Later. You mix it, and I'll be back. I have to go up and see where you'll be sleeping."

"Sleeping?" he said suggestively. "In a house like this I'll need protection from all the weird goings on. Will you protect me?"

"Well... we'll see about that."

He nodded toward Cliff Murphy. "From what we hear I'm going to be needing a lot of protection tonight. But tell me seriously—it's just a lot of bull, isn't it?"

Sheba looked at Murphy. He was sitting relaxed in his chair, watching with amusement the two in front of him. The girl was asking something which Sheba couldn't hear. She leaned forward, elbows on knees, for his answer. But the answer she got was a careless shrug.

The feeling of resentment that rose in Sheba was confusing in its severity. She, in fun, had advertised the house as haunted; but now she felt angry that people had come to make fun of it. She felt all at once that the atmosphere in the house, the slightly damp and musty air, the house itself, was in some way feeling their mockery; the hate was building, growing like a storm—couldn't they feel it?—and it would retaliate. In some way, soon, it would retaliate.

She was cold, and she shivered.

"Hey," Dennis said, "you need a drink. I'll warm you up if you'll let me. I could go up and help you find that room."

She sipped the drink he gave her and deliberately pushed away the other thoughts and fears and concentrated on the suggestive eyes of the man. She had no doubt that he was much younger than she, but it didn't matter. "Later," she said.

"Tonight?"

"Sure, why not?"

"In my room or yours?"

"Mine. It's isolated from the others."

"I think this is one night when I'll go to bed early." She smiled at him, put her drink back on the cart, and went upstairs to help pick out the rooms. One thing for sure—they had to be far enough away, but not too far, from hers.

Sheba went back along the hall after seeing that Donna and Wanda had gotten rooms ready. Darkness had fallen rapidly so that the corner at the end of the hall, where a kerosene lamp hung on a wall bracket, blended into a deep, grayish twilight. Sheba paused long enough to light the lamp. The light it cast, though, was limited and closed in, as by increasing fog and mist, so that the hall seemed even more shadowed and dark, leaving the landing of the stairway dangerous to those who didn't know the house. She stopped on the top step and looked back at the light in its isolation. It reminded her of a street scene about eighteenth century London where the streetlamps were said to have been tiny islands, dim and fog-shrouded in the black, enclosed world of walls and alleys. She went on down the stairs, pausing again at the sharp turn to light the lamp there. The globe, she noticed, felt misty— damp in her hand. She replaced it and wiped her hand on a tissue from her pocket, then went on down and into the living room.

Cliff Murphy was lighting the third lamp, and the three guests were standing closely together by the stove. Silent. Wishing they hadn't come? Had his purpose been to entertain them or scare them away?

"The rooms are ready," Sheba said, and the girl, who had been watching Murphy, gasped in startled fear as she had earlier and whirled to stare wide-eyed at Sheba before she collapsed weakly for a moment against her boyfriend's chest.

Sheba tried to make up for it with her brightest smile. "I'll show you around the house if you'd like. It—"

She had intended to tell them it wasn't so bad, that it wasn't really haunted, but the girl quickly interrupted her. "No, thanks! Just the rooms will be enough. Only, don't go away. Stay with us."

"Of course. After we have dinner we'll have a card game or something, okay?"

"Okay," the girl said, looking for approval at Randy, who had his arm around her. "If it's okay with the guys." They answered in the affirmative and followed Sheba up the sharply angled stairs. When they reached the rooms the house was quiet; Wanda and Donna had gone. But they had left lamps lighted in both rooms. Sheba stopped in the room with the twin beds first.

"The bathroom is just across the hall. And your room," she said to Dennis, "is next door. I'll show it to you now if you like."

"I like," he said, and put his hot hand on her back. They left the girl and her partner for the night, looking in dumb silence around their room.

Dennis didn't bother to look at his room. The moment they crossed the threshold he pushed the door shut and slid an arm around Sheba's waist. With his mouth on her neck he whispered, "Are you one of those lovely vampires that disappear in the sunlight? If so, I'm all yours to feed upon this night...."

"Not here," she said, wishing they'd all cut the spook nonsense. It was about to turn her off for some dumb reason. She knew she didn't like it, and she didn't think it was funny. "Come to my room, later, after everyone has gone to bed."

"After midnight?"

"Just... later. We'll try to get them to bed earlier than that. There's really nothing to sit up for around here. Come on, let me show you where it is." She pulled away from him almost impatiently. She wanted him, wanted to know how good he was in bed, but later, not now. She wished she could tell him so, but was afraid she'd turn *him* off and he wouldn't come to her room at all.

He let her lead him by the hand, around the corner where the lamp seemed to be throwing even less light into the increased darkness. She pointed to her door.

"That one. Give me ten minutes after everyone is settled."

She noticed the heaviness of his breathing, but assumed it was the labored breathing of sexual need, until he put his hand to his throat and looked back at the lamp.

"Kind of stuffy in here, isn't it?" he asked.

"Is something wrong?" she asked.

"Naw."

He turned on her the smile of self-confidence of a male who has conquered his woman, not seeming to know in his immaturity that in her case it was just the opposite. She returned his smile softly, knowing she was the ideal of femininity, letting him think he was the irresistible male. As he would be—when the time came.

Together they went down the stairs. The living room had been vacated, and the lighted lamps quite successfully cast out all but the most persistent of shadows. They got out the card table and set it up, and Dennis mixed more drinks just as Diane and Randy came back into the living room in a half-run, giggling.

Donna came along the hall and foyer lighting lamps, and announced that dinner was ready to serve in the dining room. They went gaily along with her, the drinks obviously having overcome any nervousness on the part of the girl. She chattered, giggled, and flirted with Randy.

For the first time dinner was served in the large dining room at a table that could easily have held twenty guests. The six people who ate there took up only a small portion of one end of the table.

Immediately after dinner Cliff Murphy excused himself and disappeared beyond the dining room door, and after a few more minutes the others went back into the living room. Donna remained with them only until they were settled at the card table, then she said good night and left.

The conversation continued in a light vein, led by the girl, until her partner began to look slightly droopy-eyed from too much liquor and too little sleep. Diane, evidently feeling that the evening of cards had brought Sheba into intimacy with them, leaned toward her and asked a question in a hushed voice:

"Will you tell me something, honestly and truthfully?" Sheba didn't like personal questions, and for a moment she hesitated, then she said, "I'll try."

"Was he putting us on? That man."

Sheba wasn't sure she knew what the girl was talking about. She tried to recall some of the things that Murphy had said at the dinner table, but none of it had anything to do with the house. Not then. And Sheba had a strong feeling that the girl was referring to the house. "What did he tell you?" Sheba asked.

Dennis groaned slightly. "Man, what didn't he!"

But the girl paid him no attention. "I mean about him being a psychic investigator, and him being here to find out about the things that happen at night."

The card game had stopped, unfinished. Sheba said, "I don't know what he is. He may be a psychic investigator all right, but he isn't here to find out what goes on in the house. He's here because he was the last owner and he came to get some personal things that were left behind. It has nothing to do with the house." Diane leaned back in her chair. "That's what I thought! He was just putting us on."

"Well, I can say this," Randy said, "he's damn good at it. He ought to be in movies. He just about made a believer out of me."

The three of them laughed a little, but Sheba asked, "What all did he tell you?"

"Oh gosh," Diane said. "I can't remember it all, but mostly it was how really dangerous it is to be here after dark. You know—like maybe people are, well, murdered in their beds or something. But then I got to thinking that after all, the rest of you are here. And you're still alive."

"*Murdered?* He said that?" Sheba felt hot with rage suddenly. What was the guy trying to do, run off all her guests?

"Naw," said Dennis, coughing as he lighted a cigarette. When the coughing subsided he said, "He didn't really say that, he just said if we valued our lives perhaps we'd better get out of here before dark. But I wasn't fooled by it. I just figured it was another put-on, you know, like the haunted-house bit to start with. I think he was just layin' it on us."

"Pretty heavily, if you ask me," Sheba said. "I'm glad you didn't take him seriously and pull out before dark."

"So am I," he said, looking at her with eyes that spoke their wanting. "Why don't we try out our rooms now and listen for spooks in the night."

"Don't get that started again, Dennis, for Christ's sake," Diane said. "I'd just as soon not have any dressing to go along with this dark, old, horrible house. It's bad enough just the way it is. I'll be glad to get back to the dorm at school."

They pushed chairs away from the table and prepared to leave the room, and Sheba looked at the profile of the girl and decided she really didn't like her very much.

"The house isn't so bad," she said. "Not when you get used to it."

"I'd never get used to it. Come on, Randy, hold me close and never, never let me go."

They waited for Sheba to blow out the lamps in the living room, and then said good night in the turn of the upstairs hall. Into Sheba's ear Dennis whispered, "Remember, ten minutes."

In the pale light of the lamp at the corner Sheba looked at her watch. It was ten minutes to eleven. She went into the closed darkness of her room and lighted the lamp.

She had changed and was wearing a black, sheer, hip-length top and narrow bikini panties, and was beginning to shiver in the chill in her room when the knock came softly at her door. She opened it and let Dennis in, and with no word spoken closed the door again and turned to meet the eagerness of his arms and body.

The kiss was long and well done, and gradually she eased him toward her bed. The only sound in her ears was his heavy breathing; her only awareness the hardness of his arms and body and the caressing hands that moved over her bottom and pushed away the thinness of the panties. She liked sleeping with a virile man, and it had been so long—so long. He turned her, his back to the door, her back toward the bed. And then, without moving his mouth away from hers, began to push her down and back, holding her.

Even in his arms she fast became chilled and started shivering.

She opened her eyes and immediately saw the door, and the thick, white, misty substance that was pouring in around it; not oozing, not moving slowly as before, but rushing, swiftly and in deadly silence.

The scream choked to a low groan in her throat and she shoved hard at the man whose arms were around her. She was aware that he stepped back to stare without speaking at her, but the white had now covered the door and the fear of it had covered her, and just as the man who might have become her lover for a night turned to see the thing at which she stared, all awareness began leaving her and once again she knew she was losing consciousness. The whiteness was replaced by darkness as all strength went out of her body.

At first, when she awoke, she couldn't remember where she was. It wasn't her bedroom in the apartment. This room was so dimly lighted it was nearly dark. The ceiling was too high and too plainly that of an old, old house. And the bed was larger and not as soft. She sat up, leaning on her elbow. On a table by the bed a lamp burned, casting into the room a kind of sickish, yellow light that did not reach the corners.

Suddenly she remembered. Dennis. The door... And—

She stared at the door, but the thing that had been there was gone. Dennis, too, was gone. The door was closed. The silence in the house was the silence of the hour before daybreak.

She lay back on her bed, looking with apprehensiveness about her, moving slowly so that not even the squeak of a rusty bedspring would break the silence. What had happened to Dennis? Had he seen what she had seen, or had he simply put her into her bed when she'd fainted and then gone on back to his own room?

And what had she seen? Something angry and rushing at her as if—as if— She covered her face with her hands, wondering how much more of it she could take. In the daytime she didn't want to leave the house. And at night, she didn't dare.

She was afraid. Sickeningly, horribly afraid. And she didn't know what of. She had no name for it.

Curled into a small knot at the far side of her bed, away from the door, she waited for daybreak.

CHAPTER 9

Donna's alarm went off at seven, a shocking, irritating sound crashing into a soft, dreaming sleep. She turned over and grabbed for the clock, knocked it off the table, and then hung head down off her high bed to drag it out from under the table where it had rolled. When finally it was shut off and only its echo left ringing, she put it back on the table beside the lamp that had been left burning low. Since the night of her turning doorknob she had left a light going, always a bit uncomfortably aware that she was the only one left in the row of bedrooms on the east side of the central stairway. There was a growing sense of security in knowing that Cliff Murphy's room was not far down the narrow hall south of the balcony.

She dreaded the day when he would be leaving.

A familiar clang came up through the warm air register from the basement. Esther building up the fire. Donna quickly made up her bed, then wrapped a robe around her and went out to wash up as best she could in a bathroom that would still be cold, in water that had only begun to warm up a bit again after the dying down of the furnace during the night. Those hard facts she knew from her several days' experience of living in this house which was increasingly a stranger to her. She had thought she would be getting used to it, would begin to start liking it, but each day found her with an added conviction that leaving her job had not been the smartest thing she'd ever done. Of course, it wasn't really the job that mattered. It was their dark and dreary house that was getting to her. Ceilings seemed higher each day, and walls closer. Rooms smaller, and in some way difficult to breathe in. Windows too few and too narrow. Instead of width they had height. And who needed height? She liked modern terraces and walls of glass. And she had a feeling that she would smother completely in this house once Cliff was gone.

Yet she couldn't walk out and leave Sheba because Sheba depended on her to stay on as manager of the lodge.

Lodge. If it weren't so depressing it would be funny.

Night lights were still burning at the corners of the hallways on each side of the balcony. Lights that lighted nothing, serving only as beacons in the dark.

She passed by the one on her side of the stairway and as she turned down the hall that led into the unoccupied east wing she glanced over toward the small glow of light at the far side of the stairs. That something lay on the floor beneath the lamp didn't at first register in her mind. Then she stopped.

For a long moment she stared at the shadowed thing that did not belong on the floor of the hall, under the light in its bracket, a rolled lump of darkness that was hardly visible in the round shadow thrown by the bottom of the wall lamp.

Slowly the feeling of distinct uneasiness rose in her. Without speculating on what it was she went toward it, and when she stood at the top of the stairs, with the darkness of the lower hall and foyer falling away to her left, and long corridors stretching away both front and back, the time when she began to absorb in her mind what lay before her seemed as endless as the darkness. She saw first that it was a man, lying face down, dressed in pajamas. There was no sound coming from him, and no movement.

She began backing away, then in stark silence she turned and ran around the balcony and down the corridor into the darkness where Cliff's room was. A window at the end of the corridor had coming through its misted panes the first gray touch of dawn.

She found the door to his room and began pounding on it with both hands, her voice still frozen somewhere in the back of her throat.

The door opened suddenly and she fell into his arms. She was faintly aware that he was naked from the waist up, and that the arms that held her so tightly for a moment were strong and well-muscled. She was securely close in his strength. And she could breathe. But there was something on the floor—a man. With her hands on his chest she pushed herself away and looked up into his face. To her surprise her voice came, sounding quite rational and calm.

"Something's wrong," she said. "There's a man lying in the hall."

With long steps he passed her. "Show me," he said tersely.

She ran at his side to the edge of the stairway, then stopped and pointed. He went on, bent down on one knee, and turned the body over gently. Donna could see that the eyes were open, staring in still blankness upward toward the bottom of the lamp in the bracket. His mouth had twisted sideways, as though he had been lying cold for long, long hours.

Cliff Murphy's hands moved quickly and deftly, touching the temples and wrists for pulse. Over his shoulder he said softly, "Can you bring me a sheet or a blanket?"

Donna ran around the far side of the balcony to her room and grabbed the folded spare blanket off the foot of her bed. When she returned to the hall and went near enough to hand the blanket down to Cliff she saw the face of the man and recognized the guest who had said his name was Dennis.

"What's wrong with him?" she asked, shocked into not being able to really believe what she saw.

"He's dead."

In silence Donna watched Cliff spread the blanket over the body and then rise. Thoughtfully he looked down at the spread of the blanket, and then at the closed doors of the bedrooms.

"We can't move him yet," he said quietly. "But neither can we leave the others to come out and find him here. I suggest we wake them and ask everyone to go down to the kitchen, and I'll get to town as fast as I can and bring back a doctor. If you know where their rooms are, will you get them please? I'll wait here until everyone is downstairs."

Donna moved in numb stiffness to Sheba's room. She knocked once, then turned the knob. The door opened, to her surprise. Sheba hadn't locked her door?

Sheba sat in her bed, on the far side, huddled into her blankets with only her face showing. Wide, fear-darkened eyes showed in her small, white face. Her full lower lip hung lax, and her hands trembled against her cheeks. When she saw Donna her eyes closed briefly and she slumped a little, as though she had held her strained position for too long.

Donna rushed toward the bed and pulled a robe from the back of a chair where it had been carelessly hung. She held it for Sheba to slip into.

"Hurry, Sheba," she said. "You have to come downstairs." How to tell her, she wondered, that someone lay dead in the hall not twenty feet from her door when she already was white with fear. Or did she already know?

Without speaking Sheba pushed away the blankets and climbed over her bed. She was entirely nude.

The robe was not exactly a heavy one, so Donna asked, "Don't you want to put something else on, Sheba? You might get cold."

Sheba stopped suddenly and looked down at herself and touched her bare breasts lightly. Her hands moved down her body and away, and her eyes came alive and suddenly gave the room about her a swift inspection. They stopped, staring in dumb silence at something on the floor.

Donna looked, and saw the sheer, black, lace-trimmed shorty nightgown, and several feet away, nearer the door, the almost-nothing bikini panties. Sheba continued to stare as if she couldn't move, and Donna finally went over and picked up the nightgown. To her amazement, the garment was coldly damp and soggy, as if it had been rinsed out and dropped on the floor to dry.

"Why," she said, "it's wet."

She looked at Sheba and met eyes that mixed misery with fear, and expressions that Donna could not understand. Sheba's lips trembled, but still she did not speak. Donna tossed the damp nightgown onto the chair.

"Well, you can't put that on. Nor this. Don't you have a heavier robe?" Sheba didn't answer, but even as she was asking Donna recalled the old fuzzy, heavy thing Sheba often had worn around the apartment. She opened the wardrobe doors and pulled it down off the hanger.

Sheba held out her arms and Donna helped her into it. Then, while the girl stood as though in a wordless trance, Donna buttoned the robe and tied the belt. Without telling her why, she led Sheba from the room.

Cliff stood in the hallway by the body of the guest, leaning across him as though to hide him, one hand against the wall for support.

After one brief glance at Sheba's face, he said, "Why don't you take her on down to the kitchen and then come back for the others?"

Sheba was staring at the lumped blanket with the same expression the nightgown had provoked. She had to be led like someone unable to move without help.

To avoid the long front stairs and still, dark foyer, Donna took her through the service hall and down the back stairs. The kitchen had turned a sickening gray with the light of day that was being smothered by a dense fog over the marsh.

Wanda stood by the stove, yawning and pouring coffee.

"Good morning," she mumbled through her yawn. "You two want some coffee?"

Donna pushed Sheba into a chair and turned back toward the stairway. "Sheba does," she said. "Make her drink it."

"What's wrong?" Wanda asked suddenly, looking from Sheba to Donna.

"Just give her some coffee," Donna said. "You'll know soon enough."

She ran back up the stairs and down the hallway. She stopped for one moment beside Cliff to ask, "What shall I tell them?"

"Would you like me to get them?"

"If you don't mind, please do," she said, and glanced down at the unmoving blanket and that which it covered. If only he would rise... if only this weren't true. "Are you sure he's really dead?"

He touched her shoulder lightly. "Look, why don't you go back downstairs and get something to drink or eat. I'll get them up and out if you'll just tell me where their rooms are."

"I couldn't possibly eat. I...But she felt that she would give almost anything to escape this reality; to turn the responsibility over to Cliff Murphy. "Their room is the third one down." She motioned toward the hall running west from the balcony.

"All right, I'll get them and send them down, then I'll get dressed and go on to town and I'll be back as fast as I can. You just see to it that everyone stays in the same room downstairs. The kitchen would be the best place, probably."

She nodded and turned away.

When she entered the kitchen Esther had come up from the basement and was standing beside Wanda, waiting. At the other end of the room, seemingly oblivious to all, Sheba sat staring at the cup of coffee on the table in front of her.

In a low voice that she hoped Sheba wouldn't hear, Donna said, "There's been a death."

"*What?*" Esther demanded harshly.

"Who?" asked Wanda, frowning as if she didn't believe it.

"The boy, Dennis."

The two sisters looked at each other and then back at Donna.

"The one with the long sideburns," Donna explained.

"What happened to him?"

"I don't know. Cliff will go to town for a doctor as soon as he brings the other two down. For gosh sakes, don't say anything to them unless they ask. Let's just get some coffee and food in them if possible. And I'm going to drink some coffee myself."

"What's wrong with Sheba?" Wanda asked in a loud whisper.

Donna shook her head. "I don't know. Just shocked I guess. I feel the way she looks. Do you have some coffee for me, Esther?"

Esther came to action with a start and got a cup from the corner of the stove where four others were lined up neatly, warming. She poured the coffee and placed it on the table in front of an empty chair. Donna sat down and held her cold hands around the warm cup.

The door of the downstairs hallway opened and the two guests, white-faced and as silent as Sheba, came through and woodenly walked over to sit down at the table. They stared at Donna and the others as if they were something in a nightmare, and then drew closer to each other.

"Esther will get some coffee," Donna said, keeping her voice soft and calm, as soothing as possible. "And some food if you'd like to eat something."

Diane shook her head. Her voice squeaked a little. "Just coffee."

Randy's voice came in hoarse, deep contrast, as if he needed to clear his throat. "Just coffee, please."

The coffee was brought, and sipped, then Diane burst out suddenly as though she couldn't stand not talking about it. "He had asthma real bad sometimes, but I never... Is that why he's dead?" she demanded of Donna.

"I don't know. The doctor will be here and he'll tell us."

"What are we going to *do?*" she cried in a voice of despair. "Do we have to just sit here?"

"It won't take him long to go to town and back," Donna said. At least, she hoped it wouldn't.

The minutes dragged by, and gradually the sunlight penetrated the fog and shone weakly in through the east window. Then, when it began to seem as if no one would ever come, there was the faint sound of cars and then footsteps in the silence of the house.

Donna rushed down the hall and to the door, aware that others were crowding behind her. The front door stood open, and a man in a dark suit with the typical physician's bag in his hand was already going up the stairway. Behind him came two men in white, a stretcher between them. Cliff Murphy, in the lead, said something to them and they followed him up the stairway, out of sight.

Donna didn't move, nor did those who stood behind her. To her ears came the faint mumble of voices from above, and after another seemingly endless time the doctor came back down the stairs and waited in the foyer for the men with the stretcher and the burden they now carried carefully down the twisting, steep stairway.

Cliff Murphy followed, stopping at the front door to speak with the doctor for a moment before he closed the door and came back to face the silent, small group of people who waited.

He looked them over, as if deciding what to say.

Somewhere behind Donna came the hysterical cry of the girl. "I want to leave here! I can't stand it here any longer! Now that he's been taken away, why can't Randy and I leave?"

"You can," Cliff said. "But not until the sheriff comes. He should be here any minute. He's outside now with the doctor. I have to show him around and then I'll bring him back to the kitchen, so why don't you all just go on back and wait a few minutes longer."

They turned and went back to the kitchen, and Donna noticed that Sheba hadn't left the table. She was still staring at her cup of coffee, now gone cold.

"He had asthma," the girl said again. "Did he die from that?"

Sheba looked up and stared at the girl.

Cliff said, "It's possible. We'll know later. Just wait here a few minutes longer, please, then you'll be free to go."

He left, and Donna began to feel again that she too was being smothered, that she had to get out of the house and away before she died. Restless, she walked the floor, going from the window and the increasing light of the sun to the shadowed stairs at the other end of the room.

The feeling of smothered restlessness continued until Cliff Murphy came back into the room, this time accompanied by two men in uniform.

As soon as Diane saw them she cried out, "He had asthma. We should never have come here."

One of the men had a pencil and pad in his hand. "Could you give us the name of the dead man, please, and his address? His next of kin?"

Randy came forward to supply the information, and then, when asked, his own name and address. He ended it with a question of his own. "He—he died a natural death? Or was he ... ?"

The question hung in the air, and the sheriff looked sharply at him, waiting. "Yeah?"

Randy looked around him as though he had stepped into his own baited trap. "What I mean is the house is haunted.... I thought maybe—"

The sheriff put an end to his stammering with a contemptuous snort. "That give him asthma? That smother him to death?" He didn't wait for an answer. The pad and pencil were shoved into his pocket with a hand that looked as if it could use the gun that hung heavily in its holster if it had to. His deputy marched away in front of him, and over his shoulder the sheriff said, "If I need to see you I know where to find you, but I don't see any reason why you can't go on back to school. And when you get there you'd better stay."

"Yes, sir," Randy said, and no one had ever looked more relieved. He reached sideways and grasped Diane's arm. "Come on, let's get out of here."

She held back slightly. "We've got to tell his folks, Randy!" And the tears began coming then, tears of fear and nervousness repressed for long hours.

"I don't even know them, do you?"

"No."

"I guess the sheriff or someone will do that. We'd better get back to school, like he said."

He tried again to pull her, but she held back.

"We have to get dressed! We have to get our overnight bags."

He looked down at his own jeans and shirt, then at Diane in her robe. "Oh yeah." And again he was pulling her, urging her to hurry.

"I don't want to go back up there."

"You've got to go back up there, for Christ's sake, Diane, how else are you going to get your clothes on? Come on."

Diane looked helplessly at Donna, then she followed Randy, and the door closed behind them.

Esther said in disapproval, "The way these young people live nowadays. Ugh. No thought at all about spending a weekend together."

"You know so much about it," Wanda said in unaccustomed irritation.

Donna expected Esther to tell her to shut up, but she didn't. She rather wished Esther had, just to bring back a feeling of normalcy.

Esther went instead to a closet, got a broom, and began to sweep the kitchen floor, moving in a fast and energetic pace out the back door and onto the enclosed porch. Another door slammed as she went on out to the back stoop.

Donna hadn't realized she was just standing and straining her ears for sound until she heard a car start and leave, roaring and speeding, and Esther came back into the house with an announcement.

"Well, there they go," she said, adding unnecessarily, "like bats out of hell."

It occurred to Donna that no bill had been presented to them, and nothing paid. She sat down in astonishment. "I completely forgot to charge them anything! What a manager I'd make. With all the things that happened, it didn't enter my mind."

Wanda said, "How could anyone have thought of anything! I mean, after all, who expected someone to die the first night they stayed here? I never would have thought of it myself. The bill, I mean. The death, either."

Esther put away her broom. "Charge a certain amount in advance after this."

"I guess I'll have to. Of course I have their addresses, but I somehow wouldn't feel right about sending them a bill now. Especially a bill for him. For Dennis."

"You can look at it this way, you didn't lose much. Not as much as he did," Wanda said.

Donna looked at Sheba. "What do you think, Sheba?"

"Huh?" Sheba looked up at Donna as if she had been long asleep. "I wasn't listening, I guess."

Donna thought that Sheba looked as though the shock of the death had been almost too much for her, and now for the first time she wondered if Sheba had gone into the hall earlier and found him there. There must have been some reason for the state of dumb terror in which she had found Sheba. She remembered too that Sheba was supposed to act as hostess in this "lodge," and she, Donna, as business manager. It was no time to talk over the business end with Sheba.

She asked instead, "Would you like to get out of here and go into town for the day, Sheba?"

Sheba twisted out of her chair and went slowly toward the stairway. "I don't know. I'm going upstairs to dress."

The door to the front hall opened again and Sheba paused, standing near the wall, her eyes swiftly changing, lighting with the fire of dislike as she watched Cliff come back into the room.

With him, for Donna, came a security as gentle and warm as the first touch of sunlight. As protective as his arms had been.

His eyes swiftly took in each of them, then he helped himself to a cup of coffee from the stove. "The kids took off so fast the sheriff almost went after them. But he decided to let them go. Under the circumstances. Death is a shock to anyone of any age, and especially to a young person and more especially when the deceased is also young." He looked up at them again and his eyes settled on Sheba. "The doctor said it was no doubt caused from his asthma attack. When did you last see him last night, Sheba?"

"When I said good night to them in the hall, there at the corner where the light.. . where he was." Her voice was cold and sharp. "Now if you'll excuse me I'll go up and get dressed."

He watched her until she was out of sight, then he said to Donna, "Can we go into your office for a while?" They went silently down the long hall, into the foyer, then into the room across from the pillars of the living room and into the makeshift office. It had a desk, at least. Donna went to the windows and pushed aside draperies that held out the sunlight which had pushed lower the misty fog that had earlier hung over the marsh. It lay in patches now, among the grass and the water. In another hour it would be gone. She turned to see that Cliff had sat in the chair in front of her desk and was watching her with eyes that in some way seemed weary and sad.

"Something really is wrong," she said, wishing she understood all that he was feeling. "Something more than what it seems?"

"I can't prove it," he said. "And I don't know what it is, but I had a definite feeling that your friend Sheba knew more than she was telling."

Donna picked up a pen and rolled it between her fingers, wanting to tell him about Sheba, yet not wanting to betray her in any way. She trusted Cliff, Sheba did not. In a way it left her feeling slightly dishonest, as though in being physically attracted to him, in perhaps falling in love with him, she was blinded by that love. Sheba liked all men, usually. She had never known her to really dislike anyone, even Neil, whom she looked at with some contempt.

"You don't think Sheba could have possibly had anything to do with his death, do you?" Donna asked. "After all, it was of natural causes, so what could Sheba have to do with it?"

"I think you misunderstood me. I just said I think she knew more than she was saying."

She kept rolling the pencil, waiting for him to go on with whatever he wanted to say, but the room was silent except for the tick of a clock on her desk. At last she looked up to find his dark eyes steady and watchful under his straight, dark eyebrows. The look for some reason startled her. She jumped slightly and saw him smile. But still he said nothing.

"You're right," she said in mild frustration. "I constantly misunderstand you, it seems. For one thing, I'm beginning to wonder why you're really here. I assumed you came after something you wanted that had belonged to your family. Are you having trouble finding it?"

"I guess you could put it that way. There's a lot of stuff up in that attic. But I'd like to know something about your friend, okay?"

"Okay, I guess so. But why don't you ask her? I really haven't known her all that long."

"For one thing, she's not very cooperative."

"And am I?"

He smiled again, and the whiteness of his perfect teeth startled her almost as much as the beauty of his smile. It affected her more than she liked, since it was against her self-image to fall so hard so fast. She wondered if he had made a pass at Sheba, and the sudden and intense jealousy she felt was so new and so consuming that she didn't dare meet his eyes again for fear he would read her.

"You're easier to talk to," he said. "Miss Gilbert, for some reason, does not like me at all. Do you know why?"

She replied coldly, "I've no idea." And privately she wondered how he could be so sure about that. "Sheba usually likes men. Did you do something to make her mad at you?"

"Not that I know of. And that's what I figured— that she usually likes men, I mean. I think it was pretty obvious that she liked the kid that died, and I think she knows more than we do about it."

"If she does, she didn't tell me."

"Hey," he said softly, "you're not getting mad at me too, are you? I need a friend or two around here. And I choose you, if you'll let me."

She didn't look up. To do so would let him know that to be chosen by him, for any reason, would be better than anything she had yet found in life. "I said I would tell you all you want to know about Sheba, but I haven't known her long, and I will not betray anything I feel is a confidence."

"Okay, I'll accept that. How long have you known her?"

"Less than a year. She went to work in the same office where I was bookkeeper and we began to have lunch together. It turned out that she was getting a divorce and on her salary couldn't afford what she was used to. Actually, she couldn't even afford an apartment. So, because I had a three-room apartment that was taking too much of my money, I offered to let her share it. We lived together six months, next door to Wanda and Esther. Sheba used her divorce settlement for the down payment on this place. She calls me her partner at times, but I'm not. I'm only her business manager, really."

"She had a good idea about this lodge business."

Donna looked up, pleased. "Do you think so?"

"I sure do. But didn't she come alone and stay several days before you came down?"

"Well, not several days—but yes, she came one day and called us the next and we came down the day after that. But you know that. Why keep going back to that? We came when she needed us. It's that simple. We flew in."

"Why didn't you ride down with her?"

"We weren't ready to go. I had to give two weeks' notice." She paused, feeling the stir of something beyond a curtain in her mind, as if for a moment she came close to knowing the question he was searching to ask, and the answer to that question. The feeling disappeared as quickly as it had come.

"Still, you came without giving notice."

"Yes."

He leaned forward, his face serious and commanding. "Donna, you've got to tell me why! Why did you suddenly have to change your plans? Why did she want you to come on down instead of waiting?"

She shook her head. "She—I don't know. Cliff, I honestly don't know. She said she would tell me when we got here, only somehow I just never found out." Donna motioned at the room, the house in general. "She just didn't want to be alone, I guess. But then, Sheba is an impulsive person."

Cliff didn't seem to hear the last part. "She didn't want to be here alone. And it was she who wrote and placed that ad, wasn't it?"

"Yes."

"Donna—what happened to make her suddenly decide on calling this house *haunted?* She had to have a reason. Was Sheba the kind of girl who was interested in the occult or witchcraft or the supernatural in any form?"

"Good grief no. Sheba is a gregarious person. She loves parties and people. That was one reason having a hunting lodge so appealed to her— all that many men, you know." She stopped suddenly, feeling as if she had betrayed more of Sheba than she had intended.

Cliff leaned back and looked at one corner of the ceiling. "Maybe that's it," he said quietly, half to himself. "She was never alone before and one night in this house, especially after going into the water in her car the night before, was too much. At least enough to give her the idea that the place could be haunted."

Donna watched him and finally asked, "Now can I ask you a question?"

"Sure. Anything." His eyes came back to settle distractingly on her.

"Why are you so interested in Sheba?"

"Not because I'm falling in love with her," he said, and laughed softly.

Donna felt the sudden heat in her cheeks, and then when he laughed strongly, teasingly, the heat increased with the fury of having her emotions seen and known by him. She shoved back her chair and rose, holding herself haughtily straight as she looked down at him, now lazily at ease in his chair and still laughing at her.

"I think you are the most arrogant—arrogant—"

He supplied a word for her softly, "Bastard."

"Yes! Bastard! Thank you."

She went out of the room, hearing his laughter echo in the surrounding rooms. And following that was the echo of her slam of the door.

CHAPTER 10

In the rather uneventful days that followed, Donna stayed away from Cliff Murphy as much as was hospitably possible. She wasn't sure if she felt insulted or pleased that he seemed not to particularly notice her, that he began spending a lot of time somewhere else—upstairs in his room, or up in the attic, or looking over unoccupied areas of the house. There were times when she heard his footsteps overhead. And other times when she wondered where he was. She couldn't help wondering, but she made no effort to find out.

At other times he left in his car and stayed away long hours. But always he returned before dark.

One day when he had gone away in his car she took advantage of knowing for sure he wasn't in the attic to go up again, somewhat stealthily, as though seeing the attic again would reveal to her the secret of his purpose.

That he had a purpose was growing strongly in her convictions, and it was a purpose more serious than merely coming after a few things.

Perhaps, as Sheba had suggested, a purpose more ominous? More dangerous.

She left the attic door open. Esther was in the kitchen, beginning the long preparation of dinner, and Sheba had taken Wanda, with the laundry, to town. They wouldn't be back for a couple of hours. Donna had the entire upper stories of the house to herself for the first time.

And that was one reason she left the attic door open. There was something decidedly creepy about the thought of closing herself into that huge, dark space that she remembered from her other visit.

The steps of the steep, enclosed stairway creaked and groaned faintly as she moved upward with caution. No matter how carefully she placed her feet, the steps responded eerily, as though warning the attic that it was about to be invaded by one who did not belong. She couldn't recall the stairs sounding so unstable the other time she had climbed them.

A thought entered her mind that made her stop on the stairs, that caused her to look down at the step on which she stood, and at the wall near her shoulder. In amazement she wondered that she had not noticed it before—the increased falling away of the paper in the rest of the house, the crumbling of the very wood under her feet. The house was deteriorating, rapidly, right under, their eyes.

The wall of the stairway had never been papered, and looked as if it had never been painted. The mold had turned it green in places, and it was difficult to tell whether the material was wood or plaster. With one finger she gingerly touched it, and found that it was slimy and damp.

She jerked away the finger as if she had touched something ugly and evil, and held it away from her as she backed down the stairway to the hall. She left the door hanging open, her attention on the condition of the ceiling and walls in the hallway. There was no wallpaper here, either, and no paint. Not anymore, if ever there had been. The lack of light kept it from being easily noticed. She wondered about the bedrooms in the service section of the house. Wanda's room, and Esther's, and the others that were left closed all the time. She crossed the hall and opened a door, pushing it back with her hand but staying where she was in the hallway.

A smell of damp, rotting stink flowed out upon her, as the stink of decaying vegetation. She held her breath against it and looked into the room. There was nothing there to account for the smell except the strange, green stuff that had settled in places on the walls like a slimy green moss that grows at the edge of stagnant water. The one window, a narrow, dingy thing, had hanging from a rod a curtain that was gradually shredding away. The mattress on the bed was discolored with dampness and touched with the green growth.

With a shudder she left the door open and retreated from the hallway. She had seen all she wanted to see at the moment, and needed to talk about it with Esther. Had it always been this way, or was the house all at once rotting out from under them?

Esther was busy at the sink, rubbing a leg of lamb with some special mixture of spices. Her elbows jerked sharply about and as she worked she hummed a cheerless little tune. Donna stopped at the bottom of the stairway and looked at the linoleum on the floor, but it was glossy and clean and freshly waxed. The glass of the few widely scattered windows gleamed in the sunlight. Donna went around the foot of the stairway that protruded into the room to a window and scraped her fingernail along the slender wood-strip divider between panes. The wood came away in front of her fingernail, as soil before a scraper. Soft and damp. She stared at it in unexpected horror.

Esther's voice came somewhere from the side of reality, a welcome sound.

"What are you doing?"

Donna turned to see that Esther was coming across the room, both hands held carefully palm up to avoid spilling from them the spices that clung there.

"This house," Donna said, "is crumbling away right around us!"

"Huh?" Esther came up to look at the window. "Crumbling?"

"Yes. Falling away. Rotting. Look how soft this wood is." With two fingers she picked away a small portion of the wood of the window. "It's soft. There's no substance to it. We should open all the windows and let the place air out and dry out or there won't be a house left one of these days."

"I'll be darned," Esther said, frowning at the window. "It wasn't this way when we came, was it?"

"I don't know. I don't think so."

"Have you noticed anything different about your room?"

Esther looked about at nothing. After thinking it over she said, "I noticed that my shoes are mildewing. I had to wipe mildew off my good shoes this morning. I guess I don't wear them enough. At least, that was what I thought at the time."

"But the house—your room."

"To tell the truth, I don't know. I get up before daylight and get dressed and come down here, and here I stay until after dark. I don't go upstairs to bed until I'm ready to go to bed." She jabbed with her elbow toward a rocking chair that sat between the cookstove and a table with a lamp and a stack of books on it. "I spend my evenings sitting over there reading. I guess you know that, though."

"Yes, I know that. You know, Esther, I have a very strong feeling that this is just beginning to happen. That it wasn't like this when we came."

"Hey," said Esther. "How could it happen so fast?" Donna walked away, looking at the walls, the ceiling, the doors of the cupboards, all so dark and old, so unpainted, unvarnished. "I don't know. Perhaps it really didn't and I'm just beginning to notice it. I wonder if the Murphys didn't do some remodeling here? I'll have to ask Mr. Murphy about that, Cliff." she added, hardly thinking of what she said, only of what she saw. High in one corner of the room was a spreading patch of green. She pointed.

Esther came to stand beside her and look up at the patch. When she finally spoke her voice was low, as if she was afraid that her words would be heard by ears other than Donna's. "You're right. I know for a fact that wasn't there last week. Cobwebs were there. I had a heck of a time getting them down because I had to get a stepladder from the garage and stand on the top of it and then reach a broom up, and for a while there I thought I wouldn't be able to get it after all. The ceiling is so high, you know. I never did touch the ceiling, but I got most of the cobwebs."

The back of Donna's neck began to ache from the strain of looking up. She lowered her chin and rubbed her aching upper spine.

"Most of them..." Esther said dreamily. "Some were still there. But they're gone now." In a louder voice she said, surprised, "There's that same green mildew like was on my shoes."

Donna walked slowly across the kitchen, looking at the wide, old-fashioned baseboard. "Esther," she said, stopping, speaking with a purpose. "Do you have a strong flashlight?"

"You bet your life I do. I wouldn't be without one."

"Where is it? I'd like to look the rest of the house over, carefully."

"It's in my bedroom right under my pillow. Alongside my billy club."

Donna went up the stairs behind Esther, and into the room two doors from the top of the stairway. The bed was high and large, with two fat pillows. Out from under one Esther pulled a flashlight that was almost as large as a baseball bat. After one astonished look Donna laughed.

"You sleep with that under your pillow?"

"I absolutely do. I don't intend to be caught unawares with nothing to protect myself. I always figured if a burglar got into my room the first thing he'd get would be the flashlight in his face—and it's bright—and the next he'd get would be my billy club over his head. And after that if he still wanted to snoop around in my room I'd scream. There's nobody in this world that can scream louder than I can."

Donna only half heard Esther because she had pinpointed the very strong light into the corner between the wardrobe and the wall.

"Look," she said.

Esther came to peer over her shoulder, then in silence she moved in and bent down for a closer look. She adjusted her glasses and looked through the bifocals.

"What is *that!*" she finally said, moving back and away, her face pinched in distaste.

Donna looked at the thick, slimy green that had grown in the corner as if it were on a rotting log in a swamp. "I only know that I've never seen anything like it since I was in biology class. And that's been so long ago that I wouldn't be able to put a name to it."

Esther adjusted her glasses again and glanced around the rest of the room. Donna moved too, taking the bright beam of the flashlight around the shadowed baseboard. The green, slimy growth was there, too, thin and spreading, like fingers or a trailing vine, creeping through the places of darkness.

"I swear it wasn't here the last time I swept my floor, and that was only a couple of days ago."

"But couldn't you possibly have missed seeing it?"

"I might have. But I know as well as I'm standing here that it wasn't there when I moved in!"

Donna moved on, not answering. On her knees, she bent down and looked under the bed, but quickly got to her feet. The green slime was working its way up the wall there toward the head of the bed, as though reaching for a victim. Donna felt her skin tighten and tingle with warning.

"Is it under the bed?" Esther asked.

Donna bit her lip and turned away from Esther, looking at the rest of the room. She shined the light toward the high corners of the ceiling, but they were clear.

"A little," she finally said, and snapped off the light. "Let's see if we can move the bed out from the wall."

"Why do you want to move it?"

"Let's just get it away from the wall."

Esther got opposite Donna and together, with much straining, tugging, and pulling, they moved it slowly away until four or five inches separated the high wood headboard from the wall.

"There," Donna breathed weakly.

Esther was gasping for breath.

"Sit and rest a minute, then we'll go on."

"I'm all right. I'm not sure I want to see the rest of the house."

But she followed Donna from the room, and peeked over Donna's shoulder each time they looked into a room whose door had been closed.

"These rooms have to be aired out," Donna said, and left each door pushed back as she passed the bedrooms of the service wing.

Esther kept up. "I tell you I'm sure those rooms weren't like that when we came here. I'll have to tell Wanda to be sure that she gets up there and cleans that stuff out—whatever it is."

"Let's check my room. I really haven't looked at it, either, I guess. It's so close and dark back in the corners and behind all that old furniture—"

"Well, I hope we don't have to move another bed."

"Of course," Donna said thoughtfully, "I always leave my window open a little. That might help."

But the green growth was there, too, deep in the corners. This time Donna used a nail file from her dresser and, squatting on her heels, dug off a bit of it and wiped it onto a sheet of note paper.

Holding the paper carefully, Donna took it to the bright light of day in the window and looked closely at it, Esther still at her shoulder.

With the nail file she probed it and found that it was about a quarter of an inch thick, very flexible, and shining with the slippery moisture of its body.

"We're living with *that?*" Esther said. "I never saw anything like it."

"I have. But only in very damp, decaying swamps. I don't understand why it's here in the house, and I don't really know what it is."

"Do you suppose Mr. Murphy would know? He seems to be a pretty smart man in some ways. I think he must be pretty well educated."

"He might know. We'll ask him. Here, you take it down to the kitchen, carefully. I'll take the flashlight and go on through the rest of the house."

Esther's lip curled in distaste as she gingerly put out thumb and finger from each hand and held the paper as if the thing on it was poison. "I'll carry it," she said, "but I'm going along with you. If you don't mind, that is."

"I don't mind. Let's look at Sheba's room."

They went around the balcony and down the hall, Esther holding out arm's length ahead of her the white note paper with the alien green. Donna thought she looked comical in her unpleasant task, as if she were carrying from the house a decayed dead rat that under no circumstances did she dare drop; but Donna didn't feel like smiling.

She opened Sheba's door, pushed it back, and stopped. The difference was clear. Even the smell was less offensive than in the other rooms, an odor Donna had hardly been aware of until she opened Sheba's door.

"My!" Esther said. "She certainly keeps her room clean."

Donna shined the light quickly into the corners. "There's nothing here. Not a thing. I wonder why."

"This part of the house must not be as damp as the other side. What's that on the floor?"

Donna had hardly looked at the garment when she had first passed it. Automatically she stooped and picked it up, and then in silence she stared at it, feeling its wetness between her fingers, hearing the slow drip, drip, drip of the water that fell to the floor.

"It's soaked," Esther said. "Is it her nightgown?"

"Yes."

"My gracious, I'd freeze in a thing like that."

Esther's voice passed over the blank wonder in Donna's mind as the drops of water went so softly into the thin rug on the floor.

"Why is it so wet?" Esther asked.

Donna shook her head. "I don't know." She carefully spread it over the back of a chair, touching it as little as possible, a growing sense of revulsion rising in her.

In a whisper, Esther asked, "Do you suppose Sheba *wet* the bed?"

"I don't think it's that... no. If she has that problem she never mentioned it to me."

"Well, one wouldn't."

Donna wiped her hands on a tissue from her blouse pocket and backed toward the door. "I think she must have rinsed it out and then forgot to take it along to the laundry."

She didn't really believe that. She was remembering another nightgown she had found dripping-wet on the floor. She was jerked back from her thoughts by the slam of a car door below.

"That'll be Sheba. Esther, you take that sample— whatever it is—down to the kitchen and put it on the cabinet for Mr. Murphy to look at. He might know how we can deal with it. Being from the more humid climate of the South and all..."

Esther, following close on her heels as they left the bedroom, said, "I don't want the nasty stuff on my cabinet."

"Then put it on the windowsill. Just so it doesn't get lost."

"If it got lost there'd be plenty more, it looks to me," Esther said gloomily.

"All right, put it where you want," Donna answered impatiently. "Just don't drop it unless you want to go after another sample."

At the stairway, Donna started down and Esther went on toward the doorway to the service quarters but they both were stopped suddenly by the dull clang of the metal knocker. Donna stood still, her hand on the banister, and Esther looked down at her in silence. But Esther was never silent for long.

"Why is Sheba knocking? The door isn't locked. Besides, they'd have to come to the back door with the laundry."

Donna felt the pulse of amazement that always came with the unexpected. "It obviously isn't Sheba and Wanda. We must have another guest. Cliff Murphy wouldn't be knocking either."

"Oh dear," Esther said, hurrying on. "I'd better get this out of sight."

"Wait," Donna said. "Put it down in the hallway and then hurry back and look until you find a bedroom that's free from that stuff. We can't rent a room to someone with that slimy stuff growing out of the woodwork."

Esther acted for a moment as if she were going to be turning circles indefinitely. She held the paper far out in front of her, turned around, and around again, and said, "Oh dear."

The knocker clanged again and Donna went on down the stairway, giving Esther one last reminder. "Hurry, just put it down on the floor of the service hall and start looking for a room. I'll delay them until you let me know." She went on, saying to herself, "I'll show them into the living room, serve them something to drink, or show them the house down-stairs...." She hadn't looked into the rooms downstairs though, and into her mind came the sudden equivalent of a terrifying nightmare; what if she opened one of the doors to find that the walls, the floor, and the ceiling were covered with the slimy green stuff? A cushion of oozing dull green, like the padded walls of an unearthly cell.

As she passed through the foyer her glance went, against her will, to the baseboard, but the new white paint the Murphys had evidently put there was untouched with the creeping fungus.

She had a fixed smile on her face when she opened the door. Outside, standing at the far edge of the porch and looking up at an upper story of the house was a woman of indefinite age and rather plain appearance. As though she hadn't heard the door open her gaze dropped suddenly, she jumped, dropped her handbag, and both hands flew to cover her mouth. Over the tops of her fingers her eyes bugged for a moment before they squeezed shut in relief.

"Oh grief." She breathed heavily and bent to pick up her purse. "You startled me. I was beginning to think there was nobody home."

"Won't you come in," Donna said.

She came in, looking around eagerly. Donna doubted that there was much she didn't see.

"Are you alone?" Donna asked.

The woman whirled to face her. "Why do you want to know?"

Caught by amazement again, Donna motioned helplessly. "Why, so I'll know how many guests."

"Oh. I might have some friends who'll come later but right now I'm alone. I just need one room."

But Donna could see by the flush of guilt that passed over her face that she was lying about the friends. Donna smiled, but the woman glanced quickly away, as though the smile were a trick of some kind. If Donna had felt in a better mood she would have laughed. As it was she went to stand by the desk with the guest book and spoke her small speech.

"Would you sign your name and address please? And we require payment in advance. Because of the inconvenience of bathrooms we're asking only twenty dollar for each twenty-four hours, for each guest. You will be served breakfast in the kitchen at any hour before eleven, lunch whenever you want it. Dinner is the only meal that has a set time, and that is at six o'clock in the dining room. I hope you will enjoy your stay with us. The woman had taken the pen Donna offered to her but was reading the other three names on the guest book. "Only three other guests?"

"Actually, none at the moment. They have checked out." A mistake on her part, Donna thought with a glance at the book. She had completely forgotten to mark the date of their departure. Obviously the woman hadn't heard of the death of the one man. "We've just recently opened," she said.

The woman stared up at her as she leaned slightly forward over the desk, pen poised above the book. "You mean I'm alone in this haunted house?" She looked and sounded as if she were about to throw the pen and start running.

"Oh no!" Donna said, wondering if the woman thought she was looking at an apparition. Donna forced a smile, but the guest didn't respond. "I am here," she said.

The woman straightened a little, still staring. They were about to lose a potential guest, and they couldn't afford that. Not if Sheba wanted to keep her lodge and have it renovated and put in shape.

"Also," Donna said hastily, "there is the cook and the housekeeper, and also the owner of the house. Oh— and another guest." She glanced at the book. It had been purchased since his arrival and she hadn't thought to ask him to sign his name and address. "Besides, the house really isn't haunted. That was only a gimmick. Just a fun thing."

This was no time to be playing games, she saw. Not with this guest.

The woman straightened even more and said firmly, "A gimmick! Ah, but you're wrong about that. The house is haunted. It's filled with the silent spirits of death and evil, of all things beyond." She looked around warily. "I can feel it. My mother was a medium, and although I don't have her gift I do have a certain sensitivity. You may not think your house is haunted, dear girl, but it is."

She bent and wrote swiftly. April Calder. The address was a town in New Mexico.

"You've come a long way," Donna said.

April Calder straightened, dropped the pen, smiled briefly, and opened her purse. "Yes. I'm a writer. I saw your ad in a newspaper at home and got ready immediately." She handed two ten-dollar bills to Donna. She seemed to be relaxed and more at ease now. Quite self-assured. "I'm gathering facts for a book on the occult, and I'm looking for fact, not fancy. And I'm sure at last I've found it."

Donna took the bills, folded them several times, and tucked them into her palm. Then she wrote a receipt.

April Calder had walked to stand by a pillar and look into the living room. Without comment she returned and walked down the foyer and looked up the stairway.

"You haven't lived here long, have you?" she said.

"Less than a month," Donna replied, watching her, wishing Esther would hurry, trying to think of where to take April Calder to get her away from climbing the stairs.

"I think I'll be staying here for quite a while if the hold on the house isn't too advanced, too strong. If it is I will have to leave, and," she turned around and fixed her unnerving stare on Donna, "and if that happens, then I would suggest you *all* leave."

Donna now stared at her openly. She was almost ready to believe there was something strange and different about the woman. April Calder—light brown hair combed into a simple, not very flattering style, dressed not very becomingly, no makeup—began uncomfortably to take on an aspect of something that was more spiritual than physical. It hadn't occurred to Donna that the ad might draw other than fun seekers. That it might also draw the dead serious, the occult masters, the spiritualists and mediums. Nor, probably, she thought, had Sheba expected anything but joke lovers.

Donna watched April Calder walk slowly back into the edge of the living room and stand with her head tilted slightly as if listening to a sound far beyond Donna's hearing.

The strain was too much. Donna glanced hopefully at the stairway, but there was no sign of Esther yet. How could she get away before she had even shown the guest her room? "Uh," said Donna, "do you hold séances?" *That* was what mediums did, wasn't it?

The woman quickly held up her hand for silence and said, "Shhh."

Donna held her breath for perhaps ten seconds before the guest turned and smiled at her. But the smile was something one might have found in a funeral parlor. Donna glanced at the stairway again. Still no sign of Esther. What the hell was she doing anyway? Scrubbing down the walls? Or hopping around like a jack rabbit looking for a perfect room in a house that was becoming a damp and cold and slimy ruin?

"You can relax," April Calder said. "The living room is all right."

"What?" Donna cried, as if the woman had said that she now could rise from her grave.

"The living room is all right." She went back to look up the stairway. "It's up there," April said.

"What's up there?" She wasn't talking about bedrooms, Donna was quite sure.

"The evil spirit. More than down here it's up there. I can feel it. Ah, if only my dear mother were here, she would be able to tell you what it is that haunts your house."

As though she had in some way been called forth, Esther suddenly came into sight at the sharp angle of the stairway where it rose to the balcony. She stopped and in silence stared down at the guest. April Calder didn't move, nor did she speak; but there was a visible tightening of her body as she looked up at the severe and bony exterior of Esther, who, in the constant lack of light that was a part of the second-floor balcony, looked almost diaphanous, as if she could have been an apparition.

Donna, however, was glad to see her. She crowded around April and went up toward Esther a few steps. "Did you get a room ready, Esther? This is April Calder, our new guest. She came alone, so we need only one room."

Esther nodded, and once having started seemed unable to stop. "A room. One is ready."

"Fine. Are you ready to go up, Miss Calder? I'll show you where the bathroom is—the one that's convenient to your room. I'll get your suitcase."

Donna hurriedly went back to the foyer, got the suitcase, and led the way up the stairs. The hard, straight look that Esther settled on her seemed to have a meaning that couldn't be spoken of in the presence of the guest. "Where is the room, Esther?"

As if probed with an electric stick, Esther jumped and climbed the three steps back to the balcony. "Right down this wing. It doesn't have much light in it." She gave Donna the look again, but Donna had little choice but ignore it.

"We'll see to it that Miss Calder has plenty of lamps, Esther. She's a writer."

"Oh." Esther looked at the guest, then back at Donna. "It's down here. The third room. Quite a ways to the bathroom from here, but it's a nice room. Warmer than the others."

"Spring is on its way now," Miss Calder said. "I noticed the frogs were beginning to sing now, and birds are flying. But I also noticed something very strange as I came along the road. The birds don't come close to the house. Had you noticed that?"

Donna and Esther exchanged another look, but Donna's was of simple wonder.

"No birds near the house? No, I hadn't noticed. I just thought maybe it was too early for them to be anywhere."

"Oh no. There are a lot of birds farther out on the marsh. But not near the house. That was the first thing I noticed. The second was the lack of trees and shrubs around the house. You know, it almost reminds me of a castle I saw on a low hill in Scotland once. There, you know, are no trees anyway. But here there are trees abundantly. Everywhere except on this little knoll by your house. It's as if nothing dare try to live here." They went down the corridor of a wing that had not yet been occupied and into the third room on the right. The door was open, the bed made. Draperies at the window were drawn, and a lamp had been lighted. It was a small room, with wardrobe, two chairs, a dresser, night table, and bed. April Calder went to stand in the middle of it. Once again she turned her head slightly sideways, as if listening. Slowly then, as Donna and Esther watched her in silence, she turned.

Her lips were parted slightly and a faint frown lowered her brow and made her eyes seem shadowed and deep-set. She nodded.

Donna heard Esther sigh, as though relieved. But then Esther didn't know what April Calder was listening for, Donna thought. Of course *she* didn't either, for sure, but she knew enough to wish she could hurry and get back downstairs

"The room is all right?" Esther said.

"I guess it will have to do, but—there's something here. It's faint—not as strong as back at the stairway, but much stronger than down in the living room. However, it will do."

Esther looked at Donna for clarification and, smiling, Donna said, "There's some kind of odor."

April Calder opened her mouth to say something to the contrary, but Esther beat her to it.

"There's some spray deodorant Wanda can bring up when she gets home. That should take care of it."

The surprise on April Calder's face made Donna feel like laughing for the first time. Instead, she drew back toward the door, saying, "There are some things I have to take care of in the office, Esther. Would you please show Miss Calder where the bathroom is?"

By that method Donna managed to escape. She left the dim and dreary second floor and hurried down the stairs to the foyer and into her office. She sat down at her desk with a sigh of relief, almost ready to agree with April that the upstairs was the abode of evil spirits.

She had just finished writing down and filing the day's room rent when Esther came in without knocking. She hurried across the room to literally fall into a chair, breathless.

"Did you hear me running around up there room to room? I was afraid you'd hear me. You don't know the time I had trying to find a room without that stuff. Somethings got to be done, I tell you."

"You mean it's *everywhere?*" Donna had almost forgotten the green stuff.

Donna found she was looking over her shoulder at the near corner as if the growth was there and suddenly had grown eyes that stared and fingers that reached slowly and in deadly silence for her. There was nothing, though, that she could see from so far across the room.

"The room you gave Miss Calder," Donna said. "Was it clear?"

"Fairly. Anyway, she's settled now, or settling. Said she'd be down later." Esther rose, sighing. "I'd better get on with dinner, or it will be late. It's going to be late anyway."

Donna remained at her desk after Esther had gone, watching out the window that gave her a partial view of the bridge. She searched the road for a blue car. A rather dark sky-blue sport coupe with a white top. Cliff Murphy's car.

Strange, she thought, how even a glimpse of his car on the road beyond the bridge doubled the speed of her heart. The house, the cold winter atmosphere, all of it changed when he came in. A place that seemed increasingly dull and boring—nearly suffocating with closing her away from the world—at once became the most exciting place in the world when that blue and white car returned, bringing back into the house the man who puzzled her; who overpowered her with an emotion that she had thought didn't exist. He was becoming too important in her life, and she didn't know how to stop it. They talked often. But what of? She couldn't remember.

Restlessly she left her desk chair and went to stand by the window where she could see farther into the distant marsh. In vague half-thought she noticed the birds far away in the sky, a few scattered about. None close. And faintly she heard footsteps somewhere overhead, foot-steps that moved irregularly and slowly, as if unsure and hesitant. The new guest doing a bit of exploring in the realm of the unknown? What would she think of the unclean walls? Donna smiled, and promptly forgot her.

For a moment she lived again the touch of Cliff Murphy's arms around her, hard and tight, when she had run to him the morning she'd found the body under the light. The only time he had touched her.

The office door opened suddenly and unexpectedly, and he was there, coming toward her, closing the door behind him.

"You weren't expecting me?" he said. "I'm sorry. I guess I should have knocked, but Esther said you wanted to see me. She seemed to think it was pretty urgent."

Donna leaned forward, her feet flat on the floor, the edge of the desk pressed against her diaphragm. She laced her hands tightly together and avoided direct contact with his eyes. "I didn't see you return," she said.

He sat down facing her desk. "I just now came in through the kitchen. Esther was working like mad trying to get dinner ready on time. She mentioned something about another guest."

"Yes. A woman alone." Donna smiled. "She was rather unnerved to think she might actually be in this house alone. I don't think she considered we who work here as exactly human. She was glad to hear there was another guest. You."

"Why did she come?"

"She's a writer, she said. "On the occult. Haunted houses interest her. She's also—well, a believer." That's putting it mildly, she thought as she smiled at him. "You might have her camping on your threshold come dark."

"Great," he said without enthusiasm. "Was that what Esther seemed to think was so urgent?"

"No, it isn't." Donna hesitated, wondering if she should talk to Sheba first. After all, Sheba was supposed to be the owner. But, as Esther had said... "Do you know anything about botany?"

"A little. Why?"

"Esther didn't show you the sample she brought down from upstairs, I gather."

For a moment he looked steadily at her, almost frowning. Then he laughed. "You must be conning me. A sample of *plant* life from upstairs? In the house?"

"Yes. Come and look at it, okay?"

"Sure." He rose as she did and waited, still smiling.

"What did you find, a vine growing in through a crack somewhere?"

"Let's go first and get Esther's flashlight."

"I have one," he said. "In my room."

They went up the stairs and Donna saw that April Calder was not in sight. "I'll wait here," Donna said. "The room I want to show you is in the service wing."

While he was gone she lighted the lamp in the bracket at the corner nearest her. The glow it cast hardly penetrated the increasing shadows caused by the fading daylight hours and lack of windows in the area surrounding the rise of the stairway, and the branching of halls and corridors into the various wings.

Cliff returned with a flashlight and led the way to the room.

"Take a look, Mr. Murphy."

The room was dimly twilight, the day beyond the window having gone cloudy so that not even a touch of sunlight helped to relieve the natural gloom. He crossed the threshold and Donna followed him, standing behind him as his glance went quickly from walls to ceiling to floor.

He snapped on the flashlight and aimed the strong white beam of light at the wall and down to the baseboard. The green growth on the walls glistened under the light as with unlimited, watery, microscopic eyes. In silence he bent near the baseboard, flashed the light up the wall and down again to hold it steady near the floor. With one hand he touched the growth, feeling its surface with his fingers.

"I don't believe it," he said. "This stuff looks like pond slime."

With one finger he bulldozed a small path into the growth and pulled away the piece that lapped wetly over his hand. It lay in his palm like a small strip of soft, shiny plastic.

"Rubbery," he remarked in a low and thoughtful voice, feeling it between his fingers. He handed the light to Donna without looking up. "Hold this, will you please?"

She took the light and leaned over his shoulder, directing the beam toward his hands. He turned the sample, broke it, crushed it between his fingers, and finally smelled it. And hastily held it away.

"Wow! Strong, isn't it? I'd been noticing an odd smell in the house," he said lightly, "but I thought it was Esther's cooking."

She laughed despite the fact she really didn't feel there was anything they dared laugh at. Not here. Not in this room.

He glanced up at her with a gleam of amusement narrowing his eyes. "Don't tell her I said that or I'll get you when you're least expecting it."

The suggestion that lay behind his teasing threat made her all at once breathless. She drew back slightly, but his attention had already gone back to the growth. He dropped the gooey, crushed sample onto the floor, stood up, pulled a handkerchief from his pocket, and wiped his hands. "I'd say that of all growths I have ever seen it more resembles pond slime than anything else."

"Or something that grows on rotting logs in wet places?"

"Yes."

He took the flashlight from her and went slowly around the room. When he had completed the circle and had come back to stand beside her he asked, "How about other rooms?"

"Not as much as this one, so far as I've seen. But it's in most of them. Some rooms have only a tiny bit, down in the corners, practically invisible." They went out into the hall, where she turned to face him. "I was noticing also that the wallpaper seems to be turning loose in places, and I wanted to ask you if your mother and dad did any redecorating in the house—or was it always this way?"

"Mom had several rooms papered and painted, but not all. The house was looking good the last time I was here, which was only a month or so before their deaths. I came back for a very short time when I came to identify their bodies, but I stayed no more than five minutes in the house." They walked slowly down the hall, side by side. As they went he shined the light at the walls and baseboard. "But anyway, Mom was very interested in redoing the whole house last summer, room by room. She had finished a lot of it. A lot more than shows now. I'm sure there was no... whatever the hell it is, then."

A sound echoed through the house with a dull, ominous ring, and then stopped.

"Was that the knocker on the door?" he asked.

"Yes," she said. "Someone else must have come. We seem to be very popular today."

"Strange how that rusty old knocker can be heard so far away. Look, Donna, before you go ...""

She paused. "Yes?"

"I think you'd better take that ad out of the paper." His eyes were clearly not teasing now. She heard the knocker again.

"I can't do that," she said. "Sheba is the one who placed it. It isn't my place to remove it. After all, it's her house now. Isn't it?"

"Yes, it is. But that can be remedied. I'll be glad to repay what she has already paid me, because if the house is going to rot out she bought nothing but a burden. I'll make arrangements to get the money back to her tomorrow and we can have the house vacated within a week."

One thought came foremost to her mind: What then? Would she ever see him again?

But she asked, "Do you think it's that serious?"

In the silence of his pause the door knocker echoed again, a bit louder, with a series of impatient knocks rising one upon another like ripples of dark water against a receding bank.

Quietly he answered her: "I think it's that serious."

CHAPTER 11

Sheba looked into the mirror to brush her hair, and saw the beauty of the reflection without emotion. She might as well have been looking at a stranger who didn't impress her much, regardless of blue-black hair and striking features. Sometimes, lately, she felt as much a stranger to the inner image as to the outer. It seemed as though she had reached a level of nonexistence.

She dressed in a long hostess gown that left arms bare and slightly chilled in the never-warm room. She was twisting to reach the zipper in the back when a light tap at the door interrupted her mumbled curses at hard-to-reach zippers.

"Come in!"

Donna entered and closed the door softly behind her. "Bless you," Sheba said. "How did you know I was needing help at this particular time?" She backed toward Donna, holding the dress in place at her waistline. "Zip me, will you, dear?"

Donna eased the zipper up while Sheba held her breath.

"Am I putting on weight, Donna? I don't remember this dress being so tight."

"If so it doesn't show. The dress looks good. But you've already got goosebumps."

"I can't go around in pants and sweaters all the time. Not when there's a good-looking man in the house."

"Well, it's your goosebumps."

"Besides, it's warmer downstairs."

"Not much. Not unless you plan to sit in the hearth." Donna stood by the door with her arms folded across the front of her long-sleeved sweater. Sheba saw her in the corner of her vision, a girl who was beautifully put together and always poised and gracefully at ease— outwardly at least.

"I hung your nightie on the chair to dry," Donna said. "Did you find it?" Donna's voice seemed silky soft and insinuating, and it struck Sheba with the cold shock of a key inserted into a hidden door of her mind. She stared hard at the spot on the rug where she had this morning dropped the wet nightgown. Then at the nearby chair where the yellow nightgown was still draped over the back of it. She couldn't bear to look at it, to remember waking in the night to find herself lying on the floor cold and *wet*. And feeling as if she had been sexually ravished.

Donna came quickly to touch her shoulder. "Is something wrong, Sheba?"

"No!" She turned her back to Donna. But in front of her now was a black, reflecting, uncovered window, because the last traces of sun glow had gone and left behind a world that was dark, lonely, cold, and frightening. In front of her was fear. She turned back to Donna. "Yes, something's wrong. I don't know what it is. Maybe just nervousness because of, you know—his death."

"I understand how you feel, I think. And that's one of the reasons I came up to talk to you. I think we should leave here, don't you, Sheba?"

"Leave? But that's impossible. I've put almost all my money into this place, and I'd lose it."

"No, you wouldn't. Cliff is prepared to return your money. You won't be obligated in any way. He said we could be out of here within a week."

The mention of Cliff Murphy's name was enough to make Sheba forget the cold in the room, her fear of the dark, of being alone. No man had ever affected her as Cliff Murphy did. A strange new hatred boiled up into her throat.

"Oh he did, did he? So that's his little game! He wants to get the place back." She came close to Donna and looked up into her eyes. "Can't you see now? It's clear to me now—all of it. He stays on and on because if he can't scare me out and get my money as well as my property, then he pulls the old gentleman trick and kindly offers to buy it back—and have us out of here in a week. Great! How many *other* tricks has he pulled, Donna?"

Donna's eyes widened. She replied quickly in his defense. "He's not pulling tricks, Sheba. How could he? I was the one who—"

"How could he?" Sheba's stretched arm pointed toward her nightgown. "I don't know how. But what do you know about him? I wake in the night with my gown soaking. I'm lying on the floor, cold and freezing. I'll bet he drugs me or something and unlocks my door and does it to scare me out—and—and—well, does the whole bit."

"Sheba, that's a terrible thing to say!"

"Oh sure, you'd think so. I didn't think you were capable of it, Donna, but you're so much in love it shows all over you." Trembling with rage, and with something beyond her control, Sheba turned her back to Donna and went to close the window shade.

"Sheba," Donna said, "He was only trying to help you."

"Help me! Oh come on. By taking my home, my business, away from me?" She avoided Donna's eyes as she went toward the door. She had thought Donna was her friend. Now she was fast changing her mind. "I think we should go down now. We have guests waiting. After this please stay with them instead of bothering me with Cliff Murphy's schemes. As far as that goes, you can ask him to leave."

"Sheba, listen!"

Sheba stopped, the door open, the hallway dim beyond. "I'm listening," she said coldly.

"I haven't had a chance to tell you this, but this afternoon while you were gone Esther and I discovered that the walls in many of the second-floor rooms are being ruined by a—by a—I don't know what it is, Sheba, but it looks like a thick, green, slimy mildew."

"Where?" It was a trick, Sheba thought. Something Cliff Murphy had done.

"It's covering the walls and woodwork so fast that—"

"Where is it?" Sheba demanded. "I don't see a thing, and I haven't."

"All right, come with me. We can look in Esther's room,"

Donna went ahead of her down the hall, around the banister of the stairway, down the next hall, and left into the service area. She left the door open behind them because only one light was visible at the far end of the long, narrow corridor. The cold in the corridor had greatly increased and with it came a musty, odd smell.

They entered a room that was so small it seemed boxy, with furniture too large for it. Donna went straight to the bed, dug a long flashlight out from under a pillow, and snapped on a white, strong beam of light. Then she got down on her knees, lifted the bedspread, and aimed the light under the bed. Then she looked up. "Okay," she said, as if entirely out of humor herself, "take a look."

"How the hell can I look when you won't hold the light still?" Sheba reached out and snatched the light from Donna and pointed it for herself.

"Look at the baseboard," Donna said.

Sheba drew a long breath of resignation and leaned farther down. She pointed the light at the baseboard and saw the dull green, wet, shining stuff that was spreading there. "So? Mildew. Or something. We live in the middle of a large and lovely marsh, with a lake nearby. What do you expect? Especially in cold weather. It's damp here. I'll just go to town and see what people do to dry it out of the houses, that's all."

She snapped off the light, got up, and tossed it onto the bed.

"That's not all!" Donna said. "You should see the room next door. Sheba, it wasn't like that when we came here. Didn't you go through all the rooms when you first arrived?"

"Well... yes, we looked the house over, as I told you. Except for the attic."

"Then you saw that room, didn't you?" Donna pointed at the wall. "The one next to this one. Did you see any so-called mildew on it?"

"No, I did not. And I don't want to now. Let's go downstairs."

Donna had picked up the flashlight again. "Not until you take a look at that room. If this stuff under Esther's bed doesn't convince you, then maybe that will."

"Donna, damnit, I'm cold." She hugged her arms; her fingers felt like sticks of ice. It only made her colder and more irritable. But she followed Donna out into the hall and to the next door.

"Somebody closed this again," Donna said, opening it.

She didn't go in, she merely stood queen-like beside the door and pointed the light.

Sheba didn't go in either. She didn't have to. She could see the fingers of green that spread upward toward the ceiling. After one glance she backed away.

"No one's using the room anyway. Close the door. I'll see about it the next time I'm in town. Meantime, we have guests waiting. Are you going down with me, or aren't you?"

They joined the group at the stove, with the new man, whose name, Sheba remembered, was Tommy Kirsten, leaping up like a jack-in-the-box to get a chair for Sheba and make sure it was placed next to his. Sheba noticed that Cliff Murphy also rose and moved over nearer to the wall to make room for Donna. The married man, who sat with his arm on the chair in which his wife sat, made a half effort to rise, but then slid back.

The heat from the stove was like a touch of warm sunlight.

"You're so lovely in that dress," Tommy said, and Sheba smiled at him. He sat down near enough that his arm brushed hers, adding, "We've been hearing how haunted your house is. How do you stand living here?" Although he had spoken softly, he had gotten the attention of the entire group. Sheba looked around at them, seeing all eyes upon her—from the strange, staring eyes of the oddball guest April whoever-she-was, to the dark intensity of Cliff Murphy's.

"You've been hearing *what?*" she said quickly. "From whom, may I ask?"

"Miss Calder says she can feel the spirit moving in the house," Tommy said, amusement creeping in between the words.

"Oh really!" Sheba forced a laugh that she hoped would make April Calder less sure of herself, but the stare didn't change. "Maybe Miss Calder had better be very sure she doesn't anger the spirit by telling its dark secrets. It might come and attack her in the middle of the night."

The anger was there again, mixed with fear, perhaps—she wasn't sure. But it made her voice tremble slightly. She knew only that she didn't like April Calder. Fortunately, Tommy laughed aloud and in delight; and it covered the quiver behind her words. His hand touched her arm and pressed, and his fingers were thick and warm. She felt the urgency of time going, going away. Make love tonight, quickly. Tomorrow they would walk together and hold hands and fall in love and the world would be lovely for a while.

And then he would be gone and someone else would come by. For a while.

"I don't laugh about things like that," April Calder said.

Quietly Donna said, "Sheba was only kidding. Do tell us some of your experiences. Miss Calder, Sheba, writes on the occult, you know. Have you read any of her books?"

Sheba realized that Donna was trying to get her out of a spot she shouldn't have gotten herself into. These people were paying guests. And keeping the house, turning it into a hunting and fishing lodge, depended at the moment on people like these. Guests. Any breed or type. Besides, it was her own fault that guests were making fun of her house and calling it haunted. She had called it that herself; and in newspapers in several cities, besides.

So she smiled as sweetly as she could at April Calder. "No, I haven't. But I certainly will."

April said, "I haven't had a book published yet. Just articles in magazines. But I'm compiling a book."

"You'll be writing about my house, then.'" Sheba said, her smile straining the muscles in her cheeks. The effort was too much, and she let it slide away.

"I certainly hope to. With your permission, of course." Sheba couldn't answer that. As if she had been hypnotized by the big, protruding eyes of April Calder she returned the stare.

Cliff Murphy said suddenly, "The sale isn't necessarily going through, is it, Sheba? I may be buying back the house, and if that is the case I'm afraid you'd have to get permission from me."

Sheba switched her stare from April to Cliff. As always, he looked totally relaxed in his chair; and, as always slightly disdainful. The smile on his lips was so small as to be almost no smile at all, and his eyes were as narrowed and dark as the upstairs corridors. That his statement had been out of place and slightly premature was beside the point. It had succeeded in getting Sheba off the hook for the moment. She hadn't wanted to give April Calder permission to write anything, and she had a strong feeling that Cliff Murphy knew that.

The other female guest said, "How long have you owned the house, Miss Gilbert?"

"Please call me Sheba. As to your question—about a month."

"Oh, is that all?"

"That's all."

The woman looked up at the ceiling. "I think it's a delightful place. Reminds me of pictures I've seen of those old gray castles in Ireland and Scotland. If I owned it, I wouldn't sell it at all."

Sheba smiled deliberately at Cliff Murphy. "I don't intend to," she said. But if she had hoped for some sign of surprise, or regret, there was none.

"Then," April said, "with your permission…

"I'll think about it, Miss Calder, and let you know." Sheba had a sudden, malicious urge to get them all out of the house, her house. Get them out and never let anyone return. The feeling swept through her with a power that left her weak, silent, and stunned. She had wanted a lot of people around her. She had publicity. What better way to get it than through a writer? Calling her house haunted would bring one type of guest, but a duck hunter or a fisherman wouldn't be disturbed by any such thoughts. They would scoff at it and go on about their own particular pleasure.

That was what she had wanted, and now she sat leaning back in her chair, hearing the low conversations of the people and yet not hearing it, watching them and wondering. And it seemed that the strong feeling of hostility had not been hers at all, but a cold draft from beyond the warmth of the stove that swept through and touched her for a moment.

She looked toward the foyer and saw its shadowed hugeness, and was aware of another feeling. She dreaded going upstairs alone tonight, back to that bedroom where last night she had awakened out of bed, on the floor, in a nightgown that was unaccountably wet. She understood none of it. Only her fear.

Once, she had tried to tell Donna of the mist, the fog, of that other presence, but Donna hadn't listened. Now Donna had shown her a reason why the house should go, and she wished she had said yes, yes, yes. But she hadn't. She was torn and pulled, as if something invisible and more powerful than she was urging her to stay, to send the people away. But stay, always stay. Never leave.

Never.

After dinner, and after another long discussion beside the stove, the only warm place in the house, guests began drifting away to bed. April Calder was the first to go. She stood near a pillar by the foyer and said, "Listen. Everyone listen."

And when everyone grew so quiet that the soft sound of rain against the window behind the stove was the only sound to reach Sheba's ears, April said:

"Can't you hear that?"

She seemed to be listening toward the stairway and the rise that went up beyond the lights into the darkness of faraway ceilings.

Cliff Murphy said very softly, "What do you hear?"

"A kind of pulsing. Like a heartbeat. Or a rhythmic rush of blood. Or other nonlife substance. Can't you hear it?"

Sheba saw from the corner of her eye that the woman whose name she now remembered as Kim Jones, a woman who was in her thirties or so and seemed quite impressionable, shook her head.

"Where is it?" Cliff asked. "The heart of it."

Sheba looked at Cliff in surprise. Did he actually believe that stuff? He had seemed to be silently laughing at everyone. Teasing. Had something happened to make him change his mind?

"The heart of it," April repeated, as if she had gone into a kind of trace. "I don't know, but it's up there somewhere."

"Second floor or attic?"

April was silent again, and no one seemed to be breathing now. The rain touched the uncovered window like soft, sliding fingers. Donna stood up and her chair creaked. Kim Jones squealed and then clapped both hands over her mouth. Her husband laughed at her. But only briefly.

Then Kim laughed a little at herself and explained, "That scared me. When Donna moved, I mean."

Donna stood still beside her chair, smiling, watching Kim. She asked, "Is it all right if I move again now? I was going to close the drapery at the window."

"Of course. I'm sorry. I don't know why I screamed like that."

Sheba knew. The atmosphere in the house had become charged almost to an exploding point.

Cliff Murphy said, "Miss Calder—you were telling us—"

She interrupted, "I wasn't aware there was an attic, Mr. Murphy. Of course most houses do have attics, but... I honestly don't know. I haven't located the center of the power yet. But listen closely and you will hear it."

Sheba shivered violently, and her arm was suddenly touched by the warm hand of the man who sat in the chair beside hers.

"You're cold," he whispered, leaning toward her "Would you like me to bring you something to put around your shoulders?"

She shook her head.

April's voice sounded frustrated and impatient, "How can I get the answer when I'm constantly being interrupted? I don't think anyone here is really serious about it. Not even you, Miss Gilbert."

"Of course not," Sheba said. She didn't like the woman anyway. "It was only a gimmick, Miss Calder. I thought you knew that. I would think that anyone would know that! Haunted houses and ghosts belong in another century."

The smile on April's face was small, cool, and superior "I'm afraid, Miss Gilbert, that you have a surprise coming. To phrase it lightly. Now if you'll all excuse me, I'll go up to my room."

After she was gone, her steps creaking upward on the stairway, Kim Jones said in low-voiced amazement "She actually believes that stuff and yet she goes up there alone? Good Lord, Ralph, don't you dare get ten feet from me. I thought it would be fun to come here, but now I don't know."

"Ahh," he said, scolding, "don't be a goof, Kim." He glanced at Sheba. "That Miss Calder was probably a gimmick too. To make icy fingers crawl up and down your spine."

He grabbed his wife suddenly and started tickling her while she twisted and squealed; then laughing together they said good night and went out. After that they all left, with Sheba holding back to turn out the lights.

"Shall I help you?" Donna said.

"No. I plan to leave a light on tonight."

Donna and Cliff Murphy left the room and Sheba went from lamp to lamp, blowing out the small yellow flames. She was aware that Tommy was waiting for her.

"I'll walk you to your room, okay?" he said.

"Yes, I don't want to be alone. April Calder is not a gimmick, you know. I didn't bring her here, and she gives me the creeps."

"She would anybody."

He came to her and in the shadowed corner of the large room he kissed her. His body was warm and she needed him for many more reasons than one, tonight.

"I'll protect you," he said, "if you'll let me."

"Yes..."

"Can we go to your room?"

She started to say yes again, and then she remembered the last time a man had been in her room. She pressed closer to him, pushing away the memory. She said, "No. I'll come to yours, later, as soon as I can get ready. Just show me where it is."

At the top of the stairs he pointed out to her that his room was the fourth one down the right-wing hallway, and she was glad to hear that the other wing, the one where the first guests had stayed, had been left empty this time. "I'll be there," she whispered, and went around the balcony to her room.

She changed to a nightgown and when she opened her door the hall was so still that she could hear the pulse herself, just as April Calder had. A soft, rhythmic beat, like the beat of a heart.

Her own heart pounding in her ears. The stupid nut of a woman who believed in... The memory of a white substance oozing in around her door came clearly to her mind and Sheba began to run, lightly, around the dark well of the staircase and down the hall toward his room. She didn't want to think of that other time, so many weeks ago now, when she had seen something she had felt was in its strange way living and dangerous.

In running to the arms of a man she ran not only from the nightmare of that night, but the nightmare of nights since.

He was waiting for her.

In the pale light of his room he took her into his bed and undressed her, and his skin was hot and smooth against her, his body heavy. His mouth felt her. His hands moved upon her. And her mind was suspended and she existed in her body, in need, wanting and waiting for fulfillment.

Breathing became more difficult. She was gasping, gasping for air. He seemed not to notice. His own breath was the gasp and grope of passion, and with his mouth at her breast she looked over his head and saw it.

At the closed door. Rushing, foaming through in thick, white, smothering speed; through the old-fashioned key hole, the thin crack around the door, coming through like smoke, thickening ominously.

In sudden, terrible panic she shoved her lover off and ran. First into the corner, away from the white at the door, and then straight into it, where she groped for the doorknob and jerked it, shoving the door back against the wall. In blind, silent panic she fought her way through a hallway that was filled with thick, white fog.

Her hand touched a wall and she followed it, and when it turned sharply left she went forward, her hands out, feeling for the banister of the stairway. The fog thinned for a moment and she saw the pale light at the corner of the hallway across the wide way between wings, and ran for it. The fog closed in again, thick, impenetrable. But she knew now where her room was. First door around the corner.

First door.

She found it, opened it, and stumbled forward, searching in the fog-filled room for her bed.

Choking for air, she fell weakly across her bed, the cold, damp air covering her naked body like the water in the marsh.

WHEN SHE WOKE it was gradually, as though becoming aware of a dream. She was standing, holding a lamp in her hand, looking up into the face of a man she had never seen before. He was tall, with thick brown hair and moustache, and he was smiling down at her and not moving or speaking. She noticed that he was wearing a hunting jacket and that he held something in his hand. A black, double-barreled gun. But he stood at ease, with one hand on the gun butt, because the gun's muzzle was resting on the floor.

Reality snapped in her mind and she realized she was standing in front of a world that was edged by a gold frame.

A painting.

She jerked backward, away from it, staring in horror. The lamp in her hand tilted and she almost dropped it. With both hands she grasped the bowl of the lamp and looked again at the painting. A nearly life-size painting of a man wearing a brown hunting suit with a shotgun at his side.

Where was she?

She turned away, looking, and saw boxes and trunks; and farther away, against a post, a broken chair. She whirled back to look at the painting, and the face kept smiling at her.

The attic?

How in God's name did she get into the attic? It had to be the attic.

She had never seen the room before, not ever. And she wanted nothing more than never to see it again. But how could she get out? The darkness surrounded her in all directions, so that she was in the small center of light thrown by her lamp.

The memory of the night flashed suddenly to mind... she had been on her bed, naked.

She looked down at her body and saw that she had put on a robe. And then she had gotten her lamp and come up into the attic!

A scream for help trembled threateningly for a moment in her throat,but she held back. Why bring the wholehouse up when she hadgotten into the attic without help and could surely get down. Besides, what explanation would she give?

She took several deep breaths to still her fear and began to look for the stairway that would take her down, out of this God-forsaken place.

It seemed hours before she found it, hours in which always she was aware of the painting smiling, smiling, smiling at her. She ran down the steps and out into the corridor and on to her room.

Lock the door? What good did it do? She leaned against it, tears rolling down her face; and finally she simply let herself sink to the floor, where she rested her face on her knees and sobbed out the fear and frustration of not knowing what was happening to her.

After a long while, when there were no more tears, she put her lamp on its table and went back to bed. Robe and all. She was afraid to sleep, but too exhausted now to stay awake. Day would be here soon. It had to be.

She couldn't stand much more of the night.

CHAPTER 12

Donna went downstairs to breakfast in the kitchen to find that Sheba was already there nursing a cup of coffee. Her eyes were circled darkly and seemed to have been driven back into her head. She looked up at Donna but said nothing. Wanda was yawning by the stove, as usual, and Esther was busily frying ham.

"Didn't you sleep either?" Donna asked Sheba after saying good morning all around.

"Why do you ask?" Sheba demanded.

"Because I was restless all night. I think it was that spooky stuff that April Calder gave us before she went up to bed."

"She's a nut," Sheba said, lowering her face into the steam of her coffee.

Wanda asked as she came over to the table and sat down, "What was that? Tell me."

"You've seen her, haven't you?"

"The one who looks like a bird?"

Donna glanced at the kitchen door. "Shh. She may be coming in any moment."

"I doubt that," Esther said. "I haven't sent Wanda up to wake any of them yet, but you'd better go, Wanda, and tell them breakfast is in the kitchen and just about ready."

Wanda motioned impatiently at her sister. "Just a minute. Tell me what this April—what a funny name— did."

"She was telling us she could hear the house's heartbeat. Or something," Donna said.

"What?" Wanda yelled. "It's heartbeat!"

"Uh—not exactly. She feels the house has a power within it that—"

"No!" Sheba said suddenly, violently, looking up at them. "Don't talk about it. I don't want to hear it. The woman's nuts. So let's just leave it that way, okay?"

Sheba's outburst left even Wanda quiet. Donna looked at Sheba and wondered what was happening to the girl she had known. Outgoing, excited, ready to live life to its utmost, Sheba was now becoming quiet and withdrawn much of the time, and violently angry at others. She wanted to ask her what was wrong, but not in front of Esther and Wanda.

The door opened then, bringing in the freshness of new good mornings and some mention of the weather as Cliff went to rub his hands by the stove and look to see what Esther was cooking for breakfast. Sheba raised her head only for a second. She didn't speak.

With his coffee cup in hand, Cliff came to sit beside Donna. "How are you this dull, foggy, drizzly morning?" he asked.

"Wanda," Esther said, bringing a plate of ham and eggs to the table. "Go up and get the others now, will you?"

But just then the kitchen door opened a bit and a rather timid but smiling face came in view.

"Uh—excuse me," Ralph Jones said. "Is this where we're supposed to come for breakfast?"

Donna got up to bring them on in. "We were just going up to get you. Didn't your friend come down with you?"

The husband and wife looked at each other, and he answered, "No, we haven't seen him."

"Then perhaps you'd better go on, Wanda. If he'd prefer not to eat now, that's fine. Esther can make his breakfast later."

They were seated again, and the platter of ham and eggs was making the rounds. Sheba shook her head and stayed with her coffee, silent, apart from the others. Watching her, Donna knew that after breakfast she must try to draw her out.

The two men were talking about a springtime that seemed to be delayed when the scream vibrated through the upper story of the house, far away, unreal at first but louder as the pounding, running steps shook the ceiling.

Wanda almost fell down the stairway, her hands clinging desperately to the railing, her scream dying away. The men were up and running. Cliff took the steps several at a time and stopped beside Wanda, supporting her with his arms. She pointed upward, silently. She seemed capable only of pointing and shaking her head.

Cliff gave one rapid order: "Esther. Come and help her down."

Esther ran, and the moment she reached them Cliff released Wanda to Esther and went on up the stairs.

They crowded past Esther and Wanda, all of them. Donna went behind Ralph Jones, aware that Sheba was just behind her. And behind Sheba came Ralph's wife. Donna had to run to catch up with Cliff, and behind her she heard the thud of the other running steps.

"Where is his room?" Cliff asked, as if he knew what had sent Wanda screaming back to the kitchen.

Ralph passed him without answering and opened a door. There he stopped, staring into the room.

He backed out, blinking.

Cliff went into the room with Sheba right behind him. and Donna heard the soft cry of rejection of what Sheba saw. Then the cry rose higher, louder, forming into hard-to-understand words: "No. No! Not again, my god, not again, not again."

Donna reached the threshold to see, first, Cliff's arms go around Sheba as he pulled her back toward the door; and next the form on the bed. He lay nude on top of the blankets, his body a sickening bluish-white, as if frozen and now thawing in places that left purple blotches; and over his head was a pillow.

At Donna's shoulder a feminine voice asked, "Is he dead?" incredulously. High-pitched and unnatural.

Her husband said, "Kim. Come on. Please don't go in there."

Cliff, one arm dragging Sheba back to the door, reached out the other, put his palm flat against Donna's breasts, and pushed her gently backward into the hall: In astonishment, only half aware of Sheba's growing hysteria, Donna looked up into his eyes. They told her nothing.

When she stood in the hall he pushed Sheba toward her.

"Can you take careof her?"

Donna nodded and put her arms around Sheba. She seemed suddenly aware of it and clung to Donna, her hands clutching Donna's sweater. But her words were as unintelligible as before.

"Why is this happening to me—it can't happen again —it can't—he can't be dead—"

"Ralph," Kim's voice was on the verge of a scream, "what's she talking about?"

"I don't know."

Cliff raised his voice suddenly, in a tone of demand. "All of you—go on back down to the kitchen. Get some coffee. Get out of here!"

In the kitchen Donna pushed Sheba into a chair and went to get coffee for her.

"I can't just sit here, I can't." Sheba cried piteously.

Donna put the coffee under her nose. "Please. Just drink, okay?"

When Cliff came downstairs not long after, he was wearing his suede jacket and on his way out the back door.

"Hang in here, all of you. Stay together until I get back. I'm going after the sheriff and all the other people something like this requires."

The door closed, its brief opening letting in a draft of air that was colder and damper than that in the house. Kim Jones looked at her husband.

"What did he mean by that? Ralph—how—is Tom dead?"

Ralph answered, "Just try to drink some coffee or something."

"I can't."

"*Try.*"

Donna looked at the people in the room. Sheba bent over her stomach, as if she hurt; Ralph and Kim Jones looking as if they were caught in the quicksand of a nightmare; Esther by the stove finding something to do by shoving coal into it; Wanda—Wanda walking.

Donna was on her feet suddenly. "Where's April Calder?"

Everyone, except Sheba, stared at her as if they'd never heard of April Calder. In the silence came the sounds of metal snapping dully under hunks of coal as they rolled to a resting place in the stove.

Donna crossed the long room and looked up into the darkness of the second floor, and hesitated.

"She never came down, did she? I don't remember seeing her this morning."

"No," Esther said. "I don't believe she did. Wanda, did you go call her this morning when—did you go when —" As though all at once disgusted with her own weakness and nervousness, Esther's voice strengthened: "Wanda, go with Donna and look for that woman!" Wanda's voice quivered an answer: "I—I've forgotten where her room is."

"I haven't. Come along, Wanda." Donna didn't want to go back up there alone, to find only God knew what. That was too much.

But April Calder had to be found.

Donna waited until Wanda had reluctantly crossed the room to stand beside her, then she climbed the steep, twisting flight of stairs.

The light of day was left behind them. Up the corridor on the landing a small, kerosene wall lamp flickered on as if day hadn't arrived, would never arrive in this twilight world where dampness ruined and death happened for no comprehensible purpose.

They stopped to listen, but the whole house was still except for sounds drifting up from the kitchen, magnified against the high, dark ceiling. A cup put down in a saucer. The quick footsteps of a woman. More clunking of coal into the stove.

"That's Esther," Wanda whispered shrill in Donna's ear, breathing warm air on her neck.

Donna nodded. "We'll have to check on April's room."

"Is it—close to his?"

"Yes. But come on." Donna moved away from the warm breath.

The service door had been left open, and beyond it a wisp of pale daylight moved through the mists that lingered in the hall.

"It's foggy in here," Wanda said.

"Yes, so I noticed."

She also noticed that Wanda stopped and remained standing by the banister, her gaze moving down the left-wing corridor but her feet planted firm and flat. And Donna remembered that it was Wanda who had once this morning gone alone into the fading light of that corridor to the fourth room.

Gently, Donna said to her, "Just wait for me. It's only the third door."

Wanda nodded, staring toward it.

Keeping her eyes and her thoughts away from that other door as much as was humanly possible, Donna went to April's door and listened for a moment. Something moved within the room, a sound that was more the whisper of material than the reality of a footstep.

Donna knocked lightly, calling, "Miss Calder?"

The sound stopped immediately, and then there was nothing.

"Miss Calder? It's Donna, and Wanda." She glanced at Wanda and saw that her eyes had widened and her hands were tightening and loosening on the banister railing. In another minute she would be running again. Screaming again.

In a burst of anger against a woman who wouldn't answer her door, Donna twisted the knob and found the door locked. She called again, "There's been a—there's been trouble in the house, Miss Calder, and we've come up to see if you're all right. Now I insist you open this door. This minute!"

Donna waited, listening. The minute stretched out, but then there were hesitant footsteps. The lock clicked and the door opened.

The eyes that peered out at Donna seemed enormous in the white face. The lips had thinned down to almost nothing. Donna shoved back the door and saw the suitcase on the bed.

The woman seemed nearly paralyzed with fright, so Donna gentled her voice. "There's been a death just next door."

"I know."

"Then why didn't you come on down, rather than stay up here alone?"

"I plan to come down. I'm leaving."

She whirled back to her bed, grabbed up the suitcase, a coat that lay on the bed, and her large handbag. Then she shoved Donna out of her way and started down the hall.

Wanda, still clinging to the banister, evidently surprised the guest. April Calder stopped abruptly.

Donna touched her shoulder, and she leaped in surprise and stared over her shoulder at Donna, drawing away as though Donna was a part of whatever had frightened her into leaving suddenly.

"I'm sorry, Miss Calder," Donna said. "But I'm sure you'll have to wait with the rest of us in the kitchen until the sheriff and the doctor, or coroner and ambulance get here. We'll all have to be here."

"Why?" she demanded. "I didn't kill him!"

"I'm sure you didn't. Neither did the rest of us. But..."

April's chin began to tremble with emotion. She turned slightly to look at Donna without having to look over her shoulder. "I'm getting out of this house. I'm not staying another night. I was a fool to come here in the first place. I'm not even sure now that the rest of you are—are *human*."

"Don't be ridiculous!"

Donna took her arm, but April Calder jerked it away. However, she began to walk, turning at the corner where Donna turned, going back through the service hall toward the back stairs. Wanda had released the banister and rushed to follow them.

"Of course we're human," Donna said. "I think it might be a good idea if you did leave. But first you have to speak to the sheriff."

"Well, if he's coming then I won't mind staying until he does. Provided, that is, he comes today."

"Of course he'll come today. Cliff Murphy has gone after him."

"How long will it be?"

"I don't know. An hour maybe."

"Good Lord." She clomped on, as though in her footsteps she could expel some of her feelings. "Not that a sheriff is going to help much. Nothing is going to help this place. And if you people *are* human, you're doing others a great disservice by trying to use this horrible house as a way to earn money, because it's filled with—with something that I can't even describe. I never felt it so strongly before, never. And furthermore, I didn't sleep a wink last night because the house was filled with it."

"Filled with what?" Donna asked. "Did you hear something?"

"No. Well, yes. But I think I'll save that to tell the sheriff."

With her head high she went on down the hall, looking neither right nor left. But suddenly she stopped.

Behind her, Donna stopped too, then Wanda came to a halt. April Calder slowly swiveled her head sideways to look at the closed attic door.

"What's that?" she demanded in a whisper, as though something behind it could hear.

"It's the attic door," Donna said. Adding, because the woman got on her nerves and seemed startled by the door, "Would you like to go up? It's a very large attic, a very dark one. But it has many, many interesting things left there by previous owners."

"That's it," the woman said in the same whisper. "That's it! That's where it is."

"Where what is? I really think we should go on downstairs."

"The center of the energy. The spirit, the power. I have no name for it, but, my dear girl, that's where it is."

Donna reached over and started to open the door, wondering at last if whoever had turned her doorknob that first night in the house had actually remained in the house, hiding in the attic. There were so many hiding places, so many. She didn't think beyond the opening of the door, only of the sudden realization that it might be possible. And April Calder, with an unusual degree of clairvoyance, had in some mental way detected it.

But April Calder grabbed her arm and jerked her hand roughly away from the door, and when Donna looked at her in astonishment, she saw in the eyes and face a terror that was worse even than the trembling helplessness of Wanda.

"No," she whispered. "Don't open it. Don't ever open it. Come and let's go on downstairs."

Without comment they went on, but Donna was busily thinking about how to make sure that no one escaped. Fortunately, the house had only two doors. At one time she had felt it odd and very inconvenient that a house so large should have only two doors, but now she was glad it did.

As soon as they reached the kitchen she told Esther, "See to it that she stays in here with the others. I'm going to my office to wait.

She closed the kitchen door behind her, feeling that it would be a relief to get away from all those varied, strained expressions, people who seemed to be suspended in a kind of hell as they waited the long, dragging minutes for release. But the moment the door closed her away from them she became eerily aware of the large, dim, silent house. The death was there, so close and yet so far away in the room upstairs. If only Cliff hadn't gone. He seemed to be the only person capable of keeping any kind of self-control or control of others; of doing what had to be done.

The front door was closed, but she opened it and stood or a moment in the light drizzle that came down from clouds thick and gray. Shivering, she returned to the interior, locked the door, and leaned against it, letting her gaze go from the wide foyer past the arches and pillars into the living room. The stairway rose crooked ahead of her, fading into the darkness and silence of the second floor. Where a second person had died. Where the attic door was...

"The woman's *nuts*," she said as she went toward the safety of her office. At least it helped a little to call her nuts. It was more than a little disturbing to have someone around who claimed to have superior powers of knowledge. Especially when it was about things like powers of the supernatural.

Donna didn't like it. Something had turned her door knob one night, and it wasn't a... At least, she hoped it wasn't. A human, she could fight. But something as intangible as what April Calder suggested?

She stood at the window and suddenly the cars were there, coming fast. Cliff's car went out of sight toward the garages, but the sheriff's car spun to a stop near the front of the house. The back end slid sideways on the rain-slick grass. Behind it came the ambulance. Men were leaping out from all of them, and Donna rushed to open the front door.

Cliff had reached the small porch by the time Donna had pulled the door back wide to make room for the men with the stretcher.

The sheriff nodded coldly at Donna and said, "Where's the room? You people seem to be getting an awful lot of deaths here in the short time you've been around."

Men moved into the hallway past her, and Cliff paused long enough to touch her cheek lightly and comfortingly. He said to the sheriff, and the others that were waiting to go upstairs, "I'll show you the room."

"All right." The sheriff told Donna as he started up the stairs, "Go where the others are. Keep everyone in the same room until we see what happened up here. Too many deaths going on around here. I don't like it one goddamned bit."

She found the faces just as she had left them: strained and in various poses of shock and fear. Esther was still at the stove, but her hands shook, and she seemed to be moving pots and pans about just to be doing something.

"It will be over soon," Donna said to reassure everyone. "The sheriff and his crowd have arrived. Cliff is here. They're all upstairs now."

April Calder looked at the ceiling. "Strange. I don't hear any sounds. No footsteps."

"No—well, they're there, anyway."

She'd be glad when April Calder did go, paying guest or not. And furthermore she hoped that this would at least change Sheba's mind about taking her money back and leaving. On the other hand, what would

Cliff do with the house? She knew one thing: she didn't want Cliff to stay in it.

Not now.

She was afraid for him.

"Do you want some cof-coffee?" Esther managed to ask.

"Thank you, yes." Why not? At least it would help to stop the nervous shiver that had started when she was in the cold rain and had stayed with her since.

The cup was warm in her hands, and she went to sit at the end of the table near Sheba. The black hair fell forward over Sheba's white hands, her face hidden from the others, her elbows on the table to help support her head.

Donna wanted to say something to her, but didn't know what to say or where to start. She sipped her coffee instead.

A couple of doors slammed upstairs, then came the faint sound of voices that grew nearer and louder, and footsteps that seemed now to be everywhere.

The sheriff, accompanied by his deputy and Cliff, came down the stairs. The little notebook and red pencil were out again, and the sheriff's hard eyes swept the group at the table, lingering for a moment on the lowered head of Sheba and going finally to the suitcase on the floor by April Calder.

In a surprisingly mild tone he asked, "Going somewhere?"

She sat up straighter. "Yes, sir. Home."

He smiled a little one-sided cold smile, and asked for her name and address. After he had gotten the names and address of the other guests he let them have it, in the same mild voice.

"This time it's murder. Nobody's going anywhere." For a moment there was total silence in the room. Donna didn't feel surprised at his words, but she knew when she heard them that she hadn't really faced the possibility of death by means other than natural. She noticed that Sheba raised her face and slowly turned it toward the sheriff.

The deputy stood with his arms crossed over his chest.

"I guess you all know," the sheriff finally said, "that one of you here did the killing. What I want to know is which one."

His unfriendly eyes went from one to the other, excluding only Cliff and Esther at the stove. As if Esther were a piece of the kitchen equipment.

Sheba demanded suddenly, "How do you know that?"

"How do I know that? Several things tell me that. First, the man is dead. Smothered to death by a pillow over his face. Second it happened sometime between ten o'clock last night and four this morning, more or less. Third, this old place is a long way from the road and nobody was here but your bunch that's here in this kitchen!" At the end of his small speech his voice burst out loud and clear and furious.

Donna jumped to her feet, flattened her hands on the table, and shouted back at him, "And how do you know we're all that are here! Have you bothered to look the rest of the house over? Have you looked in the other rooms, or the *attic?*"

April Calder jerked around to stare at Donna. "No," she said in deep fervor. "Oh no. Don't let him open that attic door!"

The sheriff came toward the table, pushing empty chairs right and left out of his way like a bulldozer, and stopped within arm's reach of April Calder. When she saw him there she pushed back into her chair to get away from him.

"And just what do you mean by that, Miss April Calder? Do you know something that I don't know? If you do, spill it!"

His last words were louder and April shuddered visibly. She pushed so far back against her chair it almost tipped backward.

"She doesn't know anything," Donna shouted again "She's only a guest here."

"So," the sheriff pointed out to her with his pencil, "was the dead man, lady! Now if you'll kindly shut your mouth and let me handle this my own way we'll get along a lot *better!* Do you follow me? Your kitchen is a lot bigger and more comfortable than my one little eight-by-eight jail cell, and I'd rather ask my questions here. But one of you is a killer and I aim to find out *who!*"

Cliff Murphy had slowly ambled forward to stand at the sheriff's side. "Look," he said, "lay off her, okay?'

"Lay off her?" The sheriff pointed the pencil at Donna again. "Sit down there and try laying off *me*. I'll handle my own affairs, and you can talk when your turn comes. Now, as for you, Mr. Murphy, I'd just like to know exactly what your business is up here for so long. Seems to me you sold this place along about the first of January, and here it is February already. You hit town asking questions. You found out everything you could not only from me but everyone else who knew anything about the old Bleeker place. What I want to know is why. And don't give me any hogwash, because I can check you out anyway."

The sheriff poised his pencil over his notebook and waited, outwardly with all the patience in the world.

"Well?" the sheriff said. "I suppose you're on some kind of secret mission."

Cliff asked, "Would you accept that?"

"No!"

"Okay, okay. I'm a parapsychologist and I'm here as an observer and, possibly, an investigator. I work with—or for—Dr. Steven at—"

"Now wait a minute! You're a *what!*"

"A parapsychologist."

"Break that down into ordinary language."

Cliff shrugged, as though he felt he was getting himself in deep but couldn't stop it. "Okay, okay. I go around where strange things happen and try to find out why they—"

"Hold it right there! You go around where strange things happen?"

"That's right."

"Strange things like murder?"

"Yes, and other kinds of—"

"You go around where murder happens, and it dawns on me that you came here a month ago. You knew it would happen before it did? Since you have been here two men have died."

Kim Jones cried out, "Two? Two men?"

The sheriff glanced quickly at her. "I'll get to you," he said. "Right now, Mr. Murphy, I want to know exactly how you thought you were going to investigate murders that hadn't happened yet. Or do you know something that I don't know?"

"I know that you're forgetting something!"

"Oh yeah, what?"

"A murder had been committed here, and you were the one who told me about it. Plus several people had gone off the bridge and died there—"

"They weren't murders. The bridge part."

"Are you sure?" Cliff asked quietly.

It was the sheriff's turn to stare. "Huh? What are you talking about?"

Cliff shrugged and walked away. He got a chair that was abandoned to one side and brought it over to sit beside Donna. Like the deputy, he crossed his arms over his chest. Unlike the deputy, he relaxed and leaned back in the chair.

"Anyway, you now have my occupation and you can check with the doctor and the university if you want to."

April Calder said, her eyes on Cliff as if at last she had found a friend, "I didn't know you were a psych investigator!"

The sheriff said, "A what?"

Cliff nodded. "We do exist, you know, Sheriff. Sorry about that."

"Now I know what you're talking about. But I think you're all a bunch of lunatics."

"That's your privilege."

"I suppose in a minute you'll be trying to tell me a ghost murdered the man upstairs."

Cliff didn't answer. Donna was looking at him with new feelings of awareness rushing through her. She wasn't sure how she felt about it—he had seemed so practical. One of her own kind. No, that wasn't true. She had felt the mystery, and it was that which had first attracted her to him. Now, his narrowed dark eyes remained steadily on the sheriff.

Speaking so softly that no one else could hear, she said, "I thought you were teasing those kids. Do you really believe that stuff?"

"I didn't," he said, not taking his eyes from the sheriff but leaning slightly toward her, "but I'm beginning to wonder about a lot of things."

The sheriff pointed his pencil again. "Cut the whispering."

Cliff said softly, "I'll tell you later."

"I said cut the goddamned whispering. Tell me this doctor's name and address!" He wrote as Cliff gave the address, and when he had finished he cut it off with a sharp jab in the air with his pencil and came back to start the questioning with the first person on his right. It happened to be Wanda.

CHAPTER 13

At last in his room, Cliff hastily jotted down in his own peculiar variety of shorthand the odd set of facts the sheriff's questioning had brought out. Hours of questioning and threats on part of the sheriff had actually revealed very little. Unless you could find the common link that Cliff felt strongly was there, somewhere.

First, Wanda reported having heard nothing last night but she finally admitted to hearing footsteps outside her room her first night in the house, and a short time later Donna had come to her room to see if she was all right because someone had tried to open her door and found it locked.

No one was supposed to be in the house at the time but the four women and they had all been in their rooms.

That was enough to practically convict one of them so far as the sheriff was concerned, and the sooner the better, to hear him tell it. However, he finally brushed that night aside and came back to the present.

Next, there was last night. Who had been where and heard what? Of course, April Calder. It was there, she said, in the attic. What? She didn't know what, but it was terrible, whatever it was. At that the sheriff almost burst the blood vessels in his forehead and God only knew where else.

He wrote for a while, and then sat back to try to read what he had written. To try to make sense of it. And after going through it once he saw why the sheriff had finally thrown his notebook at his deputy and told the guests to get the hell out and stay out but to be available and he meant *available.*

Cliff took a deep breath and slowly struggled through the notes again. But a distracting sound was shuffling about overhead. The sheriff and his deputy obviously were still searching the house. Someone, though, must have stumbled over something and fallen flat on his teeth, from all the rattles, and someone else had come running to pick him up. Who had fallen?

Cliff couldn't help the grin of satisfaction. He knew, and he had told them, that they wouldn't find anyone upstairs. But that was all he had said because he couldn't be absolutely sure that some room in the house did not harbor a killer, and it was a more comforting thought to the girls than knowing that one of them was responsible.

Yes, one of them.

That was the only thing in the mess of notes that kept coming straight and clear to Cliff's mind. One of the women in the house had committed the murder last night. And now he was wondering about the first man who had died.

But no one admitted to having heard a sound last night except, of course, April Calder. She had heard running steps in the hallway, and the bedsprings on the dead man's bed squeaking just before that.

But no one else knew a damned thing about it.

And Cliff wondered.

He didn't want to be prejudiced, and he couldn't say for sure why he was, but his thoughts kept going back to Sheba.

He tossed the notes onto his bed and left the room.

In the hallway he met the sheriff, looking like a tall, disgruntled cluster of cobwebs, and behind him his stubbier deputy.

"Didn't find anything, huh?" Cliff said amiably.

The sheriff glared at him and went on to open a bedroom door. He didn't cross the threshold, he only looked in. Cliff knew the bedrooms had already been searched and he wondered what the sheriff was looking for now.

Cliff said, "I see you got the attic cleaned up."

The sheriff slammed the bedroom door. "And I see you got one hell of a sense of humor, boy." He pointed a long finger toward the bedroom. "What I want to know is what the hell is that green stuff growing in this house!"

Cliff spread his hands. "You sound like you're blaming me for it."

"Somebody here murdered that man, and you don't need to think I'm not coming back, boy. And you had better be *here*."

Cliff raised his eyebrows and nodded a kind of half nod. It was a little trick he used on people who got too uppity with him; but on the sheriff it didn't work. With considerable dignity, considering the layer of cobwebs, the tall, angry man went on down the stairs and out the front door. His deputy trailed along.

The slam of the door echoed twice somewhere in the high-ceilinged rooms of the house in a dull and muffled way, as though the green growth's purpose was to eventually close out all sound and bring into the house a world without sound. Without life.

He looked around, at the branching, twilight corridors, at the closed bedroom doors, and for the first time since his arrival he went to the door of the room where his sister had stayed.

He closed the door behind him when he went in.

So this was where Judy had lived, and in her nightmares had found something that was unbearable. So unbearable that she had moved into her parents' room. And then her prediction had come true after all, and the three of them had died before they could get away from Bleeker house.

As he stood in the dimness of the room those deaths seemed more a reality to him than the death that had occurred during the night before. The bed was still made. A bottle of perfume was still on the dresser. He picked it up and saw that it was one he had sent her for her birthday. Seventeen years old. So bright that she had been on her way to college a year ahead of most youngsters. He remembered his mother wondering, via letter, if her intelligence was on the borderline of madness so that her high powers of visual imagination had gone over the line into the realm of madness.

Where had they been going the night of the accident and why had they left so quickly in the middle of the night?

He looked at the ceiling. The room had been repainted and papered, he knew that for sure, yet the ceiling was showing cracks in the plaster, and in the cracks was growing the green stuff. Lower, below a molding about eighteen inches down from the ceiling, where the paper began, it was streaked as if by water, and one section of paper in the corner had turned loose and was folded back upon itself. He went near it and saw the green edging out from beneath the paper like moss slime at the edge of a stagnant pond.

There was an odor in the corner that was suffocatingly strong, a musty, damp, unclean smell.

He crossed the room to the wardrobe and pushed back the door. It squealed, tortured on rusted hinges. The clothes were still there-part of them at least—and had been pushed back against one end of the wardrobe. Someone had shoved them tightly back to make room for something else?

The door moaned and squealed again as he closed it. And then he caught from the corner of his eye another movement in the room; another door slowly, quietly opening.

The silence of that opening door, and the slowness, struck him as decidedly eerie, and his body tensed as he waited.

A head appeared rather slowly around the edge of the moving door, a head that was bright with blond hair so pale it was almost platinum. A forehead high and white, and gray eyes oddly silver, beautifully luminous.

Now, large with silent fear.

When Donna saw Cliff her eyes smiled and she sagged in relief against the door frame, her hands clutching the door as though she had lost her equilibrium and had to have support.

He suddenly felt needed, and it was a good feeling. He pulled her away from the wall and into his arms and she let him, and for a moment was soft and yielding against him.

She looked up at him. "Oh Cliff, you don't know how glad I was to see you. My room is just next door and I heard footsteps in here and that awful wardrobe door and I was almost afraid to look in."

He considered her side of the situation, and her actions. "You shouldn't have," he said. "It might not have been me, and if not... well, the next time you hear someone looking around in here, or any movements at all in here, you get downstairs and yell for me. Okay?"

"Well, okay, but why?"

"You just never know, that's all. We've had at least one recent murder in this house, and possibly two, and there could be more. You just can't go around checking up on strange noises."

"Two?"

"Yes. The kid. They said he died of asthma, but he smothered to death the same as the one last night." He walked away from her and picked up the bottle of perfume on the dresser. "I came in here because this was my sister's room. I gave this to her." He put it down and moved on, looking at other tables and chests of drawers in the room. "But all her personal things... diary..." He opened a drawer in the desk and found it empty. The second and third were empty too. "Everything else has been put away."

"I know," Donna said. "Sheba boxed up some things and put them in the hall. I think Esther or Wanda carried them into the attic. She might know where they are."

"Why didn't she box up her clothes too?"

"She probably would have but she didn't stay in this room long. Two or three nights perhaps, is all."

That information struck Cliff as somehow significant. "Sheba had this room," he repeated. "But only for two or three nights. She didn't like it?"

"No, she didn't."

"Why?"

For a long time she looked up at him before she answered. And when finally she did answer it was slowly and thoughtfully. "She was afraid here."

"Why?" He put his hands on her shoulders. "It's important, Donna, because this is the room where my sister stayed. For some reason, Sheba won't tell me a thing. But if something scared her here, it's twice as important that I know because my sister, Judy, was so terrified that she finally moved to a small bed in Mom and Dad's room."

Donna's expression changed to one of sympathy. "She did? The poor kid. What scared *her*?"

"It's a bit hazy because I wasn't here. I have one letter from Mom that tells something about it. Judy, she said, had a sense of something invading her room at night. She felt that whatever it was was going to kill them all. She wanted to leave the house, but she wouldn't leave without Mom and Dad. She felt they were all going to be killed. Then, Donna, to go further back, there once was a young couple who rented the house. That was back in the thirties. The wife murdered the husband, then said he—

Andrew Bleeker, who was the last owner—made her do it. She was to end her life in the state hospital for the mentally insane, and my checking has turned up a couple of things. For instance, she seemed to be in a hypnotic state the rest of her life, which was only a few months. The only words she was known to speak were 'he made me do it,' and when asked who 'He' was she would answer, 'Andrew.' "

"I don't understand this," Donna said.

"Nobody does. Andrew Bleeker at that time was dead. He was the first to drive off the bridge and drown. However, his body was not found. Sometime later a skeleton was found in the marsh that was assumed to be Andrew Bleeker."

Donna looked over her shoulder and lowered her voice. "Are you saying he might still be alive? That he's doing this?"

"Donna, I don't know. That's what I'm trying to find out. There seems to be no doubt the skeleton was his. It was declared to be, and given a proper burial by the town. But I want to know what it was that sent Sheba from this room."

"All right, I'll tell you why. The reason I didn't was because I thought she probably would. That first night we were all four here, Wanda heard footsteps and I went to her room to check because someone had tried to open my door. Remember, we told the sheriff?"

He nodded.

"Well, I checked on Sheba, too. And she told me something that I didn't believe, I guess. But there was no doubting her terror, and maybe there was something to it. A thick, white substance, she said, had come in through the cracks of her door and formed into something that moved toward her. She fainted. Her door was locked when I tried to get in, and I've no doubt she probably did faint. She said the same thing covered her car and caused her to drive off the bridge. But that could have been ordinary fog. The whole thing could be ordinary fog, couldn't it?"

"Fog. Yes, of course. What else could it be?" He looked about the room. "Listen, Donna, let's get out of here."

"I would like to. I would like to leave the whole place."

Her words took from his mind all else. He closed the door before he asked the question that was so important now. "Where do you want to go when you leave here?"

"I don't know."

"You don't have someone special you're going back to?"

"No. No fiancés, no lovers, not even a special boyfriend, if that was what you meant."

Into the gloom of the surroundings came a sudden, special light. He smiled at her and took her hand. "That was what I meant. Have you ever been to New Orleans?"

"Never."

"Go with me to New Orleans when I leave," he whispered. "Go with me, Donna."

"I don't live in, Cliff. I want one man, forever. I like traditions, and families. And pictures of a great-grandmother and great-grandfather taken on the fiftieth wedding anniversary."

He laughed and tipped her chin upward and held it while he kissed her lips lightly.

"Good, I'm glad you do. I like traditions and families too. Now will you come to New Orleans with me? And will you wait there for me while I bring Dr. Steven back up to see what in the hell goes with this place?"

"No," she said.

He drew away to stare at her. "I'm only asking you to live in the same town long enough to give me a chance to see if I can get you to love me enough."

"That's not why I wouldn't go with you. I can't leave Sheba."

"You can't leave Sheba," he repeated. "I suppose we can take her along then, if you want her."

"She won't go. You heard her say she's not selling the place back. And she told me nothing doing. She's keeping it. Of course, since this new... this death, she might have changed her mind."

"If we can get her to leave, then would you?"

"Yes."

He kissed her again, still gently.

"That is," she said, "if the sheriff will let us leave."

"He let the others go. If I promise to come back, he might let you girls out too. I'll talk to him—after I've talked to Sheba."

"But why would you have to come back, Cliff?"

The concern in her voice and eyes incongruously cheered him.

"It will be all right, Dr. Steven would be with me."

"Why would anyone have to come back?"

"Because there's something unsolved here, and I'm beginning to think that Dr. Steven just might be in his glory in this house. He's been searching for a monstrously haunted house all his life. And every time he thought he'd found one I fouled it up for him by disproving it. He's lived for the day when he would find it because he's been positive that they do exist in the depths of all evil. And I'm afraid we might have found it."

She shuddered. "I'd rather believe that Andrew Bleeker still lives and is trying to run people out of this house."

"Of course that would be the simple solution. But is it the most logical? If he escaped the car that night, why spend all these years in hiding? What has he been living on? He died in nineteen thirty-two. That man would be in his nineties now."

"You think *that* is less logical than saying the reason for everything here is—is a ghost of some kind?" she asked incredulously.

He saw her point. "I guess I've been living around Dr. Steven too long. You're right. I was about to lose my head. Okay, let's say we've got a flesh-and-blood murderer. Who is it?"

They began a slow walk around the balcony to the stairway.

"Andrew Bleeker? I don't care if he is ninety."

"Ninety-eight to be exact. And anyway, Andrew Bleeker is dead."

"If he is that leaves...

She walked beside him down the stairway, and the steps creaked softly under their feet. He waited for her to go on speaking but she didn't.

"Yes? Who does it leave, Donna?" The question was quiet, low, and very deliberate.

She raised her head and stopped. "As the sheriff said," she answered with a sadness he had never heard before, "as he said, it leaves the four of us."

He was standing one step below her so that their faces were on the same height. "Wrong," he said.

She looked directly into his eyes. "Yes. Wrong. It leaves the five of us. It leaves you, too, doesn't it, Cliff?"

Her hands touched his shoulders lightly and moved to his neck. She pulled his face to hers and kissed him, and then she moved away from him. Two steps down she stopped and looked back.

"And that's why Sheba wouldn't tell you anything, Cliff. She doesn't trust you."

Then she ran down the rest of the stairway without looking back. She left him with the effects of her kiss moving in waves through his body and mingling with the knowledge that not one, but two women sensed a danger in him.

And to accomplish his aim he had to conquer both of them.

CHAPTER 14

Sheba was standing at one of the windows in the living room when she saw the sheriff's car leave. Slowly it went down the low bank that surrounded the house and where the road turned toward the bridge the car stopped again and she could see that both men were looking back at the house. She backed away from the window, into the deeper shadows of the corner, even though common sense told her she couldn't be seen.

When the car finally went on she began to walk the floor again. The house was quiet now that the guests were gone. Wanda and Esther were still in the kitchen, she supposed. And she had seen Donna go into her office and close the door a few minutes after the sheriff had gone out the door. Just exactly what the sheriff and his deputy did after they left the house, but before they got into their car, was a mystery to her. They simply had disappeared for a while. Back toward the garage? She didn't know.

She stopped in the middle of the room and looked at the round stove and the chairs that were grouped around it. The first day she had arrived had been one of the better days. She had thought it quite terrible, but at least she had felt some optimism.

The decision struck her suddenly, and she left the living room and went to Donna's office door and knocked.

"Come in," Donna said, her voice sounding dim and far away behind the heavy door and thick wall.

Sheba went in talking. "I've made up my mind, Donna. I'll take Cliff Murphy's offer and we'll get the hell out of here. Okay? We can be packed and ready to go by dark, can't we? And we can stay in a motel somewhere on the road. I don't suppose we can get our old jobs back, so maybe we could go west somewhere and buy a ranch. Yes, sure! Donna, how about a dude ranch? I used to read about those. Do they still have such things as dude ranches?"

Donna sat behind the desk like a very dignified schoolmarm at her throne. With her pale hair drawn back from her classic features, and the ruffles of a white blouse right at her neck, she could have come from the last century. She looked at Sheba as if of all people she hadn't expected *her.*

"What's the matter?" Sheba asked.

"Uh ... a dude ranch?"

Sheba flung her hands out impatiently. "Dude ranch, smood ranch, I don't care. I just decided I want to get out of here, and now. Don't you? This house is... I don't know what it is, but I can't stand any more of it." Donna rose and came around the end of the desk. "I'll tell Cliff that you've decided to accept his offer."

Sheba watched in puzzled silence. Donna wasn't acting if she cared whether she left or not. In fact—

At the door Donna turned and said, "Would you mind waiting here? I don't know where he is, but when I find him I'll bring him back."

Alone, Sheba began to walk the floor. Nothing better to do. The day was going in a hurry, and soon it would be too late and they wouldn't be able to leave. She glanced at her wristwatch and saw that it had stopped running again. She took it off and shook it and then held it to her ear. After a few half-hearted ticks it stopped. A close examination showed that moisture had settled heavily on the tiny face so that it was becoming discolored.

Fog. Damn the fog. She didn't like it.

But it wasn't fog that had killed Tommy Kirsten.

She couldn't think of that. Not if she wanted to control herself enough to not run screaming from the house.

Donna's desk was covered with papers, which was unusual. Donna ordinarily was so neat it was sickening. Every time she turned around, if she didn't watch Donna, she'd be picking up clothes and putting them on hangers.

The note pad drew Sheba's attention. Doodles? Somewhere she had read that you can tell a person's character by their doodling. And at times she wondered what went on in Donna's mind. Was she really as much a perfectionist as she seemed, or was she just closed-mouthed? She liked Donna, but sometimes she wondered, anyway.

She saw circles and stars on the pad, and a few dollar signs. And she laughed. Yeah, that was Donna. She always got around to those dollar signs eventually. But then why not? She was a bookkeeper. It was her job. Sheba wasn't even sure whether she liked her work very well because Donna just never talked about it.

Below the more common doodles, and written in tiny, hard-to-read letters was the name Cliff Murphy, repeated many times. And tiny hearts and flowers and pairs of birds flying away. Donna was in love? Well, that was no surprise. She had more or less known that anyway—or at least suspected it.

The next line of words was another name. Sheba. Sheba. Sheba. And beside that was a small group of drawings. A nightgown. A door, with the knob heavily drawn as if it had been circled many times. And another thing: a pillow.

A pillow.

Sheba drew sharply back from the desk. The entire room, the top of the desk, all were blanked out; all but the white face of the pad with the black ink drawings. The pad stared up at her, accusing. Silent, and screaming in its silence.

The door opened suddenly and Sheba nearly cried out, but the two who entered didn't seem to notice. Donna came on to sit down at her desk and Cliff remained standing.

"I told him you would tell him yourself, Sheba," Donna said, and Sheba noticed that she tore the top sheet of paper off the pad, wadded it, and threw it into the wastebasket. Not once had she looked at Sheba.

Cliff Murphy said, "Sheba, why don't we sit down?"

She saw his smile, but she couldn't respond to it. When he gestured toward a chair she obeyed and sat down.

"You have something you'd like to tell me?" he asked in the soft, voice that she felt was for some unknown reason deceptive.

"I do." She looked at her hands, her long nails so carefully manicured. The nightgown she understood. And the pillow? And why the doorknob? The pillow. Donna thought she had killed Tommy Kirsten?

"You were saying..." Cliff Murphy prodded gently.

His voice startled her and she jerked involuntarily, her muscles tightening. "I was—yes. I have decided to accept your offer to take back the property. There is entirely too much fog coming in from the marsh and it's ruining the walls. I don't see how the house stood as long as it has." She felt she should thank him, because it was, after all, a kind and considerate gesture on his part. "I appreciate your offer to take it back. Could we manage to get it over quickly so that we could leave tonight? I mean before dark."

She saw him look at Donna steadily for a moment, then his eyes came back to her.

"Of course. I can go on in and make the arrangements. It won't take you long to get Esther and Wanda ready to leave?"

"I don't think so."

"Okay. I don't know if Donna told you, but I'd like to take you all down to New Orleans. Would you go there?"

"New Orleans? No, she didn't tell me."

Donna said, "I didn't think she wanted to sell the property. Then, Sheba was thinking of going west and buying a ranch instead."

"Oh."

For a while silence hung in the air, but gradually into the silence, or perhaps because of it, Sheba became aware of another sound. A rhythmic, soft throb, as the beat of a heart. Not inside her, but surrounding her. She looked at the wails, at the ceilings, and saw the patches of green that were spreading up from the corners and down from the ceiling and the throb was like the throb that surrounds the womb and protects the fetus.

The quiet peace that descended upon her was shattered suddenly by the jarring sound of a human voice.

"A ranch," he said. "Are Esther and Wanda going with you?"

Sheba looked at him, and gradually her vision cleared and he ceased being the shimmering mass he had been, as though he had risen from beneath water to stand in sharp reality in front of her eyes. She was aware of Donna just as sharply, sitting at her desk, thinking thoughts of murder —and blaming *her*. Why?

"Not necessarily," Sheba said, "I haven't said anything to them. And as far as that goes, Donna doesn't have to go with me. She can go wherever she likes."

Donna said suddenly, "Can't that be decided upon later? We haven't much time left to get the packing done and get out of here before dark."

"Will you be staying in a motel in town for the night?" Cliff asked. "I might not be able to finish everything before the bank closes."

Sheba hesitated. Suddenly, now that her mind was made up, she wanted to leave and leave quickly. A longing to drive toward the sunset rose in her. To drive and keep driving. Alone.

"Yes," Donna said. "We can stay in a motel. Sheba?" Sheba started to answer when the noise of the car pulling up outside the front of the house took their attention. All three of them got up to stand looking at one another, and Donna groaned softly. "Not another guest I hope!"

Cliff started toward the door. "If so, just tell them the lodge is closed."

They followed him into the hall and stood grouped as the front door was flung open. Standing on the threshold was the tall sheriff, and behind him, still climbing steps to the porch, puffed the deputy.

"You're back already?" Cliff said. "I wouldn't have thought you'd have time to get to town."

"I wouldn't have thought so either," the sheriff said, reaching behind him to fling the door shut right in the face of the deputy. He came forward without knowing he had almost knocked the man behind him back down the steps. "Show them what you've got, Sam."

The deputy struggled with the door a moment, finally got it open and closed, and came on to dangle something that was pale blue and very sheer. Sheba recognized it immediately. The nightgown she had worn to Tommy Kirsten's room last night. She had forgotten all about it.

Where had they found it?

"Whose is it?" the sheriff demanded, jerking it out of the hands of his deputy and swinging it toward them. "It's a woman's nightgown, and it was found under the dead man."

Cliff said, "If it was found under the dead man, why didn't you know about it before?"

"Because those goddamned clumsy idiots carried it off with the body, that's what. Don't touch a dead man, they tell me. Let the coroner do it. All right, I didn't touch him any more than I had to, and this, they tell me as soon as I hit town, was wadded in a little ball under his body. It's not much bigger than a good-sized handkerchief anyway, so I'm not surprised it was missed. But what I want to know, is it yours, lady?"

Donna shook her head, and the sheriff swung the small nightgown at Sheba.

"Is it yours, or does it belong to anyone in this house? Have you ever seen it before?"

All eyes were upon her, and there was nothing she could do. If she said no Donna would know she was lying, because Donna was with her the day she bought the tiny nightgown.

"Yes, it's mine."

The sheriff seemed at a loss for words for about three seconds, then he yelled, "Why the hell didn't you tell me you were in his room last night?"

"Because—because I couldn't see what it had to do with his death."

"You told me you didn't see him after you went to bed!"

"I didn't. It—was before."

The sheriff's neck was turning red and cords there stood out hard and angry. "What in the hell is this? Your bed, his bed, I don't give a damn whose bed it was! Were you in his room or not?"

"I was."

"In his bed?"

"Yes."

Cliff stepped forward to stand between her and the sheriff. "Hey look, fellow. So she went to bed with him awhile."

"Mind your own damned business!"

Cliff's voice was calm and mild in contrast. "You are intimidating her, you know, and you also know that's a no-no."

"Oh come off it, boy! Don't talk baby talk to me."

Suddenly Cliff's voice was cold and taut. "Then don't act like a baby. If you've got questions to ask, calm down and ask them, otherwise—"

"Otherwise she goes to jail, where I can ask them in peace. And if I have to I'll have you bound and gagged and stuffed in a box in the corner till I'm ready for you."

"You know, I believe you would."

"You're damned right I would. Now stand aside, boy, and let me get on with this."

But Cliff didn't move. "I'm telling you, you'll have better results if you stop acting so damned jumpy. We'd like to get out of this house before dark, if you don't mind."

"What! If I don't mind, he says! I sure as hell do mind. You people don't seem to realize there was a murder committed here last night."

"We do, and that's one reason we want out. Now. Can't you continue this questioning in town?"

"I sure could! Right in my jail cell, where I could keep up with all of you. The only trouble is I got only one cell and you know it. Now do you want to go there, or do you want to stay here?"

Cliff turned and looked at Sheba, then at Donna. Back to Sheba again, he asked, "If you were to go into the living room with him where you could relax, do you think you could tell him about last night?"

"I'll do it standing right here," she said. "And then I would appreciate being left alone. If I have to stay in the house, I'd like to go to my room."

The sheriff nodded. "You have to stay in the house, at least for the time being, and you can go to your room as soon as this is explained."

"I went to his room last night by prearrangement, after everyone else had gone to bed—so far as I knew, that is. Anyway, the house was quiet. I went to bed with him, that's all. And then I left."

No one said a word for a long moment, then the sheriff asked, "You went into his room wearing this and left wearing *what?*"

She returned his stare. "Nothing."

"You left wearing nothing?"

"That's right."

"Why? For God's sake, why walk back from his room to yours naked as a newborn jaybird?"

She remembered the reason: the fog. The fear of it. The feeling at night when it came that it was more than fog. And her rejection of the memory in the daytime. Who would know if she lied again?

She looked down, trying for a girlish modesty. "What I mean is, I just forgot the nightgown and put on my robe. I wasn't really naked when I went to my room." She looked up into the sheriff's eyes. "Please, sir, I swear he was all right when I left him. Why would I— why would he not be? I'd like to go to my room now. I'm not feeling very well."

"I don't wonder!" he said, but added, "Go ahead. Only don't leave this house under any circumstances. I want to talk to you again. And that goes for all of you. As for this," he shook the nightgown in her face, "it goes back to town with me. Evidence."

Sheba turned toward the stairway, went quickly past Donna, and ran up the steps. On the landing, out of sight from the group in the foyer below, Sheba stood and listened.

There wasn't much more. The sheriff asked Donna and Cliff if they knew anything about *anything* they hadn't told him, and when he got negative answers he slammed out of the house.

Sheba went on, quietly.

The dim and narrow corridor closed her in, away from the world, away from people. So she wouldn't be allowed to leave the house? She paused, looking at the closed door that led back to the service wing and the stairway to the attic. There was no feeling of surprise, nor even of regret that she couldn't leave. As though she had known from the day of her arrival, she now accepted her destiny as a prisoner of the house.

She opened the door to the service corridor, closed it behind her, and quietly went to the attic door; that, too, she closed behind her. She stood in the darkness of the narrow lift of the steps and looked up toward the ceiling of the attic. In the pale, filtered light of day she could see the cobwebs and the rafters and the steep pitch of the roof.

Slowly she began to climb.

He was there, as he had been, smiling, smiling, smiling at her. Tall, rugged, virile, ageless. And she went to stand before him, he in his ornate frame yet in some way not confined by it. She could almost hear his laughter, low, amused, with never a touch of tenderness.

The kind of man who took what he wanted, and kept what he took. In one way or another.

She heard steps behind her, coming up the stairs and across the uneven boards of the attic floor, but she didn't look around.

Cliff Murphy's voice said. "Impressive painting, isn't it? Very lifelike."

"Yes."

"Do you know who he is?"

"No. Who is he?"

"Andrew Bleeker. He was the last owner of the place. My folks bought it from his estate."

"Andrew Bleeker," she said musingly, remembering the woman at the laundry. "He's the first man who drove off the bridge, isn't he?"

"Yes. He's the first who died there."

Her laughter came unexpectedly and seemed to be not a part of her. She cut it quickly. "Dead? That man dead?"

The eyes of two men were upon her, one smiling and hypnotic, the other dark, unreadable, but not smiling. She turned away from both of them and walked slowly about the attic.

"Gosh, big, isn't it?"

Cliff Murphy followed her. "Is this the first time you've been up here?"

She hesitated only briefly, then she said, "Yes."

"I would have thought that you, being the owner now, would have been interested in seeing all the stuff that had been left here."

"Why? To me it meant a hell of a lot of work. It meant cleaning it out. I just thought I'd wait until spring. I think the others came up. I know Esther did —or Wanda perhaps. Anyway, I packed away some of the things in the rooms and someone carried them up." She ducked under a low rafter where the roof dipped sharply inward before it rose again. "I wonder why the roof was made like this. Why not just straight?"

"For water shed, I expect."

"Oh yeah."

She came face to face then with a wood case that had a glass front. In it were several types of firearms, but the one that caught her eye was the long shotgun. She turned the small knob that opened the glass door. There was a faint squeak of the rusted hinges, but the door opened. She touched the double-barreled gun timidly. "Is this it? The one in the painting?"

"It looks like it."

The feeling it gave her was similar to the one she had felt last night when she'd found herself looking into its owner's eyes, but without the fear. She was aware of a confusion of reality, of being in part away from herself, and somehow she returned to a day when she stood in the grasses of the marsh, wearing hip boots. She saw the gun raised slowly and fired.

But she wasn't there, she told herself in silence, she was here! Her hands pressed tightly against her cheeks to push the other away.

"Are you all right?" Cliff Murphy asked.

She tried to laugh at herself, and couldn't. "Yes. I think I paid too much attention to that April woman and her ESP experiences. I just had the oddest feeling that I—" She stopped. A voice silent but forceful, as forceful as the power of the gun, spoke to her: *say nothing, tell the man nothing. He can't be trusted. He can't be...*

"That you what?" he asked softly.

"Nothing," she said, and to her relief the feeling was gone, and the time was confined to the present and the moment.. And she saw something that aroused her curiosity. "Look they're not rusted. They look as if someone has been taking recent care of them."

"I've noticed that too."

She touched the double barrels, running her fingertips caressingly down the groove toward the stock.

And another thought suddenly came to her. "Oh! Your father liked to hunt, didn't he? Perhaps he used them? Maybe some of these are his?"

"No, none. He kept his guns downstairs. Actually, I think he's the one who brought these up here. He was going to sell them, but hadn't yet. He too was interested in the fact that they had never rusted."

Sheba stepped back and looked at Cliff. She saw that the guns had taken his interest to the point that he was frowning from concentration. He reached for the shotgun, then changed his mind and removed a slender rifle instead. He turned and pointed it toward a window and sighted down its length, then held it and felt the smooth barrel with his hand.

Sheba said without thinking, "Show me how you open the shotgun, will you?"

"Sure."

He replaced the rifle and removed the shotgun carefully. With it in his hands he stepped over so closely to her that his arm brushed her shoulder. "Like this, see? You turn this little jigger up here with your thumb and push the barrel down, that's all there is to it."

The gun clicked open, disjointed now. He peered down both of the barrels, then held it over so that she could see. It was like looking down long, long round tunnels that glistened dully with light at the far end.

"They're remarkably clean," he said, raising them to his own eyes again. "Someone has recently oiled them. Otherwise I don't see how they could possibly stay this clean."

Sheba thought of herself last night with the lamp, standing and looking at the painting as if she had been called. But it couldn't be so! She didn't even know how to open the damned thing. How could she have oiled it? The tremble of nervousness edged sharply into her, as though Cliff Murphy might be able to read her mind if she weren't careful.

"How do you load it?" she asked.

He pointed at the twin holes. "Right here. It will only hold two shots at a time."

"What gauge?" she asked.

He looked down at her. "I thought you didn't know anything about guns."

She stared at him, too mute to answer. But as he clicked the gun shut again she glimpsed the letters on the barrel: 12 ga. choke.

"I have to go," she said quickly. "I need groceries, and I want to get back before dark. That awful sheriff surely can't keep me from going to the grocery store, can he?"

"I wouldn't think so."

When she left the attic Cliff Murphy was replacing the shotgun and closing the door of the gun case.

She put it all out of her mind then and took the list Esther gave her and drove straight to a supermarket. The list completed, her grocery basket full, she spent a few minutes looking about and enjoying the crowd of people who hurried or strolled by.

And then she found herself in front of a small rack that held small boxes of shells. Well, she told herself, this was hunting country. Sportmen's country. Why not?

Surely and deftly her hand reached for a box that read on its top: 12 ga. shot size no. 2.

Sufficient for large animals at short range.

CHAPTER 15

"Are you still in here?" Cliff asked as he crossed the threshold into Donna's office.

"I'm back again."

She was glad to see him. The hours seemed to go slower each day until now even a minute seemed an hour.

"I wonder how long he will make us stay here?" she asked.

"Until he has his murderer, probably. Can I sit down?" The seriousness in his eyes didn't help dispel the feeling of gloom that was increasing as the sky clouded over and the day drifted toward nightfall.

"Is something wrong?" she asked, and immediately answered the question herself. "Of course something is wrong. That was silly to ask, even. How could it be right, after last night."

"Do you know where Sheba went—for sure?"

"For sure? I know where she said she was going. To the grocery."

"Did anyone go with her?"

"No. Why?"

"I want to tell you something, but I can't give you any specific reasons just yet. Will you just accept my word and promise me you'll be very careful, at all times?"

"Yes, sure."

"Okay, here it is. Watch out for her. I think she's the killer."

Donna half rose from her chair, and was only half aware that she did so. "Oh, Cliff! Why? Why would she make love to a man and then kill him? Why would she want to kill *me*?

"I thought you said you'd just take my word and promise to be very, very careful. I mean it, Donna, I'm scared half to death about you."

"Since when?" she demanded.

"Since I heard about that first night here and your doorknob incident. That's when." His voice sounded harsh and angry. "Now when I say this I damn well mean it. Don't—and I emphasize *don't*—under any circumstances open your door to Sheba after dark! Promise me."

Donna sank slowly back to her chair and leaned on one of the strong, wooden arms. She picked up her pen; the feel of it comforted her and returned her to the reality of a life where a girl was wary only of muggers, burglars, rapists... not a friend with whom she had shared a small apartment for several months. She shook her head.

"I can't accept it, Cliff. What proof do you have?"

"Proof? I told you I couldn't prove it. If I could I'd just simply turn it over to the sheriff and get you out of here."

"You surely have something—some reason for feeling as you do. Something other than someone trying to enter my room."

"You said you'd accept my word and be careful. That was all I asked." He left his chair and leaned down with his palms flat on her desk. "Just don't let her in at night. Please?"

"Cliff, it just isn't reasonable!' If she comes to my door, scared and asking to come in, how could I refuse her?"

He slapped the desk with one palm, and the sound crashed through the quiet room. "Donna! Don't be a goddamned fool!"

"You're forgetting something, Cliff," she said in cold, tight anger. "I lived with her for months. She has no reason to—to do what you said."

"I didn't say she'd do it. I said she—oh hell."

He turned his back in frustration or disgust and went to look out a window.

Donna looked at his back for a moment, at the way he leaned slightly sideways with the thumb of one hand hooked in a trouser pocket. She wanted to tell him she was sorry and that she'd do anything he asked, and then her thoughts went to nighttime in the dark, damp, forever-cold house and Sheba at her door wanting in... How could she tell her no? If Sheba needed help, of any kind, she couldn't turn her away.

She drew squares on the pad on the desk. Then rectangles. And then the rectangle became a door with a knob that turned. A door that was locked.

"Cliff," she said, pleading for understanding.

He twisted sideways on one foot to look at her. "Yes?"

"Talk to me. Please."

He watched her in silence for a while before he came to sit on the edge of her desk. "Would it do any good?"

"I want to understand. I really do."

"All right. Everything is so confusing and seems to go so far back—all the way back to things that have absolutely no connection with any of the present suspects—that I was ready to call in Dr. Steven. Remember? You helped me see I wasn't being logical. So I set out to be logical. Of all the people in this house last night, only two had alibis. The married friends of the dead man. So they're eliminated. From there I started at the least likely and moved up, discarding as I went. Esther? Cross her out. Wanda? Cross her too. Me? I know damn well I didn't. You? Of course not. That leaves April Calder and Sheba. April Calder likes to think ghosts and evil spirits and haunted houses are the really dangerous things—the destinies some can't escape. The cold reality of footsteps, light and running, in the hallway at night, was more than she could accept. Then a murder? No, she couldn't take it. Okay, now we have Sheba. Facts? She admits to being in his bed. But she didn't admit it until her nightgown was found. One mark against her. Why did she run from his room? She isn't saying. But she was the only one in his room, Donna."

"But you don't know her, Cliff!" How could she make him understand without completely betraying her friend? She was feeling more helpless and more confused by the moment. "Sheba has—well, she has always been quite promiscuous. I would have been more surprised if she hadn't gone to his bed."

"Okay. So she sleeps around a lot. So he was alive when she left him. Now, I'm going on something you won't like and looks farfetched even to me. But I want you to listen. First, Andrew Bleeker had a young wife who disappeared. Ran off, it was said. He was the sort who didn't like visitors. No one crossed his bridge if he could help it. He had a double-barreled shotgun that he used on anything that moved. The bridge became known as Bleeker's Bridge. Then he returned late from town one night and ran his car off his own bridge. No one really knew it had happened for a long time, because by the time his car was found it was in bad shape. His body was not found, as I told you."

She nodded, quiet, listening; and drew a car on her note paper. And beside the car a rectangle with a doorknob that turned. And a hand that had the grasp and fingers of a human's hand.

"Then two years later the skeleton was buried. Andrew Bleeker. And a young married couple rented the house. The first murder occurred, and the girl was the killer. After that people began to slowly come this way to hunt and fish. And a few tried to come at night. And every one of them who did—to the knowledge of the townspeople, at least—drove off the bridge and drowned. More and more it became known as Bleeker's Bridge. A place to avoid after dark. The house, and nearly worthless marshland, was for sale. Cheap, considering the number of acres and the size of the house. My folks bought it. Mom and Dad liked it, but Judy, the only young girl in the family, didn't. She was afraid. For the first time in her life she became what I felt was mentally disturbed. Psychotic. She swore something was invading her room. She was so afraid Mom and Dad were going to be killed that she wouldn't go away to college, she stayed home, and even slept in their room. Dad had fortunately made a couple of fishing buddies. They came nearly every day to fish. And that's how my folks were known to have gone over the bridge during the night, because the two fishermen left late one evening and came back early the next morning. All evidence—the way their few things had been thrown into only a couple of small suitcases, and their bed left unmade—pointed to a very hurried departure."

He paused and she looked up. She knew what he was going to say, but she couldn't admit it even to him; not yet.

"Then Sheba Gilbert bought it," he said softly. "And unfortunately she came at night. But for her it was different. She lived. Why, Donna?"

"She was able to escape before her car went under," Donna said, her throat aching with the strain of tenseness.

"Don't you know that all four of her doors were locked? That not even she knew how she got out?"

"She was probably so scared she couldn't remember."

"Maybe. But let's go on. You said she called, urging all of you to come down because she needed you. You dropped everything and came, and that first night someone tried to enter your room. Wanda also heard someone in the hall. You said that Sheba told you fog had entered her room, or something thick and white. That the same thing had forced her off the bridge. We call it fog because we can't face the fact that something could exist that isn't as simple and harmless and natural as fog. But Judy saw something that literally caused the deaths of all three of my family. Your friend Sheba saw something too, Donna. And whatever it is fills this house at night to the point where it's ruining the walls and is fast making it unfit for habitation. I might add that it has happened within a month—and that before this, before Sheba was chosen to live, this house stood in good condition for over forty years."

"You're blaming Sheba for that?" Donna let the pen fall from her fingers. "She can't be blamed for the weather, Cliff!"

"No, of course she can't. You're saying it's the weather then? Perhaps a very unusual amount of fog?"

"Yes." She felt he was in some way baiting her, but she couldn't figure him out yet.

"Okay. That long, tangled, slender thread is all coincidence. The fact that Sheba felt the house was haunted was pure chance."

"It couldn't be anything else."

"And how about the strangulation death a couple of weeks ago? Too much dampness and fog again?"

"Ye-yes."

"In the hallway, not far from Sheba's room."

Donna felt she couldn't stand the pressure any longer. A curtain in her mind, like a dream of disconnected shadows which refused to form, hid from her something she suddenly wished she could recall. She walked the floor, her hands pressed hard over her ears, closing out all sounds but the inner movements of her own mind and body.

And abruptly it was there.

"The nightgown." She turned to him, her hands lowered to her sides. "When I went into her room she was wake and terrified, Cliff. Then another time—just a couple of days ago—I found her nightgown again, the same as before. It was on the floor, wet. But then she was always care- less, and it could have been the moisture in the house."

"What are you talking about?"

She turned helplessly and stopped to look up at him. "I don't know. I found her nightgown on the floor of her room, twice, wet. And there was something about it that had her in a kind of shock. I don't know what's wrong."

"Does she know anything about guns, Donna?"

"I wouldn't know. I don't think so. I don't think she knows a pistol from a revolver."

"I was upstairs with her, in the attic, just before she left for town, and we were looking at Andrew Bleeker's double-barreled shotgun. She asked me what gauge it was."

"Gauge? Why would she want to know that?"

"I don't think it was idle curiosity. But you have to know the gauge of a shotgun before you can buy shell for it. The gun has been oiled and cared for, Donna. And gotten in shape by someone. And whoever it is— and I agree it's no ghost—I think wants everyone out of here."

"Why? she whispered.

"I don't know why. Now will you promise me you won't open your door tonight or as long as we have to stay here?"

She nodded. "I promise."

He leaned down and kissed her cheek. "Just to make sure you're okay I'm going to be sleeping in my sister's room, next door to you. If you need me, yell."

"But what about Sheba? What if she needs someone? She thought he wasn't going to give a verbal answer. His brown eyes seemed darker than usual.

"I'll talk to the sheriff tomorrow, if I can run him down, and see if he won't at least let her stay in a motel in town. Now do you feel better?"

"I guess so."

"But for tonight, lock yourself in. There are some things in the attic I want to go through before supper —and before it gets too dark. Surely there's a logical answer somewhere. The sheriff can't do a thing without proof."

"And you think you'll find it in the attic?"

He opened the door, paused thoughtfully, and said "No, not really. When I hear her car I'll come down and carry in the groceries for her. What are you going to do now?"

"I have a bit of work."

She began looking through her desk papers; an old habit she had learned to make others think she was busy. As always, it worked, and he went out quietly.

She sank down into her chair and closed her eyes. The nightgowns—Sheba's fear—and yet her reluctance now to talk. Clearly Donna saw the change she had ignored. Sheba was in some way different. But weren't they all? Even Wanda was quiet now and seemed less talkative; Esther never had to tell her to shut up anymore. And Esther? More nervous, to say the least.

No more trying to figure it out and solve the problem, Donna decided. Get on with what had to be done. If it turned out to be the wrong thing, cry later.

She left the office, walked softly past the dark and silent stairway, and straight on back to the kitchen, her steps increasing almost to a run as she went. She resisted the growing need to look over her shoulder.

Seeing Esther and Wanda huddled by the stove like two lost chickens didn't help much. They looked at her humbly as she entered the kitchen, Wanda with big worried eyes, Esther showing her worry in a face pinched and shriveled.

Neither of them said a word.

"It's even cold in here," Donna said, trying to make conversation. "The whole house is freezing."

Wanda nodded. "Esther won't go down and put any coal in the furnace."

Esther spoke up with some of her old sharpness. "I would if I had anyone with enough guts to go along and hold the lantern for me, but I'm not going down into that hole by myself."

Wanda asked, "Do you know, Donna, that is the one place the sheriff didn't search?"

"You're right!" Donna cried in a low voice, her glance going swiftly to the narrow door. She had never been down there, but she felt familiar with it because of the comforting sounds that always came up to her through the warm air vents. "Why didn't one of you say something about it when he was here?"

"I never thought about it," Esther said. "Not until he was gone. My mind seems to have gone blank or something. I guess I'd better try to get something to eat, but I don't even have any coal for the stove. I brought in a few sticks of wood from the shed, but it's about all gone. There's not any more."

"Then let's go down and build a fire and get a bucket of coal," Donna said; yet when she opened the door to the cellar and was struck by the stink of rot and dampness and saw dropping away into the total darkness of the old cellar the rough wood steps that had neither banister nor railing nor protection of any kind, she could go no farther.

Drawing courage held her immobile. She was aware that Esther and Wanda stood by the stove watching her. Donna looked back at them.

Esther said without enthusiasm, as though she couldn't deny the grasp of fate, "Well, we'll have to have light. There's a lantern I take down. Just a minute." Donna felt a rush of sympathy for the sisters, alone in the world, far away from the only home they had ever known, and now as vulnerable and helpless as children against someone who seemed set to rid the house of most of its inhabitants. Cliff had told her to lock the door, but had he told Wanda and Esther?

"I want you both to pack your things and be ready to leave tomorrow," she said. "Cliff will get the permission of the sheriff, and all you'll have to do is be sure to send him your address in case he needs you. Or if he won't let you leave you can at least stay in town. I'll make out your checks and give them to you later."

Wanda's face changed, lightening, and she rushed over to the door and called in at Esther, "Did you hear that, Esther? We're getting ready to leave."

Esther came back, the lighted lantern in her hand. "I heard," she said. "But what about the rest of you? You and Sheba?"

"We'll probably be going too."

Esther went ahead of Donna down the steps into the cellar. "You have to be careful going down here," she said, as though she had forgotten that the cellar hadn't been searched. "There's not a thing to hold on to. This stairway is just hanging here between the kitchen floor and the muddy ground. I've got boots I found, and I keep them right at the bottom step, so you just stay there on the step."

"I won't be much help to you on the step," Donna said, feeling her way ahead with her feet, carefully, one step at a time. "Gad. These steps are slick."

"I know. I just about fell one day. I've been pretty careful ever since."

Her voice had begun to sound as if it came from a barrel as she went farther down into the cellar. Donna paused to look around, and was amazed to find that it was small enough for the light of the lantern to touch each lamp wall with pale yellow. Esther had reached the bottom and was putting her feet into the large black boots. She splatted across the wet ground toward the spill of black coal that reached up to a small coal chute.

Donna said, "It's plain to see there's no one down here, unless he's in the furnace."

"If he is," Esther said in sharp casualness as she unlatched the black iron door and swung it open, "he's going to find it a bit uncomfortable in a couple of minutes." Grunting then, she threw in the first coal. It rattled against the sides of the furnace.

Donna held the lantern high, her arm outstretched, so that Esther could see what she was doing. The entire cellar was light enough that not even the space under the steps concealed anything. It was a cellar made exclusively, it would seem, for a furnace, coal and a shovel. And that was it. On the ground beside Esther sat the coal bucket she had brought down from the kitchen.

Esther finished her job, lighted the coal with a small ritual that Donna didn't question, closed the door of the furnace, and then filled her coal bucket.

"I'm ready to go. Be careful on your way up, too. A body is liable to get into such a hurry to get out of here that it would be easy to fall and break a neck." Donna backed up a few steps, then watched while Esther carefully stepped out of the boots and turned them in preparation to stepping into again. When that was done Donna led the way slowly up and back into the kitchen.

The room had darkened considerably, the few scattered kerosene lamps only spots of dull strivings to light the darkness of a too-large, high-ceilinged room. The windows now reflected the lights of the lamps, the outdoor having grown dark quickly while they were in the cellar.

Donna thought of Sheba with a lurch of anxiety. "It's dark and Sheba isn't back. I hope she didn't have an accident."

Wanda, still hovering near the stove, said, "She's back. I just heard her drive in a few minutes ago."

Esther said, "Well, you'd better get out there to help her with the groceries—"

She was interrupted by the door opening. Sheba came in, her dark hair shining with a touch of moisture beaded like dew.

Cheerfully, she said, "Hi, everybody." She had bag of groceries in each arm, and put them down on the nearest cabinet. "No one has to go out. I didn't get much. Just these two."

"Isn't it dark out?" Donna asked.

"It's getting that way fast." Sheba, with her back to the room, fiddled with the bags of groceries, balancing them, laying out a few things. "Where's Cliff?" she asked.

It was the first time she had ever asked for Cliff in that soft tone of voice, and Donna felt the tug of fear that at last Sheba was getting interested in him. And if she did, would he resist her?

"I don't know," she said slowly. "Upstairs somewhere I guess."

Sheba turned and went toward the stairway, where she paused long enough to reach up and remove the lamp from its bracket. "Replace this, will you, Wanda?" she said, then started on up the stairs.

Donna noticed that in one hand she was carrying a small box.

Sheba stopped on the fourth step and looked back. "Oh yes. I forgot to tell you, Donna, there's a car coming. I could see its headlights down the road. If it's a guest, tell them to go away. There will be no more vacancies for anyone. The house is no longer a lodge of any kind. Nor is it haunted. Please tell anyone who comes to go away."

Donna stared at Sheba and wondered about the sudden decision; but at the same time came the dull, faraway sound of the front-door knocker.

Donna turned to look at Esther and Wanda just in time to see Wanda jump slightly.

"What's that?" Wanda asked.

Esther said in disgust, "You ought to know by now. It's that old metal knocker on the front door. It's odd to me how that thing can be heard in the kitchen so plain."

Donna went into the hall and along its dim length toward the pale light on a table near the foot of the stairs. Someone was at the door, though, and her mind was more on that than on the irritatingly uncomfortable fact that the house was growing more hideous each night.

She opened the door to find that a young couple, a tall man and a slender girl, stood closely together, her hand tight in his.

"Uh—" he said, almost stammering, "is this the haunted house?"

"No," Donna said. "I'm sorry, but there are no vacancies. The lodge has been closed indefinitely."

He seemed confused, and the girl simply looked at her with innocent round eyes. "Lodge? We saw an ad in the paper—we—we're on our honeymoon and thought it might be fun to stay one night in a haunted house. Could you tell us where it is? I guess we turned on the wrong road."

"No, you didn't." She looked at them closely, saw him shift the girl's hand into a tighter hold. "I'm sorry, really I am. Didn't you stop in town?"

"No."

"I suggest you go back to one of the motels there. You'll probably hear why we're not taking guests anymore."

They started backing away. The man nodded, smiled, and turning put his arm around the waist of his bride and guided her down the steps.

Donna closed the door and latched it. Her eyes went toward the stairway, and a pale, pale glow of light from somewhere on the balcony above told her that Sheba had lighted the lamps in the corners there.

And then she had gone in search of Cliff. Had she found him?

CHAPTER 16

He sat on the side of his bed, leaning on one elbow holding toward the thin lamp light a sheet of paper. It was one of several he had taken from the metal box he had found deep in one corner of the attic. Other boxes had covered it, as though someone once had wished to hide the small metal box. He had found it locked but breaking the lock was simple. And now the content of the papers so absorbed his attention that he forgot where he was.

He read and reread a paragraph. Crazy. Fantastic. What kind of mind believed in that sort of thing? Immortality by a perfect and natural death would halt time, and time forever would stand for that individual at the moment of death, and ...

Someone was in the room with him. Suddenly and with a tingle of warning he knew that someone had entered the room, though he hadn't been aware of a sound.

He whirled toward the door, rising as he moved.

Sheba stood there, leaning against one side of the door frame. The door stood open. And she stood smiling, her eyes steady and narrowed on him. With the intensity of a snake charmer.

The warning that sent ripples of coldness over his body said in silent swiftness, *Be careful. Careful, buddy, or you're gone.*

He fixed his gaze on the tip of her cute nose and said in a friendly, southern drawl, "Well, howdy. I guess I didn't hear you knock."

Softly and intimately she answered, "I didn't knock." Her steady gaze moved without blinking toward the box on the bed. "What have you got there?"

"Just a little something I found."

"Can I see it?"

She started toward the bed and he closed one hand firmly on her soft arm and stopped her. The face she turned toward him was still hypnotically flirtatious—or hypnotically dangerous, like a cat ready to pounce at any time. He wasn't sure which.

One thing he was sure of—it was being done with a definite purpose in mind.

And with her mind, whatever the purpose, he felt the results would be dangerous.

"You don't want me to see it," she teased, smiling. 'Why? Is it some of your favorite porno? If so, don't worry. I've probably seen as much, or more, than you have. And I assure you it won't ruin my morals."

"I don't doubt that," he said, hoping she would let it go with thinking it might be pornographic; knowing that anything done by Andrew Bleeker seemed to have a strange and fatal effect on young female minds. "But I wouldn't want to show you, or any other girl I respect, any of it."

Her eyebrows raised, giving her a decidedly wicked look. She laughed. "You respect me?" Even with the short, soft laughter, she sounded surprised.

"Of course," he said cautiously, thinking, *now what?* Her hand touched his rib cage, gentle and caressing, moving around toward the front of his belt. Breathing became increasingly difficult. He wanted to release her arm and get out. To stop looking into her eyes.

She moved against him suddenly, stretching up. Her hands pulled his face down, and for a brief moment he felt the sensuous fullness of her mouth. But he was aware too of a foulness and slimy wetness, and he jerked away and looked over Sheba's head straight into the eyes of Donna as she stepped into view in the doorway.

The stare of Donna's wide gray eyes paralyzed his voice. The hurt he saw there, her movement backward, away from his room, brought up an emotion he hadn't known existed. She couldn't leave—he wouldn't let her leave thinking he would make love to Sheba or to anyone—not now—now that he had found her.

But suddenly she was gone, her footsteps echoing hollowly as she ran down the hall.

"Donna!" he called, running after her.

At the door of her room she stopped and faced him, pale and trembling in the dim light of the balcony. Her voice shook faintly as she spoke.

"It's all right. I—I might have expected too much."

"Never mind that bull," he said with an unaccountable rush of anger. "Get into your room, and don't say another word."

He opened the door and pushed the surprised and dismayed young woman into her room and crowded behind her. With the door shut behind them he held her the way he had wanted to, and kissed her the way he had wanted to, and felt the yielding of her response.

Against her neck he whispered, "I love you, you nutty little girl. What would I want with anyone else?"

"Do you really mean that?"

"I mean it."

He held her face between his hands and looked at her.

"You're beautiful, you know it?" he said. "You're everything, all over, inside and out. That kiss, it didn't amount to anything. I mean, you know, it wasn't my idea. And I think she's got something else in mind, too, Donna. She's sick, I'm sure of it now, more all the time. And I am, after all, a psychologist. I must try to help her." He looked down at her gray eyes, soft now with sympathy. "She really does need help."

"Then do what you can."

"I need to get her to a hospital but—"

Suddenly he remembered the box, and the papers. He had read only a few of the pages, not enough to let him into the strange theory. Andrew Bleeker had come up with over his years of isolation. Sheba had shown curiosity about the contents of the box, and she would be sure to look. Then what?

"Is something wrong?" Donna asked.

"I left something on the bed. Wait for me."

He hurried back to his room, but one glance from the door gave him the answer. Sheba was gone, and so were all the papers and the box.

He went back along the hall, around the balcony from Donna's room toward Sheba's. Donna stood in the open door of her bedroom, watching him across the hole of the stairwell. Sheba's door was closed, and he knocked.

There was no answer.

Donna came slowly around to stand by the newel post at the top of the stairs. After a few more tries he stopped knocking and went to join her.

"Was it important?" she asked.

"Well, perhaps not greatly important, but it was damned interesting." He took her arm and they went together down the steps. "I don't know what Sheba wanted with it especially, but it's something I don't feel she should have, anyway."

The lamps had been lighted in the living room and Sheba was lounging at ease in a chair that faced the foyer.

"I heard you knocking on my door," she said smiling at him. "Would it be indecent of me to ask what you wanted?"

He didn't feel like returning her smile. He looked for the small box, but didn't see it. "I think you took something off my bed."

"Yes," she said. "I took it because it didn't belong to you. It belongs to me. I bought this house, and all contents except those that were personal items of your deceased family. And that box did not belong to your family."

There would be no getting the box again, he could see that. And since he had a bad habit of forgetting details if he didn't write them down there was nothing to do but go back to his room and try to recall all he had read.

"Excuse me," he said to Donna. "There's something I have to do."

He heard Sheba call after him, lazily and with amusement, "If you're going to look for that box, forget it. It's not in my room, and it's not in the attic, either."

He went on without answering, trying to keep in mind the details of all he had read.

When he reached his room he remembered to lock the door before he opened the drawer where he had tossed the small notebook and pen. He wrote quickly, grabbing at fading words.

Andrew Bleeker's theory on entering another time zone as follows: Death, by any nonmutilating method, but absolutely without interment, cremation, or otherwise. Essential that body be allowed to be absorbed quickly and naturally by nature, at that specific time of mortal life that is most desirable. Physical prime. Mental prime. That which has been absorbed by nature, then rises to a timeless existence, and lives forever. His powers are the powers of supernature. Complex, controlling. His world unchanging...

Cliff sat trying to remember, digging the top of his pen into his closely trimmed beard. He'd read here and there, grabbing a gist as he went, planning to go over it all carefully later. Then he had let Sheba get her hands on it. After weeks of digging through old junk in that stinking attic, crawling among the spiders and their webs, he had let Sheba slip it right out from under his nose!

Did the man really believe he had figured out a kind of immortality? Psychopathic, no doubt about that. Brutal, selfish, inconsiderate of others. Egotistical.

No wonder people didn't try very hard to cross his damned bridge.

And no wonder his young wife left him.

He had probably wanted to try out his theory on her.

Strange, though, his influence on young female minds. Strange as hell. Weird.

Especially considering that he had been dead so many years.

What was it the man had written about the woman to spend his eternity with him?

Young, wild, full of fire and hell. A woman to be mine and mine only, to be broken to work my will, and then come to me willingly to live with me forever in this paradise which I have discovered.

Cliff didn't write down that part. He didn't have to because there would be no forgetting it. He wondered what power it would have on a mind as vulnerable as Sheba's. He wondered, and his tension and uneasiness increased.

He could see no solution except to get Sheba to a hospital before it was too late to save her; and especially now that she had the metal box with its possibly mind-bending contents.

On the other hand, he could see no point in having Dr. Steven make a useless trip down in hopes he had found a haunted house. There was the green mold, or mildew, or whatever the devil it was, but otherwise the house seemed no more mysterious than any old house would be. And there was nothing exceptional happening outside of a group of coincidences, and a murder that had not been done by a ghost. Not even old

Andrew could have gained that much power, as he had seemed to think he would. It had taken human hands to put that pillow over that man's face.

Sheba, he was sure.

Still, that was not in Dr. Steven's line.

He dug from a compartment in his suitcase a box of stationery and wrote the short letter that was sure to disappoint the doctor.

No point in wasting your time up here. Tell you about it when I see you...

CHAPTER 17

For the first time since she had known Sheba, Donna felt tense and uncomfortable in her presence. Shadowed as she was in her chair, Donna couldn't be sure that Sheba was staring. But she felt she was, steadily and with no friendliness whatsoever.

Donna went with forced casualness toward the stove, where a bit of warmth remained. Was Sheba mad at her because of the interrupted kiss? Because he had followed her and left Sheba alone in his room?

It was something they couldn't talk over. No, not this.

Donna said, "I told Wanda and Esther to pack and be ready to go tomorrow. Surely the sheriff won't object to their leaving the house, staying in a motel if necessary."

"Good idea. What about you and Cliff?"

Donna turned and looked at the small figure curled and hidden in the large wing chair. "Leave you here alone?" she asked in amazement. "Do you think I'd do that, Sheba?"

Quietly Sheba said, "But I'm not leaving, Donna."

"Oh, he was furious, that's all. Cliff will talk to him tomorrow and persuade him to let us, and you, get out of here. I'm sure he will."

"You don't understand, Donna. I'm not leaving at all. I've changed my mind about letting Cliff take the place back. I'm going to stay here—

forever. It's my home now. So of course you must go whenever you get the chance."

Donna tried to see Sheba's eyes, to read them, to find in them the truth. Did she mean what she was saying, or was she being protective in her sometimes generous and surprising way?

Ordinarily Donna would have felt free to ask her. But tonight there was a feeling of restraint. "I'll go," she said, "eventually. But not for a day or two."

"I don't need anyone," Sheba said.

Donna got up, opened the stove door, and dumped in part of the coal from the bucket. Just enough to keep the fire from going out. Then she went back to the kitchen to help Wanda and Esther with dinner.

Tomorrow morning, Donna hoped, would see a change of mind again in Sheba.

BUT IT DIDN'T.

The night passed slowly, in cold, damp silence, with Donna sitting up in bed half the time trying to keep her mind on the magazine in her hands, the stories, the ads, anything; but aware always of the silence, the doorknob that now had taken on a kind of dull menace, and the small green patch that glistened darkly in the corner of her room. She could almost feel it growing toward her.

The morning came and Donna packed her things before she went downstairs—just in case the sheriff gave her permission to leave. In case, too, that Sheba had changed her mind. Because she couldn't leave Sheba alone in this house.

But Sheba's mind hadn't changed.

She stood in the middle of the foyer, looking sophisticated and very sexy in a long, slinky hostess pajama. She smiled goodbye at Esther and Wanda, both in coats and in dowdy contrast to Sheba. Donna, shivering in a heavy sweater and pantsuit, watched it all in silence.

Sheba explained it with a casual, "The sheriff said I couldn't leave, so I'm not. But I'll see you girls in town. Cliff will know where you're staying."

Wanda said, "I hate to leave you here."

"Why? It's my house."

The smile was there on Sheba's face, but to Donna it seemed like the smile on a mask.

"Of course," Wanda said, "you've got Donna."

Sheba glanced at Donna. "There's no point in you staying, Donna, really there isn't. I'll be all right alone. I don't mind at all."

Cliff leaned against a pillar, his eyes on Donna. He seemed reluctant to go at all. Now, for the fourth time, he said, "Won't you at least ride along with me? Please?"

Donna wanted to, but to go would seem like deserting Sheba at the most crucial moment. "You won't be gone long, will you?"

"No longer than it will take me to drive in, leave the girls in the motel, and get back."

"Aren't you going to see the sheriff?" Sheba asked. "So that Donna can leave too, without a guilty conscience?" Donna looked closely at Sheba's smile. A guilty conscience? She wasn't sure she liked that, or even knew what Sheba meant by it.

Cliff said, "Oh yeah, sure. The sheriff." He straightened in an easy and almost lazy movement and went toward the door. "You're damned right I'm going to see the sheriff. And I'm going to get this thing settled today. I may even bring him back with me."

While he held the door open for Wanda and Esther he gave Donna a long look that was serious and a bit fatherly, and in the confusion of Sheba telling the girls goodbye he said to her, "Be careful."

Donna nodded.

The door closed and Sheba came back still smiling. Together they went into the living room.

Now that they were alone Donna began to wonder if she had been right in staying with Sheba. The smile was getting on her nerves, making her nervous with touches of faint panic as though if Sheba should start toward her the panic would send her screaming in flight. She remembered all too clearly that Cliff had said he felt sure Sheba was responsible for the murder.

She, Donna, had not believed it.

Or, more accurately, she hadn't accepted it; and there was a difference.

Sheba said something in polite conversation, as though trying to form some kind of communication with a stranger, and Donna replied. None of it disturbed the stronger flow of thoughts that persisted uncomfortably deeper in her mind.

The front door opened suddenly and Cliff came into the foyer. Donna, startled by the unexpected, left her chair and walked a few feet to face him.

He stood with his feet widespread and a light frown on his face. "There's a car under the water by the bridge," he said. "Who the hell's is it? All you can see is one side and the wheels. They took the whole railing off again right in the middle of the bridge."

Donna felt for a short moment that she would collapse. She had forgotten all about the young couple who had come to the house last night. "My god," she whispered. Oh my god."

Cliff came to her. His hands were warm on her shoulders, and gentle. His voice, too, was gentle. "Donna, do you know who it is?"

She nodded, and the panic rose to a nearly unbearable joint. She was aware that Sheba had come to stand near them, and her smile was gone.

"Who is it, Donna?" Cliff asked.

Sheba said quickly, "There were car lights coming up the road when I got to the house last night. I didn't see who was in it, but I gave Donna instructions to send whoever it was away."

Donna's voice came back in a rush. "You've got to get them out, Cliff, before—before—oh my god—you've got to get them out!"

He shook her. "Donna! If they went under last night just after dark, and if they're still in the car, they can't possibly be alive."

"Yes, they can! If there is an air space—Cliff, hurry and get someone. Hurry!"

He pulled at her. "You come with me."

She looked at Sheba, who stood like a horror-stricken, half-nude goddess. And she shook her head.

"Sheba wouldn't have time to dress, and I can't leave her now. You go, Cliff, and hurry. Please!"

She went with him to the door and stood watching as he ran to the car, where Wanda and Esther sat huddled in their coats. The car spun on the slippery grass and down into the drive. It didn't pause on the bridge. Within minutes it was out of sight, hidden by the tall grass of the marsh beyond the bridge.

Donna stared where the car might be, but she couldn't see it. She was able to see the missing railing. The cold dampness of the cloudy, misty morning finally penetrated her clothing and she turned back into the house, closing the door softly.

After standing by the door for a while she moved slowly over to a pillar—and then she noticed Sheba.

The girl sat in a chair, one leg drawn up, looking at the stove. She seemed unaware that Donna had come back into the house and the smile that played around her lips, coming and going, sent into Donna a far deeper coldness than she had ever known before.

Cliff had said Sheba needed help, and now Donna was sure of it. There was something about the look on Sheba's face that was not sane.

And Donna was afraid of her.

She wondered if there was any way to cross the foyer and get into her office without being seen. Once in there, she could lock her door and stay there until Cliff came back.

Sheba's head turned slowly to look straight into Donna's eyes and she laughed softly, as though she knew exactly what Donna was thinking.

Nervously, almost incoherently, Donna began talking: "I wish they hadn't come last night—I wish I had remembered that no one ever crosses that bridge at night and lives."

"I did," Sheba said with soft laughter.

Donna started backing toward the doorway. "I'm going down there. Maybe there's something I can do. I just can't wait here in the house knowing that someone is in that cold water. I just can't!"

Sheba rose languidly, stretching, still laughing ever so softly. Donna turned and went quickly out the door.

When it closed behind her she paused only long enough to draw a deep breath of the freedom of fresh air, and feel the release from being trapped with something she didn't know how to handle.

Sheba didn't follow her. Often, as Donna walked down the lane toward the bridge, she turned to look back at the house. But it remained closed; a great, ugly pile of gray stone that looked as if it belonged in medieval fantasy of Europe rather than the upper South of modern North America.

At the edge of the bridge she stopped and stood looking at the two black tires, now coated with a light film of ice that would soon melt when the sun pushed away the early morning fog. The water lay dark and dangerous and still, with only the side of the car visible in the darkness.

There was nothing she could do but wait. And she could see there would be no breathing space in that car.

She stood staring at the water until the cold began to be too much. She didn't want to walk on the bridge, so she walked a short way back toward the house. And in looking at the house she was reminded of something.

Sheba had gotten out of her car even though it had later been found with both doors closed. Maybe it had happened again, and the young couple was lying somewhere in the grass.

With a purpose now she began to look, eagerly, down the banks on each side of the bridge, parting the tall grass with her hands, working her way back toward the house. And finally giving up to go back to the very edge of the water and look along the bank to see if anyone had crawled out there.

No one had.

She went back to stand at the end of the bridge, looking across. There was still the other side. She had only to cross the bridge and look there.

The boards were rough under her feet and seemed weak and unsteady. There was a faint feeling of movement that reminded her of a narrow, swinging footbridge she had once crossed. One day before long this bridge would collapse and be no more. And then the house would be isolated from all the world.

Long before she reached the other end of the bridge the cars were in sight. She immediately recognized Cliff's blue and white car, and behind it a white car that probably was the sheriff's because it had whirling blue lights on top. Behind that came an ambulance.

Tears of relief filled her eyes as she began to run to meet Cliff. She wiped the tears away with cold hands.

Behind the ambulance she saw another vehicle—a wrecker.

Cliff stopped his car on the bridge, got out, and caught her up into his arms. Without a word he hugged her tightly, then pulled her to his car and opened the door for her. He got in beside her, drove over the bridge, and parked.

"Stay in here," he said. "If you get cold start the engine again."

From the warmth of his car then she saw the wrecker back down along the bridge past the parked sheriff's car and ambulance and drop a chain that had a large hook on its end. After several attempts the hook caught the fender and slowly the wrecker eased the car back through the water to the edge, where one of the men was then able to wade down into the water and attach the chain to a more secure position. The car then was lifted from the water and drawn up to lie on the bank long enough for the men from the ambulance to run to it.

The unlocked doors opened easily, and two bodies were taken out.

Donna saw the long, dark, streaming hair of the girl— and then she covered her face with her hands and looked no more. She heard the ambulance leave, and when it left she began to sob softly into her hands.

Because of her two more people were dead.

The door opened and closed and Cliff's arms were around her.

"I killed them, Cliff," she whispered. "I sent them away."

"You sent them away because that was your job," he said firmly, "But you did not kill them. Do you hear that, Donna? You did not kill anyone!"

She didn't want him to see her crying like a weak child, so she straightened and wiped her eyes with a tissue from the holder on the floor. He started the car and drove toward the house.

When she looked back at the bridge the ambulance was gone, the wrecker was gone. Only the sheriff's car was left.

And the tall, stooped figure of the sheriff stood at the edge of the broken railing of the bridge, staring down ever so motionless into the water.

Staring. Staring.

CHAPTER 18

Sheba stood in the attic in front of the handsome and virile Andrew. She returned his smile and moved in a slow, model's circle in front of him.

"Do you like my pants? I wore them just for you." She held out a small box, heavy on her palm. "Here they are. I got them."

She went on then to the gun case far back in the attic and removed the shotgun. She broke it open and inserted two shells from the box. Then she carefully closed the door of the gun case, put the box into the drawer at the bottom, and carried the gun back to Andrew. She stood it on the floor beside her. There was no smile on her face now.

For a long time she stood absorbed by him, and when she heard the faint opening and closing of the door downstairs, audible because she had deliberately left open all doors between her and the foyer, the smile touched her lips again. She raised the shotgun, nodded assent at the smiling face of the man, and went toward the stairway.

A voice drifted, echoing up from below, a voice that stopped her instantly and froze her into listening.

"I want to see her, anyway. She's got to be here in the house, because I saw her car out there and there's no way out of here but along the road."

A much lower voice said something about seeing if he could find her... but he didn't matter. It was the first voice, the loud voice of the sheriff that caused her to frown in annoyance and hurry back to slip the shotgun out of sight behind the painting.

Once it was safely hidden she hurried out of the attic and closed the door so that no one would guess she had been there. Then, running quickly and lightly, she left the service corridor, slipped into the main hall, and closed that door.

She was standing near the banister of the balcony when Cliff Murphy's head came in view above the sharp turn in the stairway. When he saw her he stopped.

"Are you looking for me?" she asked. "I thought I heard the sheriff yell."

"He wants to see you, yes."

Sheba went down the stairs with conscious grace, her chin held high as she had learned from watching Donna. With Donna it was natural. With her, as Andrew's chosen, all things would be natural now. As soon as she got rid of the rest of the people.

The sheriff stood in the foyer looking sour and gloomy and perhaps a bit sad, too. She smiled to cheer him up.

"You wanted to see me?" she asked sweetly.

For a long time he said nothing, just looked at her. She wasn't sure, but she thought he looked puzzled. While she waited for him to make up his mind what he wanted to see her about she looked for Donna.

And found her sitting near the stove, her eyes fixed on something on the floor.

The sheriff coughed for her attention, and she looked back with her smile.

"You can't blame me for the car going off the bridge," she said, and remembered that they would expect some emotion from her along the line of sorrow. She dropped he smile. "I really am so sorry. If I had remembered that the bridge is so narrow that people can't seem to cross it at night I wouldn't have told Donna to send them away. But you said no more people here—that is no more guests, and I really was trying to carry out your wishes, Sheriff."

She saw the flicker of pain on his face and was glad she had thought to say that. But she didn't smile again.

"Well," the sheriff said, "I never thought of it either. I guess if anybody is responsible for it, I am."

"Don't torture yourself about it, Sheriff," Sheba said with sham sympathy. "We all make mistakes."

It seemed to throw him. He looked toward the stairway, the living room, the back of the house. And rubbed his face hard all over with one large hand. "I guess you don't have to stay here. If you can get a place in town that would be all right."

"Sheriff," Sheba said, "I can't afford a place in town. And although the house may not seem a very pleasant place after all the terrible things that have happened, it is a house. And it's mine. I really don't mind staying here. At least until you solve your case. Perhaps one of these days you'll see that it is possible that the friends of that poor man were responsible. Really, who else could it have been?"

He began to bristle again. "Now I'll do the figuring out of who did what, and if you want to stay here that's your business, but you'd better not pull out and me not know it."

"I have nowhere to go anyway."

The sheriff eased toward the door, and asked nobody in general, "Do you happen to know where that young couple came from? They had Mississippi tags, I noticed, but did they mention where?"

Donna seemed to straighten a bit, as if her name had been called and her straying attention demanded. Her long, deep breath, inhaled and exhaled, was audible in the silence and was returned by soft echoes that went on and on, absorbed and returned by the house. Sheba wondered if the others heard it too, but they showed no signs of it. She smiled, glad that only she could hear the breathing of the house. Of Andrew.

"No," Donna said. "They didn't say. I didn't ask."

"Well, I'll find out in town. Hang around."

Cliff opened the door for the sheriff, and then followed him outside. To talk to him in private, Sheba was sure. To talk about her.

The anger boiled sudden and fierce in her as she turned to Donna. "Are they accusing me?"

"I don't know," Donna said blankly, then seemed to realize the depth of the question. She came alert. "Of course not! How could you possibly be blamed for that? Cliff is probably only convincing the sheriff that you'd be better off in town."

"Can't anybody understand?" Sheba cried furiously, releasing the feelings that caused her body to tremble by going to the drawer of the desk in the foyer and taking out a cigarette and lighting it. She breathed deeply of it. Then, calmed, she turned again to face. Donna. "Can't anybody understand that I don't want to leave? I want to stay. I bought this house, and I'm beginning to like it here very much. Furthermore, I'm going to like the privacy here. Yes, I'll like it. I don't want anybody living with me anymore."

"But... what about the money, Sheba?"

"Money! Don't you ever think of anything else, Donna?"

Donna drew the long breath again, and the house answered, and answered again, mocking. "You owe money still, and you were going to pay for it by making a lodge, don't you remember?"

Sheba shrugged. Cliff came back into the foyer and stood quietly by the door, watching and listening. She didn't want to talk in front of him.

"I'll manage," she said, and crushed the cigarette to bits in the clean ashtray on the desk. "Besides, that's my business now." She glanced at Cliff. "What were you two plotting? My execution?"

Cliff moved and walked slowly toward her. "No, of course not. Nobody is going to hurt you, Sheba." His hand, warm and firm, touched the back of her arm. "Why don't we come into the living room and talk awhile?" Something was up, that she could see. Her suspicions drew her eyes toward the front door. "Is the sheriff gone?"

"Yes, he's gone. You don't have to worry about him anymore, Sheba. He's not going to bother you, ever."

"Ever? What do you mean by that? He thinks I've been going around murdering people."

Cliff skirted her statement as if she wouldn't see what he was trying to do. "He's quite willing for you to leave. I told him that I intended to return your money in this property, and he has more or less put you in my care."

Sheba let Cliff draw her along into the living room and toward the group of chairs around the stove, but she returned his smile with a stare of hostility. He had something in mind. Sneaky, like a cat padding softly after its prey, he was after her. Well, he wasn't the only clever one.

"In your care," she said, and sat in the chair where he more or less pushed her. "Like how?"

He waited until Donna had sat down and then he sat on the hearth in front of them, his hands clasped and dangling loosely between his knees. For a while he looked down at his hands. Sheba leaned back in her chair, put her legs over the arm of it, and relaxed, and watched him. And waited.

"Sheba," he finally said, "I feel that you need to see a doctor. Would you consider going into a hospital for while?"

That, of all things, was the most unexpected. She yelped with a burst of laughter, her head back against the chair. "A hospital! What for? Murder? Is that what they do with mad, mad murderesses these days?"

"Sometimes," he said.

The lack of humor in his voice stopped her amusement instantly. She stared at him. "You're putting me on!"

"No, I'm not, Sheba."

"You think I've gone on a far-off trip? You're crazy, that's what—you —" She stopped suddenly, listening hard.

The house was breathing, breathing, and the whisper grew into a soft command. No... no... no... Sheba felt the comforting touch of cold dampness on her cheek. She looked carefully at the other two for an indication that they might have noticed, might have heard or felt anything, but they seemed unaware. "Sheba," Cliff said, "it would save you from jail."

"Is somebody taking me to jail?" she asked, calmer now.

"He will, I'm afraid, if he can't find out that someone else was in the room of the murdered man. And so far you seem to be the only one who was there. This is your way out, Sheba."

"I see. Tell it to me straight."

He moved and changed his position, raising one foot to the hearth and letting his hand dangle over his knee. "I will take you to a hospital where you will receive psychiatric care, that's all. Will you go?"

"Under one condition," Sheba said.

"Name it."

"That you don't take back the house. I want to keep it."

He hesitated, thinking, then said, "What say we just let it ride while you're in the hospital? We can talk about it after you're out again."

Sheba nodded. "All right. After I'm out."

"Good girl. Now, can you get your things together so that we can leave this afternoon?"

"Not this afternoon. I have much too much to do. But I can be ready to go by tomorrow."

For the first time Donna spoke up. Her voice had gained a bit of animation so that she didn't sound like a speaking robot on a Japanese horror movie. "I'll help you pack, Sheba. It won't take that long to do it, surely."

Sheba slowly stretched out of her chair, then stood with her face turned slightly away from them. For effect. Let them see her thoughtful and sad. "Going into a hospital where people will think I'm cracked is not something I'm looking forward to. At least give me the privilege of getting ready at my own speed. I'll do my own packing. I want to. And I promise I'll be ready to go tomorrow morning."

Cliff said, "I think that's fair enough, Donna, don't you?

"If she'd rather. But I'd be glad to help."

Sheba said, "I know you would, but I'd like to be alone for a while. If you'll excuse me I'll go to my room and start sorting out the things I want to take."

She left them standing together by the stove, and she went up the stairs into the sweet comfort of the coldness and darkness of the second floor and back into the service corridor. She closed the door carefully behind her.

And when she went into the attic, she was very careful to close that door also. They would follow her eventually, wondering, looking. And they would come into the attic.

She was prepared to wait.

CHAPTER 19

"Try not to let it get to you," Cliff said, touching Donna's hand with a gentle caress. "If you don't think you can stand it here for one more night we'll rush her along and get her out this afternoon anyway. What does she have to do that will take so long?"

"I don't know. She was never like this before. I feel I hardly know her anymore, Cliff."

"That happens when mental illness strikes, Donna."

Donna walked the floor restlessly, going to the window to look out but seeing the bridge. She turned quickly away, and the vision of the young couple on the porch in the dark last night returned clearly and sharply. "If only I had let them come on in!"

"Donna," Cliff said, coming over to take her hand in his and draw her back toward the stove, "look, your hands are freezing. Let's talk about something else, all right?"

"All right."

Time passed quietly and slowly, and Donna was aware of waiting, of listening for the sound of Sheba somewhere above. A footstep, a suitcase being slammed shut, a door closing, anything. And there was nothing but the quiet conversation in the still house. She looked at her watch and saw it had stopped.

"Do you have the time?" she asked.

"No. I left my watch off this morning because it had fogged up."

There was a moment of silence as Donna looked at the rusted face of her watch. "Have you noticed," she asked softly, "that a clock or watch does not run for very long in this house?"

"I've noticed," he said.

"What do you think it means?"

He smiled, teasing. "I think it means we're having a lot of damp weather."

It was an effort to cheer her up, she knew. But it didn't help. The passing time, and yet the feel of time not passing at all but standing quite still, made her nervous. "I think I'll go upstairs and see if Sheba is all right."

"I'll go with you."

She didn't object. Being alone now was not what she wanted, and she couldn't understand Sheba's wanting solitude. Not Sheba, the gregarious one.

They went up the stairs and around the balcony to Sheba's door. Donna knocked and listened, but there was no answer, no sound of movement at all within the room. She looked up at Cliff. He had a wary frown of concentration on his face as he looked at the door.

"Cliff," Donna said with growing anxiety, "could something have happened to her?"

He reached past her and knocked sharply on the door, calling out loudly, "Sheba!"

The knock and the name echoed away to silence in the house, and still there was nothing. Donna turned, looking over her shoulder, feeling their aloneness, yet aware more than ever of the surrounding walls and high ceilings of the old house.

"Cliff," she said in a soft undertone, "I have the most terrible feeling that we are all alone in this house. Do you think she might have gone out the back door and driven away? Could she have gone without us hearing her?"

"We'll see."

He pushed open Sheba's door and left it standing open. Donna waited while he went into the room and back out again.

"She's not there," Donna whispered.

He seemed to be listening, his head turned slightly to one side, his eyes narrowed and searching all visible places, corridors, stairway, closed bedroom doors, and finally the closed service door.

"I think I know where she is."

And as he spoke he began walking in long strides, fast, around the balcony and down the hall toward the service door. Donna managed to keep up with him.

He flung back the door to the service area and left it as he had Sheba's bedroom door, and then Donna knew where he was going.

At the attic door he stopped and looked back at her. "I wonder if you should wait here," he said, more to himself than to her.

"But why do you think she's up there? Why would she go up there?"

"I'm not sure she is up there, I'm just going to look."

"Then I'm going with you."

"Maybe that would be better. At least I would know where you are."

They went slowly into the musty darkness of the attic and stood at the top of the stairs. The wood posts held the roof and supported leaning tables, old chairs, boxes. Shadows deepened into more shadows, tiny windows here and there let in enough light to show the webs that hung waving in coordinated rhythm down from rough rafters. Corners, deep and dark, held stacks of boxes and old furniture behind which death itself could lie hidden and waiting.

Cliff began to walk, carefully choosing his steps without looking down. He went straight to the painting of the tall, smiling man and paused; but he only glanced at it. After a moment he passed it and went back toward the wall. Donna hurried to catch up with him. He had stopped now, and was looking steadily at something. She came up to stand close by his side.

"Cliff," she whispered, "what is it?"

He turned suddenly, his eyes going beyond her, moving quickly in a searching sweep of the attic. His hands closed hard on her shoulders and he turned her toward the stairway.

"The gun," he said. "It's missing."

"What gun?" she asked, feeling the tightening of fear in her throat.

"The shotgun. The one she was asking about. Come on, let me get you out of here."

She went beside him back toward the stairway, but she said, "I don't think she's up here, Cliff, she—"

The voice came from behind them, cold, amused, interrupting, "Ah, but yes I am!"

Donna whirled toward Sheba, and at first it seemed she was seeing two people—a small and slender girl holding against her shoulder a gun large and black, and behind her a tall smiling man who rested the same gun on the floor beside him. But the vision was cut sharply off by an arm throwing her to one side and the instantaneous explosion of sound.

The push threw Donna to the floor and in the wild confusion of the next moment, the next instant, there came the second explosion, rebounding against the ceiling and the walls. And mingling with it was a scream.

A scream of fury and pain and hatred as Sheba fell backward into the unbanistered hole of the stairway.

As the sounds continued to shatter the silence of the attic Donna sat up to see Cliff throw the long, black, heavy gun to one side and then run to the head of the attic stairway and down. Donna crawled, voiceless, to the edge of the stairwell and looked down.

Cliff was running down the steep steps toward the small twisted body that lay head down on the bottom step in the hall beyond the attic door.

Donna's voice returned to her, trembling with a scream of terror that she quickly suppressed with her hands. For a moment she felt sick, then she found the top of the stairs and clinging weakly to a wall that was slimy wet she stumbled down where Cliff was kneeling beside Sheba.

He lifted the still form gently off the bottom step and lay her on the floor of the hall. Donna heard the sound of sobbing.

"She's not dead! Cliff, she's not dead after all!"

Then she realized the sobbing was her own. Sheba's face was still and white.

"Donna," Cliff said. "I'm sorry."

The sobbing stopped and became a hard and constant pressure in Donna's throat. She spoke with an effort. "Then she is dead?"

"I think her neck was broken in the fall. Yes, she is dead. But of course we have to get her to a hospital anyway. And right away."

Donna looked for a moment into Cliff's eyes over the body of Sheba. "She tried to kill us, didn't she?"

"Yes, she did. But that's over. Come on, let's go get the car. Then I'll carry her down and—"

Donna objected hoarsely, "No, Cliff. Let me stay with her. Until you bring the car around." When he didn't answer, when he looked as though he might object, Donna said, "Cliff, I can't leave her here alone. Whatever happened, whatever caused her to do this, is over. I'll sit here and hold her —or just be with her."

"Donna, she doesn't know…"

"Cliff, please."

Reluctant in his movement, he rose and looked down at her. "All right," he said at last. "I'll only be a few minutes. I'll bring the car around to the back and be ready to come after you as soon as I can prepare a bed for her in the back seat." He touched her shoulder with reassurance. "Are you sure you want to stay?"

Donna nodded. "I'm sure, Cliff."

When he had gone she kneeled beside Sheba, not thinking, feeling only a numb weariness. Later would come the thoughts, the wondering. Later the sharpness of pain again, of facing reality. But the moment was numb, as though she kneeled beside a sleeping Sheba, a…

But it wasn't a dream. Across the hall was the open door of the bedroom where Wanda had stayed. It was there Wanda had heard footsteps go into the attic that first night. And now it seemed clear that only Sheba could have gone there. Sheba had come back and turned her doorknob and tried to enter her room. Had Sheba meant to kill her then?

But that was long ago… forever ago…

Hot and burning tears filled Donna's eyes and the door of Wanda's room blurred and shimmered into a world that had no reality. Donna put her hand out and down in her blindness and touched Sheba's arm. Cool. Uncovered.

She removed her sweater to cover the girl on the floor and felt the sweep of coldness on her own arms, but she spread the sweater carefully over Sheba's upper body.

And then she noticed the eyes had opened slightly, and through the narrow opening Sheba was staring up.

Cold waves of shock rushed like heart throbs over Donna. *Sheba was alive.*

But no, the eyes were unmoving, and Donna knew it was a natural reflex. Unnerved, she looked away and avoided the eyes carefully.

She thought of Cliff and wished he would hurry. He would be coming soon now, she told herself in silence. He—

The house was throbbing in its extreme silence, in rhythm with the increasingly heavy beat of her own heart. She felt the emptiness in the house, but there was no feeling of being alone. Something was in the attic behind her. Something—she knew not what or whom— was looking down at her. Looking, looking, and she was afraid to move.

The intense cold reached her first, and then the smell of rotting wood, of something slimy green that crawled without movement upon the walls. She twisted, looking up into the sharp rise of the stairway.

And saw it coming toward her.

Gray-white and thick and angry, rolling like a storm cloud and gathering speed, it moved into the stairway and poured down toward her and she fell back, helpless. Able only to attempt a scream from her closed and choking throat.

CHAPTER 20

He had drawn the car up into the backyard, as close as possible to the cracked and broken cement stoop that led its treacherous path to the kitchen door. Dampness from the dreary, misty, low-hanging clouds made the path more treacherous, and he thought of the difficulty of carrying Sheba's body down to the car. The sensible way, he felt, would be to go as before and send back an ambulance; yet he felt as reluctant as Donna to leave the body of Sheba alone in the house.

He didn't know why.

The blanket he was trying hurriedly to spread on the back seat of his car slipped and fell onto the floormat. He gave it another fling onto the seat. And the sound of a door slamming came almost unnoticed.

He struggled with the blanket, straightening it, then he stopped, listening. Remembering. He had left the front door standing open because he was running and didn't take time to close it. Had the wind blown it shut?

There was no wind. Only an unending cold winter mist.

He moved away from the car, his body growing tense with the warning that something was wrong in this house. He listened, but there was no further sound.

Moving fast and with an increasing sense of urgency he went up the steps to the back door. And found it locked.

The events of hours earlier that day, when he had taken Esther and

Wanda to town, brought back a vision of seeing Esther open and close the back door once. It hadn't been locked then.

Of course Sheba, or Donna, could have locked it later.

He considered knocking and calling Donna down to open the door, and immediately discarded the idea. He jumped off the stoop into wet, dead winter grass, and ran around the house.

The front door was closed, tight. And it too was locked.

Panic seized him then. He could think of only one thing—Donna would not have locked the door. And immediately he thought of something else. She might have locked it, had she been on her way to leaving by the back door.

He retraced his steps, but found the kitchen door still locked

Something was wrong; now he was sure of it. There was no time to think, only time to act—irrationally, perhaps, but that didn't matter now.

With a boot tugged from his foot he broke the glass from the kitchen window, and in the brief silence left after the shattering of the glass, as he quickly pulled his boot back on and boosted himself up and over the window frame, he heard a cry. Choked, unnatural. Terrified beyond all reason.

Donna.

Whether he screamed her name or only whispered it he never knew. Nor did he remember climbing the stairs that reached up out of the kitchen. After that the scene evolved before his eyes like a distorted, slow-motion movie, weird, unreal. The only thing about it that was recognizable, that drew him, was Donna standing pressed hard against the wall of the corridor. And it was from her throat that the hoarse, wild, terror-maddened cry was still coming like the slow exhale of wheezing breath.

Advice from Dr. Steven came back to him like a ghostly whisper: *You will be dumbfounded. You'll think you're hallucinating. You're not. Take a deep breath, clear your mind, and look. Observe. Because, my boy, you're face to face with the unnatural, that which you and most people do not believe exists.*

From unconscious instinct he reached out, grabbed Donna's blouse, and jerked her to him. He felt the coldness of her body, and the trembling. Then he felt the clutch of her hands.

But he stared at the thing that hovered over Sheba's body like a small, thickening, rolling, impenetrable cloud that was turning gray and dark so that the girl within was veiled and difficult to see. But he saw her rise into the thing that covered her as though she were being lifted. Her head swung sideways, her arms dangled.

He heard Donna scream, "Cliff, she's alive. Get her! Save her!"

But he knew she wasn't alive. He grabbed Donna up into his arms, bodily, just as the gray and threatening mass charged toward them; and he turned his back on it and ran with Donna screaming hysterically for him to go back after Sheba.

With the strength of desperation he kicked the antique, rusted lock off the back door. Within moments he was at the open door of his car. He literally threw Donna in and pulled the seatbelt down and secured it. He slammed the door and ran around to the driver's seat.

He looked back at the house once, and saw nothing but a broken window and an open door. But the door was swinging slowly shut. The car spun sideways on the slippery grass as he pressed on the accelerator.

"She's dead, Donna!" he shouted above her screams. "Do you hear me? She's dead! I'm getting you out of here, and right now, so calm down. I'm taking you to the hospital for a sedative and a rest, but don't tell what you saw, or…" He drew a deep breath, not finishing his sentence. Donna had collapsed into a state of deep convulsive sobbing.

"Well," he finally said as much to himself as to Donna "no one would believe you, that's all."

He crossed the bridge, slowing only as much as necessary. Safely over, he pressed the accelerator to the floor

Donna finally asked in stammering sobs, "Cliff— what was *that?*"

He didn't answer. There was no time now. Later he might be able to find the answer. But at the moment he had none. He concentrated on keeping the car on the road.

THREE DAYS later they stood together in the center of the road a short distance from his car, which was the last of several that were parked on available dry land. The boats moved slowly far out in different directions on their final day of dragging the lakes and ponds among the marshes. His arm held Donna tightly against his side, and he felt a familiar shudder go over her body.

He looked down at her, seeing the pale skin and large, sunken gray eyes. He hadn't wanted to bring her back, to let her see any of it again. But she could be a persuasive woman. With her he was like a twisted pretzel that changed positions at her wish. He held her.

"Cold?" he asked.

She replied with a question, "What happened to her, Cliff?"

"Whatever it was," he said, "they'll not find her. Not until there's nothing left for them to inter."

She didn't say more.

The sheriff had spied them and was coming closer. "Good afternoon, Miss Walker, I'm glad to see you're able to get out. Are you all right? I mean, considering everything."

"Yes, thank you."

He stood beside them, looking out at the boats.

Cliff asked, "Are they about ready to give it up?"

"Yeah. We have to come to the conclusion that she wasn't fatally injured and was able to get away. Of course she's on the wanted list now and won't get far unless she's pretty darned lucky. Wonder what makes a girl like that suddenly turn on her best friends with a gun."

It was not a question, only a statement. Puzzled, wondering. The questions had already been asked. Cliff had answered questions for hours. He had told the sheriff everything the sheriff would believe. Only the other part had he left out.

He felt Donna shivering again and he looked down at her. She had turned her face toward the house. With his hand flat on her cheek he gently forced her face away.

"I think I'd better take Miss Walker back to town now, Sheriff. If we don't see you again, good luck."

They shook hands, and Cliff was aware at last that he admired and liked the man. His handshake was firm and friendly.

When he and Donna were alone in the car he sat for a moment looking at the house—gray and large, atop its small hillock like a great pile of old stones. He could almost see the green growth coming through from the interior to glisten dully deep in the cracks of the stones that coated the outside like the scales on a monster from the depths of the lake.

"Someday I'm coming back. Dr. Steven has found his house. If anybody can solve that mystery, he can. And if he can't, I'm going to."

Donna's hand clutched at his arm. "Cliff, please, no! Let it alone, please."

He patted her hand. "Don't worry. There won't be any danger to a couple of men."

"I don't want you to ever come back."

"Don't worry, okay? Donna, it's my work, remember? And now," he added as he drove the car back over the bridge and down the road, "Dr. Steven has got himself a believer. I know it's there—I don't know what it is, but I'll never rest until I find out."

The sun came through when he turned from the private lane toward the highway and he looked back for a last view of the house on the marsh.

Did he imagine it, or did he actually see them? And why did he think of it as "them"? It was only fog. Two swirls of fog rising from the lowland, drifting toward the stone turrets of the empty house, melding, twisting, uniting in a diaphanous embrace.

Like two lovers, together, at last.

OTHER NOVELS BY RUBY JEAN JENSEN

1974 The House that Samael Built

1974 Seventh All Hallows' Eve

1974 House at River's Bend

1975 The Girl Who Didn't Die

1978 Child of Satan's House

1978 Satan's Sister

1978 Dark Angel

1982 Hear the Children Cry

1982 Such a Good Baby

1983 The Lake

1983 MaMa

1985 Home Sweet Home

1985 Best Friends

1986 Wait and See

1987 Annabelle

1987 Chain Letter

1988 Smoke

1988 House of Illusions

1988 Jump Rope

1989 Pendulum

1989 Death Stone
1990 Vampire Child
1990 Lost and Found
1990 Victoria
1991 Celia
1991 Baby Dolly
1992 The Reckoning
1993 The Living Evil
1994 The Haunting
1995 Night Thunder
Pending Bear Hollow Charlie
Pending Cry of the Soul
Pending Pride of Bella Terra
Pending Animal Backtalk

www.ingramcontent.com/pod-product-compliance
Lightning Source LLC
Chambersburg PA
CBHW060602310726
48982CB00008B/1213/J